CORPUS CORPUS

ALSO BY H. PAUL JEFFERS

MYSTERIES

What Mommy Said
Readers Guide to Murder
A Grand Night for Murder
Adventure of the Stalwart Companions
Rubout at the Onyx
Murder Most Irregular
Murder on Mike
The Ragdoll Murder
Secret Orders
Portrait in Murder

CRIME HISTORY

Bloody Business: the Story of Scotland Yard
Who Killed Precious?
Wanted by the FBI

BIOGRAPHY

Gentleman Gerald: America's First Public Enemy No. 1
*Commissioner Roosevelt: Theodore Roosevelt and the
New York City Police*

CORPUS CORPUS

A SERGEANT JOHN BOGDANOVIC MYSTERY

H. PAUL JEFFERS

St. Martin's Press
New York

Library of Congress Cataloging-in-Publication Data

Jeffers, H. Paul (Harry Paul)
    Corpus corpus : a Sergeant John Bogdanovic mystery / by H. Paul Jeffers.—1st ed.
        p.   cm.
    ISBN 0-312-18558-8
    I. Title.
PS3560.E36C6   1998
813'.54—dc21   98-14625
                                                                    CIP

First Edition: August 1998

10 9 8 7 6 5 4 3 2 1

For my nephew Robert Devonshire

and with gratitude to
Rex Todhunter Stout, creator of Nero Wolfe;
the late William S. Baring-Gould,
author of *Nero Wolfe of West Thirty-Fifth Street;*
and Kevin Gordon for his insights into the Wolfe Pack.

Very few people like lawyers.

—Nero Wolfe

PART ONE

Cordially Invited

PROLOGUE

Minutes of the Meeting

WIGGINS AWOKE IN the middle of a steamy July night with an exciting brainstorm. Margaret Dane would present the Nero Wolfe Award to Theodore Janus! What a publicity coup it would be for the Wolfe Pack were he to bring together at this year's Black Orchid Banquet the lawyers whose courtroom sparring had enthralled the country for nearly a year. But when he offered the proposal to the steering committee there was a terrible row, proving the Nero Wolfe maxim that one man's flower is another man's weed.

Himself an attorney and a former district attorney, James Hamilton railed, "Theo Janus is just as bad as the gangsters he defends. Instead of getting such an honor, the bastard ought to be disbarred and run out of town on a rail."

Oscar Pendelton answered, "I appreciate that you still have the taste of sour grapes on your tongue because Janus has beaten you in court, not once but twice, but personal feelings should be set aside. We will not be honoring Theodore Janus the lawyer. We are recognizing his contribution to the cause of Nero Wolfe."

"Such hypocrisy," Hamilton retorted. "Why am I not allowed personal feelings but it's okay for a vote in favor of this from you, the very man who published Janus's book? And, I might add, the novels authored by our chairman."

"Are you suggesting I put Wiggins up to this?" Pendelton demanded. "If so, where is your evidence?"

Hamilton shrugged. "It's purely circumstantial."

The sweet voice of Marian Pickering Henry cut in with, "The essence of democracy, James, is that a person is free to cast a ballot for or against something or someone for whatever reason he or she chooses and not be called on to justify that vote."

"I take that to mean, Marian, that America's most popular writer of thrillers is joining with the man who also happens to be *your* publisher. Am I to be the only one to say 'nay' to this preposterous idea?"

"You do not stand alone in opposition, James," thundered Judge Reginald Simmons. "Theodore Janus is a national disgrace!"

"You are hardly objective, Judge," said Wiggins. "You have your own score to settle with Janus."

"Excuse me," said Harold Randolph meekly, "but may we debate Wiggins's proposal without all these harsh adjectives? I have no great love for Janus, either, but for reasons Marian Henry has so eloquently stated, and because I agree that Janus has earned this coveted award on the basis of his scholarship, I shall cast my vote in favor of the motion."

Nicholas Stamos pleaded, "Mr. Chairman, may we dispense with further discussion? Please call the roll on your nomination of Janus so that we can move on to other business. I vote nay."

Pendelton all but shouted. "I vote aye."

"As do I," said Marian Pickering Henry, quietly.

"No, no," bellowed Hamilton, thumping a fist on the table. "And if this motion carries, I may be left with no choice but to resign from the committee, and perhaps from the Wolfe Pack."

Wiggins turned to the sixth member. "Admiral Horne, with two in favor and two opposed and the chairman not eligible to vote except in a tie, it's up to you."

As tall and stately as the mast of his prized yacht, Trevor Horne had spent thirty years in the navy and had adopted a way of seasoning his speech with sea salt. "I know we're not supposed to discuss this anymore," he said, "but as I see it, we could run into heavy weather if we set sail into these uncharted waters. If we give our highest award to this notorious shyster for whom I bear personal animus because he filed a meritless law suit against me, we risk not only Hal's resignation, but perhaps being swamped in an ocean of resignations! But on the other hand, Janus's yeoman work in compiling the Wolfe encyclopedia can't be overlooked."

"If you are reluctant to vote in the affirmative," Wiggins said, "may I suggest you consider Nero Wolfe's maxim that it is always wiser, where there is a choice, to trust to inertia."

After several moments of deliberation, Horne said, "Yes, I must abstain."

Wiggins beamed. "The chairman votes aye."

1

Mouthpiece

DURING THE LONG and sensational murder trial that had held the whole country spellbound and left the majority of the people outraged at the acquittal, commentators had invoked many adjectives to describe the man who led the team of defense attorneys. He had been called gaudy, flamboyant, a dude, and the courtroom cowboy. Yet these terms had failed miserably in preparing Peter Burford for the effect of seeing Theodore R. Janus in person.

He wore a white western-style Stetson hat, a three-quarter-length shearling jacket, a red-and-black plaid flannel shirt, a yellow neck bandana, and gleaming brown and white cowboy boots. Chocolate brown jeans cinched by a wide black belt cried out to support a holster and a Colt .45 Peacemaker six-shooter. The only indication that Janus was a lawyer was his bulky brown leather briefcase, which looked so shabby it was reasonable to suppose the silver-haired character who carried it into the office had picked up a far less successful attorney's by mistake.

"Back so soon, Mr. Janus," said Burford. Long and sinewy in mechanics' coveralls and with a well-worn gray Cessna Aircraft baseball cap cocked jauntily backward on a head of thinning blond hair, he stood at a combination counter and display case. With shelves cluttered by gauges, meters, oil pumps, and other aeronautical gadgets, it would be to an untrained eye as mysterious as the shelves of fat volumes of criminal and civil codes might appear to the clients of Janus's law firm. There the visitor invariably found wood-paneled walls festooned with expensively framed diplomas and certificates and quaint old prints of wigged and robed English barristers that had become familiar in British courtroom dramas of movies and on television in the form of Rumpole of the Bailey.

In Burford's realm, as in numberless small private aviation airports, airfields, and landing strips to which Janus had flown in the thirty-five years since earning his pilot's license, the attorney found the floor-to-ceiling sheets of faux wood paneling decorated with dime-store framed photographs of classic aircraft from double-winged and kitelike planes of the barnstorming era to sleek corporate jets of a world when travel had been measured in miles not time. Except for these, the office and the young man behind the counter might have been familiar to Charles A. Lindbergh.

Burford said, "Your Mooney's all fueled up, sir."

"Thank you. What do I owe you?"

"Fuel and topping off the oil came to fifty-eight dollars."

"And the car rental?"

"Did you happen to check your mileage?"

"Seventy-four."

"The first hundred's included in the day rate, so that'll be thirty-six dollars," the young man said as he entered the mileage on the rental form.

From his wallet Janus drew a gold credit card and slapped it on the counter.

"You had no problem finding the prison, I hope, Mr. Janus."

"Your directions were excellent."

"I live not far from it, so I'm familiar with the route. And we often get people stopping to ask for directions, although most of the folks who come to Watertown to visit the prison don't fly in on their own planes."

"No, I'm sure," Janus said as he stuffed the receipt for the fuel and oil and a copy of the rental form into the bulging lackluster bag.

"I watched 'em build that place, you know," Burford went on. "That land used to be the site of a Nike missile base back in the old days when we worried about the damn Russians sending rockets across Canada en route to New York. I don't know what's a sadder comment on things, the need to build a missile defense against foreigners or us having to build prisons to protect us against our own people. Of course, nowadays they're not prisons.

It's the Watertown *Correctional Facility.* I say we ought to forget about correcting those creeps. They're guilty. Let 'em rot in prison."

Janus smiled tightly. "You're quite the philosopher, sir."

"I hope you didn't take that personal. If I ever got in a mess I'd want the best mouthpiece in the country, which is you."

"You're very generous."

"Like everybody else in the whole country, I watched you on television during the big trial out in Los Angeles. You and your associates did an amazing job getting that guy off, even though I did think he was guilty as sin and walked away only on account of he had plenty of money to afford to hire the likes of you."

Janus's smile stretched thinner.

As Burford's skin flushed from his open collar to slightly receding hairline, he blurted, "Gee, I'm sorry. 'Likes of you' was a bad choice of words. At times this old mouth of mine lands before my brain signals the wheels are down."

Janus's smile relaxed. "That's why there are lawyers."

"I understand it was your job to get him off."

"That was the jury's decision. But you are quite right about prisons. Blessed little correction is taking place."

Burford flashed a nervous smile. "Are there any changes in your plan, Mr. Janus?"

"My plan?"

"Your flight plan."

"Oh. It's still straight back to Stone County Airport."

As to the other plan, the one that had brought him winging upstate to quaint old Watertown, he had run into a stone wall by the name of Jake Elwell.

Now it was back to square one.

"How's the flying weather?" he asked. "The announcer on the local radio station said some snow is in the offing. I can't be grounded. I've got a very important appointment tonight with a friend who's bringing me a box of rare Cuban cigars."

"Well, you needn't worry about snow delaying you. There's only the usual lake-effect showers expected from a weak front moving in. You'll be home long before it gets here."

"Thanks for your many kindnesses," said Janus, lifting the

hefty bag and striding toward the door as if he were John Wayne or James Stewart going out to the street for a shootout. "You've got a fine little airport here and you run it very well."

"Hope to serve you again, sir."

Hurrying to his plane, Janus muttered, "Not bloody likely."

Flying all the way up to Watertown again in hope of finding that Jake Elwell had had a change of heart about talking would be a fool's errand.

2

Over My Dead Body

IN AN ELEGANT gold-leaf frame above an antique rolltop desk in the small, cluttered office of the proprietor at the rear of the Usual Suspects bookstore a florid red and green needlepoint embroidery proclaimed:

CLOTHES MISTAKE THE MAN

For proof of the motto one had only to observe the man who had coined it. In wintertime, donned in his tweed Inverness cloak and deerstalker cap, Wiggins was Sherlock Holmes. In spring and summer in a white suit and straw panama hat with slouching brim he was, according to some people, the late Truman Capote. Those of a slightly older generation found in him a strong resemblance to the fat man who had been the cleverest of the wags of New York in the 1920s and '30s known collectively as the Algonquin Round Table: Alexander Woollcott.

Indeed, all Wiggins needed to be Woollcott's exact replica was a little mustache and a pair of wire-rimmed spectacles. But those adornments carried with them a tiresome necessity of being taken care of. The glasses had to be cleaned and the mustache required constant trimming. But similarities between Alec, as the Round Tablers had called Woollcott, and himself went beyond the physical, for not since the days of the Round Table had the New York literary world encountered a man with the impressive knowledge of criminality, real and imagined, as that which Wiggins delighted in exhibiting for the elucidation of his customers.

In Alec Woollcott's era the newspapers had doted on the oh-so-mysterious death of Dot King, the Broadway Butterfly. It had gone unsolved, as did the killing of another Manhattan lovely by the name of Louise Lawson. Although both cases had been marked by impressive sleuthing, it had been coverage by the press that had made them sensational. Alec also had been diverted by ludicrous lovers Ruth Snyder and Judd Gray and their hare-brained plot to kill Ruth's husband. Around the same time, the un-beatable combination of sex and murder had drawn Woollcott, Damon Runyon, and a flock of other worthy celebrities of the Fourth Estate to New Jersey where one Eleanor Mills and her two brothers were accused of murdering her husband, the Reverend Edward Hall.

So influential had Woollcott been at the time that when he de-clared that a Stanford University professor had been unjustly con-victed of murdering his wife, the man won a new trial, which ended in acquittal. Then there had been the murder of Mrs. Nancy Evans Titterton, cracked by intrepid detectives who fol-lowed a strand of upholsterer's twine to a dim bulb named John Fiorenza. An arrest in the Bronx meant death in an electric chair at Sing Sing whose wooden arms had also embraced Ruth and Judd.

But while all this had been going on for the titillation of Wooll-cott's readers and radio listeners during the Depression, other fas-cinating crimes were casting spells upon the readers of detective stories titled *Fer-de-Lance, The League of Frightened Men, The Rubber Band, The Red Box, Too Many Cooks,* and *Some Buried Caesar.* Featur-ing the private detective Nero Wolfe, they had been turned out with amazing alacrity by an author whose name often led readers to the mistaken assumption that Rex Stout had to be as fat as the private detective Stout's imagination had invented.

That the writer of the country's most popular detective of nov-els and Alexander Woollcott, an insatiable reader of mysteries, would come to know one another had been inevitable. Indeed, Woollcott was so convinced, after reading *The League of Frightened Men,* that he had been Stout's model for Wolfe that he invited Stout to dinner at the Lambs' Club in 1935 and confronted Stout with his confirming evidence. First, he was fat, brilliant, and an absolutist. Secondly, in 1933 Edna Ferber had referred to Woollcott as a "New Jersey Nero." Third, Woollcott was author of *While Rome Burns,* and who had burned Rome? Nero!

Although Stout had brushed the theorizing aside, Wiggins had refused to do so, advising his bookstore clientele and associates in a universe of writers, editors, publishers, and readers of the whodunnit that Woollcott had indeed provided the inspiration, and that because of his resemblance to Woollcott, if anyone wanted to see Wolfe in the flesh, all one had to do was look at himself.

Unfortunately, Woollcott had died long before the arrival of Usual Suspects only two blocks from Woollcott's East Fifty-first Street apartment. Had its portly tenant lived in the 1990s, would there have been reason to doubt that he would be a frequent and knowing customer?

He certainly would have derived great pleasure in the lurid history of the store's address. As buildings went in a city Alec had described as having no attics and no yesterdays, the store at Beekman Place had been site of the nineteenth-century ax murder of Cleopatra Ducoyne by a notorious deceiver of wealthy women. In the speakeasy years it had belonged to the gangster Owney Madden. Then it was a safe house for a cell of Depression era communists and the naive fellow travelers of the 1930s literary smart set which included, allegedly, Dashiell Hammett. World War Two years saw it used as a brothel, while the 1950s had brought subdivision into floor-through apartments. In the sixties its basement had been a bomb factory for Weatherman revolutionaries.

Now restored on the outside to the condition in which the ill-fated Cleopatra Ducoyne had left it, the four-story interior accommodated the bookstore on the first and second floors, storage space on the third, and the owner's apartment on the fourth.

Venturing out of it occurred only for the most urgent reason and on four occasions for pleasure—to attend the convocation of the Baker Street Irregulars in early January, the Edgar Allan Poe Awards in the spring, the Wolfe Pack's gathering known as the Shad Roe Dinner, and the Black Orchid Banquet in December.

Now, suddenly, shortly before that event, Wiggins found himself talking on the telephone with the man who was to receive the Pack's most prestigious award.

"Wiggins, I need your assistance with something I must take care of right away," Janus declared. "I appreciate your aversion to leaving your store, not to mention journeying out of the city, but I hope you will set all that aside in this case and come up to see me at my ranch on Sunday."

Thinking that only Theodore Janus would refer to his small horse farm in Stone County, only forty-five minutes by car from the city, as a ranch, Wiggins answered, "I trust this isn't going to require my getting into a saddle."

The attempt at levity was greeted as mirthlessly as if Janus were summing up for a jury in one of his famous murder trials. "I assure you this is strictly business," he said, brusquely. "I'll have my driver pick you up at your door in the Rolls Sunday morning at eight and take you back as soon as we're through."

WITH A MOURNFUL sigh that lifted his great shoulders and swelled his massive chest, Wiggins found himself in the back of a marvelous automobile offering the comfort of plush seating, a bottle of champagne in a silver ice bucket, and a bowl of chilled strawberries with heavy cream. Sunday's *New York Times* had been carefully culled of the sections that nobody ever read, unless the object was finding employment through the classified ads, a rental apartment, condominium, or co-op in the real estate section, or exotic vacation ideas in the travel pages.

By the time the Rolls had glided across the George Washington Bridge and with the silence of a cat turned northward on the Palisades Parkway, he had skimmed the *Book Review* and found, as usual, page after page of tiresome critics whose reviews always seemed to be longer than the books they were assessing. Once at a literary cocktail party he had marshaled the temerity to suggest to an editor of the review that if less space were given over to windy critics about books that few would read, more authors might also be reviewed. He had been answered with the amazed glare one would expect if one showed up at a black-tie affair in a pair of faded jeans and scuffed cowboy boots—except, of course, if one happened to be Theodore Roosevelt Janus.

Presently, the Rolls-Royce left the highway for the narrow, winding country roads of Stone County. Peering through the window at the idyllic landscape, he imagined himself in the role of Dr. John H. Watson in "The Copper Beeches," listening intently while Sherlock Holmes mused that the lowest and vilest of the alleys in London did not represent a more dreadful record of sin than the smiling and beautiful countryside.

While Holmes's cases frequently drew him to the countryside, the mere thought of leaving his town house on West Thirty-fifth Street had been anathema to Nero Wolfe. On the rare occasion when the great detective did exit his abode he traveled by automobile, but grudgingly. Even with his trusted aide Archie Goodwin at the steering wheel, Wolfe would clam up and sit anxiously on the edge of the seat, gripping the strap in case he might have to leap for his life.

To ride in a taxi was invariably "a frantic dash." He had done so to visit Archie in a hospital and another time for the purpose of saving his capable assistant's life. And he had called at police headquarters when Archie happened to be locked up in a jail, prompting Wolfe to direct his considerable outrage in the direction of Inspector Cramer, along with a threat to have the police force abolished.

Like himself, Wiggins mused as the Rolls proceeded, only the most extraordinary occasions not connected to a case could entice Wolfe out-of-doors. Once a year he went to the Metropolitan Orchid Show. In 1934 he had left his residence to dine at the same table as Albert Einstein. And rarely did he go to the scene of a crime. He expected Archie Goodwin to do all the legwork and return to report back with all the pertinent details, which Wolfe then pieced together like parts of a jigsaw puzzle to produce the solution to a typically New York sort of crime.

This was not to say that other cities were devoid of stimulating murder and mayhem. Los Angeles had supplied readers of mysteries the cases of hard-boiled private dick Philip Marlowe and a handful of other latter-day fictional sleuths. And there had been occasionally notable actual crimes, such as the Menendez brothers, the O. J. Simpson case, the murder of Bill Cosby's son, and the sensational murder trial that had kept Theodore R. Janus on the West Coast for a year-long media circus. Yet it wasn't the crime that transfixed the nation via television. Its attraction had been Janus's dazzlingly effective swordsmanship in his legal duel with Maggie Dane.

Soon, thanks to his middle-of-the-night brainstorm, Wiggins thought with immense pride and satisfaction as the Rolls took him northward, there would be a grand reunion of the most exciting pairing of male and female lawyers since Spencer Tracy had battled Katharine Hepburn in the film *Adam's Rib*.

Alive with anticipation, he found himself suddenly emerging from woods at the crest of a hill affording spectacular views on all sides of the glories of the Hudson Valley. Executing another turn, the Rolls moved slowly along a dirt road that seemed little more than a cow path. Then he saw a large gray fieldstone house that seemed to crouch like a mountain lion about to spring.

Coatless but wearing a black vest, Janus leaned in the front doorway.

"I'm so grateful that you came up, Wiggins," he said, taking him by the arm and leading him indoors. "Frankly, you're the only one I could ever entrust with this matter."

Following Janus down a long corridor whose walls were hung with framed pencil and pastel sketches of him done by courtroom artists for television news programs, he came to a large office that appeared to be a museum to Janus's namesake. Displayed on every table, shelf, and wall were images and artifacts of Theodore Roosevelt as Dakota Territory cowboy, police commissioner of New York City, vice president and then president of the United States, father and family man at his Sagamore Hill home at Oyster Bay, South American jungle explorer, with his foot resting on a head of a lion on a big-game safari in Africa, and Bull Moose Party candidate for president in 1912.

"You have quite an impressive collection," Wiggins said as Janus directed him into a large Victorian era armchair that faced a life-size oil painting of Janus by the renowned portraitist Kevin Gordon. A small shelf beneath it held leather-bound copies of all the books Janus authored.

"When I'm dead and gone," Janus said, seating himself behind a massive desk that looked old enough to have been Roosevelt's, "all this goes to the Smithsonian."

"That's very generous and patriotic of you."

"Have you given any thought to what will become of your very impressive collection of Sherlockiana and your Nero Wolfe first editions?"

"Not a whit."

"You should do something about it. Life is short. My office will be happy to make all the arrangements for you."

"Maybe I'll take a leaf from the pharoahs of Egypt and have it all buried with me."

"I know several Sherlockians and a few Wolfe Pack members who would have you dug up and your grave looted in less than the proverbial New York minute," Janus said, reaching for a handsome cigar humidor. "Do you mind if I smoke?"

"Of course not. It's your house."

Janus opened the lid. "These are Cubans," he said, carefully looking for flaws. "They were smuggled in from London. Have one."

"Thanks, but being a Sherlockian, I'm a pipe man."

"The ever present briar. But Sherlock smoked cigars, too."

"With a cigar stuck in my mouth I'd look like the character Clemenza in *The Godfather*."

With the cigar lighted, Janus looked at it admiringly and said, "I'm at a loss for words to express how deeply honored I am to be this year's recipient of the Nero Wolfe Award."

"I assure you the honor is ours."

Janus puffed smoke and watched it drift away. "The way I've heard it, not every member of the committee felt that way."

"That's water under the bridge."

"Indeed so." He carefully laid the long cigar in a crystal ashtray. "But it was your nomination of me for the Wolfe award, and your persistence on my behalf, that has brought you and me to this moment. I know you have to be wondering why I've dragged you all the way up here on a Sunday morning. You have surely deduced that it was not simply to express my gratitude."

"That's true."

"I did so because you are the only person whom I can trust, and this house is the only place I feel truly safe."

Wiggins gasped. "Good lord, Theo, whatever do you mean?"

Retrieving the cigar, Janus smiled. "I have every reason to believe there will soon be an attempt to kill me."

"An attempt to kill you? By whom?"

"I have no idea. I only know someone has already tried."

Wiggins struggled to his feet. "When? Where? How?"

"Last week. I was exercising my favorite horse. The shot was fired from a passing car. I actually heard the bullet zing past my right ear." He dug into a pocket, drew out a wad of gray metal, and held it between thumb and forefinger. "This is it. I found it in a tree trunk."

Wiggins returned to his chair. "Because I did not learn of this case of attempted murder in the press, you obviously did not report this to the police. Why not?"

"I'm working on the case in my own way."

"Excuse me, my friend, but to paraphrase a well-known legal maxim, a lawyer who hires himself as a detective has a fool for a client. You must go to the police now."

"With what? An uncorroborated story that would be trumpeted by the news media as a publicity stunt?"

"You have the bullet."

"I could have fired it into that tree myself. Besides, it is in no condition to be of value as evidence. You need the gun to make a ballistic match. To obtain the gun, you'd have to locate its owner. Meanwhile, I want you to keep the bullet and tell no one about this conversation. In the event I am murdered, you can take it to your police friends."

"Theo, you can't risk your life by playing detective!"

"If this individual is to be caught, he has to be given the chance to try again."

"What if he tries and succeeds?"

Janus chuckled. "I will die with the satisfaction of having disappointed cardiologists who persist in telling me I must have bypass surgery immediately and warning me that if I do not quit drinking and smoking cigars I'll die of a massive heart attack. Well, if I am murdered, I hope before I croak there'll be time for one more drink and a last *oscuro* cigar."

PART TWO

The Wolfe Pack

3

The Reluctant Guest

"Either you're early," declared Chief of Detectives Harvey Goldstein, "or I'm late."

He carried a weighty shopping bag in each fist.

Laying aside the thick Mancuso file, Detective Sgt. John Bogdanovic rose from a butter-soft leather chair and reached for the bags.

"My heart attack was over a year ago," Goldstein said as he stepped past his rangy, muscular aide. "I appreciate that I am well past fifty, as well as a tad thin of head hair, a little saggy in the midriff, and nearsighted, and I realize we're in the middle of a cold wave, but I really am perfectly capable of toting my bags. The owner of Usual Suspects sends regards."

Bogdanovic retreated to the chair. "Has it occurred to you that you probably constitute Wiggins's entire margin of profit? How many books do you buy from him each week?"

The bags went on top of a desk. "Any amount expended in any mystery bookshop is damn well spent. There can never be too many places for a person to go to engage in the normal recreation of noble minds. In this instance, the detective is Nero Wolfe. By the way, you've been invited to the Black Orchid Banquet."

A puzzled frown creased Bogdanovic's lean face. "I had no idea you were into flowers."

Goldstein sighed impatiently. "The Black Orchid Banquet is the annual dinner given in honor of the central character in all the volumes in these bags. In addition to being the greatest detective in American crime fiction, Nero Wolfe was expert in the field of orchidaceae."

Bogdanovic's puzzlement twisted into grimace. "Oh, gawd. Is

this another gang of grown-ups like the Baker Street Irregulars who pretend detectives in mystery stories were real?"

"The Wolfe Pack is similar to that Sherlockian group," said Goldstein as he lifted a dozen paperbacks and a handful of hardcover books from bags to desktop, "only Wolfies aren't quite as serious about Nero as the BSI boys are regarding Sherlock."

Bogdanovic snorted. "Boys is right."

Goldstein's smile was tolerant. "As chairman of the steering committee, Wiggins has done me the honor of asking me to make one of the toasts that will precede the presentation of the coveted Nero Wolfe Award to Theodore Janus."

Bogdanovic lurched up. *"Janus?* These Wolfe people are going to honor the mob's number one mouthpiece?"

"In addition to being the country's most famous criminal defense lawyer, Janus is author of a Nero Wolfe encyclopedia," Goldstein said, holding up a ponderous paperback. "This is it. An astonishing feat of scholarship!"

Bogdanovic crossed the large office to a window with a view of the flat sprawl of Brooklyn beyond the East River. He stood with hands in the pockets of tan slacks, drawing back a brown jacket to reveal a tan shoulder holster holding a black Glock automatic pistol. In Goldstein's years as a sergeant the departmental weapon had been Smith and Wesson's .38-caliber snub-nose police special revolver. Clipped to the tan belt around the young detective's trim waist was a gray beeper. The left pocket of the coat contained a cell phone no larger than a billfold. Just down the corridor in his immaculate office Bogdanovic had the latest computer technology. Its bewildering array of related equipment linked him to cyberspace-traveling law enforcers against whom criminals had an even bleaker prospect of getting away with it than their kind in the alarmingly increasingly distant and uncomplicated time of Goldstein's youth.

Recognizing a stance that was invariably prelude to a John Bogdanovic remonstrance, he sighed. "All right, Sergeant. What's really eating you?"

Bogdanovic spoke without turning. "I do not think the chief of detectives should be socializing with a guy who is linked to organized crime. Especially with this Mancuso thing going on."

"Because Janus defends mobsters doesn't make him one."

"There's another reason I'm against you taking part in this banquet," Bogdanovic said, wheeling around. "I don't think you should be hobnobbing with the shyster who got Morgan Griffith off with a slap on the wrist."

"Twenty-five to life without parole is a slap on the wrist?"

The lanky detective returned to his chair and flung himself into it dejectedly. "Griffith should've got the death penalty."

Both men fell silent as their thoughts turned back two years to the murder that had introduced them to a remarkable detective by the name of Arlene Flynn.

Goldstein smiled. "Bogdanovic and Flynn! You two were great together! She shouldn't be wasting all that talent in the sticks. Working for me she could earn twice what she gets with the Stone County district attorney's squad. And she'd be more challenged."

"There are people for whom money isn't all that important. And a lot of people don't share your view that New York is top of the ladder in all things, including the crime department."

After a pensive moment Goldstein muttered, "Ridiculous!"

"I'll bet that if you asked Arlene she'd agree with me that it's not going to look right if you give Janus this silly award."

"In the first place, it's not a silly award. Secondly, I am not the person who'll give him the award. I'm delivering a toast to Lily Rowan. In the Wolfe novels she is a girlfriend of Nero Wolfe's assistant, Archie Goodwin. At the banquet Lily is being represented by someone who is an expert on Wolfe. She will be the one presenting the award to Janus."

"Well she can do it without me. Wiggins can count me out."

"Not so fast with regrets, John-boy. The woman in question happens to your favorite prosecutor from the other coast."

"Maggie Dane? She is going to be there?"

Goldstein drummed stubby fingers atop the stack of books. "Johnny, I've never seen such a look of surprise on your mug."

"I don't get it," Bogdanovic said, rising again. "How can she give an award to the guy who used every dirty legal trick there was to beat her in that travesty they had the nerve to call a murder trial out there in La La Land?"

"They go back a long way. Before she became a prosecutor in

Los Angeles, she was a junior associate in his firm right here in little old New York. I met her just after I had made lieutenant. She took my deposition in a two-bit assault case that involved an up-and-coming mobster we've all since come to know as Don Carlo Perillo, boss of bosses. I couldn't help laughing when I saw that among the legal papers she unloaded from her briefcase was the new Nero Wolfe novel, *A Family Affair.* I thought it was amusing that she'd be reading it while defending a crime-family member. That puts our initial encounter in the mid-1970s. Then she got married to an actor and gave up a promising career as a criminal defender to accompany her hubby to Hollywood. When it ended in a divorce she supported her son by going back to the law as a prosecutor. So you see, she and Janus are old friends. As to the Wolfe Pack's giving the award? One word: publicity. Our friend Wiggins is keenly aware that the reunion of Maggie Dane and Theo Janus for the first time since the big trial will bring out the press in droves."

"That is my point! Do you really want to see yourself on the front pages in a picture with him all duded up in that ridiculous cowboy getup, ever present big fat stogie in his hand, smug smile on his suntanned kisser, hugging you as if he owns you?"

"If there's to be a picture in the papers, I'm sure it won't include me. Maggie Dane is much more photogenic. And newsworthy. She is also such an authority on Wolfe that Wiggins has banned her from taking part in the quiz that is a Black Orchid ritual. That's why if I'm to avoid making a fool of myself when I get up to introduce her I'd better do some brushing up on the corpus."

Bogdanovic's expression went blank. "The what?"

"The body of work by Sir Arthur Conan Doyle is called the *canon.* Nero Wolfe stories are the *corpus.*"

"As in *delicti,* no doubt."

"It's actually a tongue-in-cheek reference to Nero Wolfe's avoirdupois. In movies long before your time he was portrayed by Edward Arnold, back in the thirties. On radio he was played by Sydney Greenstreet, the fat man in *The Maltese Falcon.* On TV it was William Conrad. He was suitably chubby, though not as immense as Wolfe. Nero tipped the scale at a seventh of a ton."

"I can see why Wiggins fits right in with that group. He's got to weigh at least three hundred."

"You're going to fit in, too, once the Wolfies learn your name. Wolfe was of Balkan ancestry. Same as you."

Bogdanovic looked up interestedly. "He was Croatian?"

"Montenegrin, actually. Now, please bring me up to speed on the Paulie Mancuso situation."

"The DA's people are stashing him until trial, months away." He made a sour face. "Evidently, they don't trust us enough to tell us where they've put him."

"I trust you're endeavoring to find out the hiding place."

"I already have. He's at the Hotel Radcliffe."

"That's pretty upscale. The district attorney's office must have gotten a sizable increase in its budget."

"Maybe Paulie's dipped into his ill-gotten gains so he can live in comfort before the wizards who run the witness protection program give him a new identity and ship him off to some town in the Midwest."

"You've done an excellent job in locating him, John. Archie Goodwin couldn't have done a better job of ferreting."

4

For the People

DESPITE THE DISGUISE of a baggy pants suit, enormous black sunglasses, and a large straw hat with floppy brim meant to further conceal long red hair that she had pulled up into a knot beneath it, she found herself recognized all the way through the airport. Suddenly, after a fourteen-year career and more than a hundred successful murder prosecutions, a television camera in the courtroom had transformed her from just one more familiar face around the Los Angeles County Criminal Court into a national celebrity. Yet amid the embarrassment of being asked for autographs as she hurried toward her departure gate, she found some comfort in the unanimous opinion of those who delayed her that the outcome of the trial was nothing less than an assault against the American system of justice and an affront to common sense and decency.

At a newsstand she bought *Good Cigar* magazine with a large cover picture of Theodore Janus wreathed in a blue cloud and a provocative headline: IS THIS MAN'S LAW ALL SMOKE AND MIRRORS?

In a bookstore she purchased the new legal thriller by John Grisham.

Although she could cite a few exceptions in crime fiction, all of them men, Los Angeles Deputy District Attorney Margaret Rosemary Dane viewed the overall lack of prosecutors as principal characters as a disappointing flaw in the mystery genre. Lawyers who did solve crimes were invariably working on behalf of someone who had been mistakenly charged with a crime or, even worse, set up by the police, often in collusion with a prosecutor. In the courtroom dramas of theater, film, television, and books, the rule seemed to be that true nobility of character resided only at the tables occupied by a Perry Mason rather than a District Attorney Hamilton Berger. For every capable exception to the rule, such as the prosecutors on *Law and Order*, television was replete with the Perry Masons.

In detective novels the officers of the law from the cops to the prosecutors were often described as dolts or impediments to be overcome. Sherlock Holmes faced inept Scotland Yarders. Nero Wolfe had to tangle with Inspector L. T. Cramer.

With a smile, she wondered what Wolfe would have made of Harvey Goldstein. And how might Harvey respond if the weighty private sleuth stormed into his office, as he had into Cramer's, and threatened to have the police abolished?

When cases moved out of the hands of investigators and into courtrooms the drama in fiction, as in real life, lay in whether the defense could outwit and outmaneuver the prosecution and get the accused off. In cases in which Nero Wolfe had investigated, Assistant District Attorney Irving Mandelbaum, who shortened his name to Mandel, and Westchester County prosecutors Fletcher M. Anderson and Cleveland Archer had no need to worry that Wolfe's case might be undercut by a defense lawyer's histrionics.

"A trial is theater," Janus had taught her, first as student and lately as adversary. "If you want to take the measure of the social, moral, and political character of a nation's people," he said, "look at their attitude toward major criminal trials. Study the great legal shows, Maggie. You can learn more from them than you'll ever pick up in a classroom."

The first trial had grabbed the headlines from coast to coast not because the crime happened in a big city where awful things were expected to occur but in the sedate and civilized town of Fall River, Massachusetts, in 1895. Charged with taking an ax and hacking to death Andrew Borden and his second wife, Abby, was the sweetly mannered and demure daughter of Andrew's first marriage, Elizabeth. In an inkling of things to come, reporters rushed from all over the country to cover what headline writers trumpeted as "the trial of the century."

Faced with a weak case put on by the prosecution, the jury deliberated for one hour and returned to court to declare Lizzie not guilty. Word of the acquittal spread like wildfire through Fall River and by telegraph to newspapers across the country and around the world. In another foreshadow of what such sensational trials in the next century would produce, many who had not been in the court during the trial, but had followed the case in press coverage, were shocked by the shortness of the jury's deliberations and so outraged by the verdict that Lizzie ultimately moved from Fall River to spend the rest of her life shunned by a public that gleefully recited:

> Lizzie Borden took an ax
> And gave her mother forty whacks.
> When she saw what she had done
> She gave her father forty-one.

A hundred years after her name got an enduring place in the annals of America's most famous criminal trials, another murder case was to end with the jury finding the defendant not guilty and a vast majority of the public in angry disagreement. Almost immediately, another piece of poetic public opinion went around:

> O. J. Simpson took a knife
> And used it on his former wife;
> And when he saw that she was dead,
> He slashed Ron Goldman toe to head.

In the hundred years between Lizzie Borden and O. J. Simpson thousands of men and women had been charged and put on trial for murder, with most convicted, but every now and then one of these cases of homicide was vaulted into such a state of intense public interest and insatiable curiosity that it, too, became "the trial of the century."

In 1906, millionaire playboy Harry Thaw's troubled mind was obsessed with the beautiful twenty-year-old model who had become his wife, the former Evelyn Nesbitt. But neither could Harry rid his mind of Evelyn's former fatherly benefactor and lover, Stanford White. If the lurid stories she had whispered to Harry were to be believed, the country's most famous architect had been a sexual pervert. Consequently, when Thaw strode up to White while New York's most celebrated people enjoyed late supper in White's magnificent restaurant atop Madison Square Garden, whipped out a pistol, and fired three bullets into the architect's body, then declared that he did it to save his wife's honor, defense lawyers claimed that such a deed could only be declared a justifiable act.

With the best defense his riches could buy, Thaw pleaded not guilty, dined on sumptuous meals catered in his jail cell by the city's finest restaurants and lobster palaces, and calmly waited for the trial to begin and its star witness—Evelyn—to take the witness stand. He expected her to leave the jurors with no choice but to exonerate a man who had defended her honor.

From shooting to verdict, the public doted on all the lurid details while viewing the drama as a lesson in morality. Unlike a morality play, however, the trial of Harry Thaw did not have a happy ending. The jurors proved incapable of reaching a verdict. With a mistrial declared, Harry faced a second trial at which the defense came to court with a fresh strategy. This time he pleaded temporary insanity and beat the rap.

In the decade known as the Roaring Twenties excess seemed to be an American preoccupation. In 1926 Connecticut's murder trial of Gerald Chapman (the first man to be named Public Enemy Number One) set a style for raucus press coverage of a man who had come to be regarded by the public as a kind of folk hero.

That same decade provided the press opportunity to tweak the public's passion for a sensational murder and a lively trial. Set against the vivid tapestry of the Roaring Twenties, a case that Damon Runyon called "the dumbbell murder" provided a boisterous and uninhibited decade with a show involving a brigade of free-booting reporters that Runyon called "the best show in town." Its seemingly mundane central character, Ruth Snyder Brown, became a national fixation.

Also on the scene was a fledgling court reporter by the name of James M. Cain, who would base his book *Double Indemnity* and the movie of the same title in part on the case. The murderous housewife was played by Barbara Stanwyck with a sultry cunning that Ruth Snyder would have envied. In the role of the hapless helper in homicide, however, Fred MacMurray had seemed much too smart to have been patterned on Ruth's hapless paramour, Judd Gray. Ruth then claimed one more niche in criminal history. She was the last woman executed at Sing Sing.

The year she and Judd began their fateful journey into the annals of criminal trials had been a time of triumphal pageantry and spotlight for a man known for acute shyness. And in a case of life imitating art, aviator Charles Lindbergh was launched on an odyssey that would validate the words of one of the 1920s' most successful novelists. F. Scott Fitzgerald had declared, "Show me a hero and I'll write you a tragedy."

In the trial of Bruno Richard Hauptmann for the kidnap and murder of Lindbergh's infant son the court proceedings were the first to be covered by newsreel cameras and radio.

Almost as sensational as the Lindbergh case was the "thrill killing" of a young boy by a pair of brainy young sons of wealthy Illinois families. But the central figure of the trial of Richard Loeb and Nathan Leopold in 1924 was their controversial defense lawyer—Clarence Darrow—whose strategy was to introduce psychiatric evidence and to challenge the use of the death penalty.

In 1943 the murder of Manhattan socialite Patrica Lonergan and the trial of her husband, a pilot of the Royal Canadian Air Force, marked the crime-journalism debut of Dorothy Kilgallen. The daughter of a respected Chicago newspaperman, "Dotty" broke the story of a homosexual relationship between Wayne Lonergan and Patricia's wealthy father. The trial provided Americans a respite from the news of the Second World War. Did Wayne really kill Patricia? A jury said he had. Many people doubted it.

Kilgallen would be at the heart of the murder trial of a handsome doctor in 1954. The case of Sam Sheppard provided the inspiration for *The Fugitive* on television and in a movie. An appeal of the guilty verdict had freed "Dr. Sam" and introduced America to a lawyer who became as famous in defense as Clarence Darrow—F. Lee Bailey. Had Dotty not been busy writing a book on the Sheppard case, had she not been in failing health, had she not been promising to reveal "the truth" behind the assassination of President John F. Kennedy, and had she not died under rather mysterious circumstances, she certainly would have covered the

1965 trial of Dr. Carl Coppolino, also defended by Lee Bailey, and the one that had catapulted to fame another brilliant young phenomenon in the ranks of defenders—Theodore Roosevelt Janus.

The arrest of Richard Edwards for the shotgun murder of one of the guards of an armored car as it made a delivery of half a million dollars to a bank in a suburban shopping mall had led to a nest of 1960s revolutionaries. The result of Janus's portrayal of Edwards as victim of society's failings rather than a criminal was transformation of the prosecution's straightforward murder case into a political show trial. Convicted only of manslaughter, Edwards served a mere eight years.

A decade after the Edwards trial another involved a doctor. This time it was Jeffrey MacDonald, a physician serving with the U.S. Army's elite "green beret" special forces, tried for the murders of his wife and two small daughters. MacDonald's case was the subject of a best-selling book by Joe McGinnis that elevated a new style for writing about such sensational cases and fostered a profitable genre of books begun with Kilgallen's tome on the Sheppard case—True Crime.

Like readers of detective novels, Americans soon found whodunits in real life as they and their system of justice met a new kind of criminal—the serial killer—in the form of Ted Bundy, Wayne Williams, John Gacy, and Jeffrey Dahmer.

When private school headmistress Jean Harris shot and killed the famed author of the Scarsdale Diet, Dr. Herman Tarnower, the 1980 case and its entourage of women reporters put the abuse of women on trial.

The trial and subsequent legal civil-trial entanglements of subway gunman Bernhard Goetz, a popular hero, was followed in the public's attention by Robert Chambers in "the Preppie Murder Case" of 1986, the next year's Billionaire's Boys Club murders, and the trials of the Menendez brothers for shotgunning their parents to death. Excuses were offered to justify all this violence. Then came the O. J. Simpson trial with F. Lee Bailey sharing the spotlight as a "Dream Team" of defenders put the police on trial.

What was hardly ever involved in a trial that provoked such wide public absorption was a weighty matter of law or some issue of historical, social, political, or economic significance. But if a case was not important to anyone but those directly involved, what explained its notoriety?

The personalities of the people in the case? Occasionally.

The temper of the times? Sometimes.

Sex was almost always an element.

But what factor could be discerned in *every* instance? From Elizabeth Borden to Orenthal James Simpson what was the common denominator? What was it that exalted one murder so that it could become a part of the warp and woof of our history, even legend? That factor, Maggie believed, was the tantalyzing possibility that through clever lawyering the accused could get away with it. The result was that heroes of America's system of justice were rarely the prosecutors. Glory, fame, and riches went to defenders like the one who had been summoned across the country to do battle with her in yet another trial of the century.

Janus had won the case, in the opinion of all the people who recognized her in the airport, through trickery and legalistic chicanery. And, as her flight to New York City was called and she pondered the purpose of her journey, she was certain that few of them would have approved of her acceptance of the invitation from the Wolfe Pack to honor Janus with its most prestigious award.

Even the chairman of the steering committee had told her he would understand if she chose to refuse to do it. "It certainly is going to be controversial," Wiggins had warned. "You could find yourself being pilloried by a press that has been depicting you lately as a saint."

As she replied with a laugh, she thought of a perfect answer in the form of a quotation from the Wolfe corpus: "The essence of sainthood is expiation."

5

Gambit

DURING THE SHORT stroll from bookstore to subway, only three passersby abandoned the taciturn demeanor that comes with being a New Yorker to remark upon the spectacle of the huge figure made larger by a billowing gray tweed Inverness cape and the matching deerstalker cap. After all, there was nothing unusual about a fat man in New York City, even one with an ebony walking stick with a silver handle in the shape of the Maltese falcon that had been a clue in the solving of a murder. But the encountering of someone dressed like Sherlock Holmes at four o'clock on a Saturday afternoon the week before Christmas, when one expected to see several portly men in Santa Claus outfits, was more than enough to turn the heads of even the most blasé New Yorker.

The first, a gentleman with a chesterfield overcoat and a hurried expression, had muttered, "Good afternoon, Sherlock," and kept on walking.

A block farther, one of a gaggle of giggling schoolgirls had blurted, "Hey, get a look at him!"

The last, an elderly black man with a grizzled gray beard, extended the ubiquitous panhandler's paper coffee cup and said, "I don't have matches to sell like Neville Sinclair had in *The Man With the Twisted Lip,* but I could surely use whatever spare shillings you might have in your pockets, Mr. Holmes."

A dollar poorer, Wiggins descended into the subway and took up a position at the end of the platform in the expectation that the last car of the train when it pulled in would not prove to be so crowded that there was no room for a large man. Only then did he chuckle in admiration of the street begger's savvy in having quickly deduced upon encountering a man dressed up like Sherlock Holmes that reference to a classic Holmesian story concerning another panhandler would result in the windfall it had succeeded in producing.

When the train arrived and the doors of the cars opened, the Wiggins strategy in choosing to ride in the last was vindicated. Side-by-side unoccupied seats amply accommodated a posterior as formidable and expansive as the behind of Stout's brainchild, although the very idea of Wolfe taking a subway was preposterous in the extreme.

As for trains in general, Wolfe had said, "No publication either before or after the invention of printing, no technological treatise and no political or scientific creed, has ever been as narrowly dogmatic or as offensively arbitrary in its prejudices as a railway timetable."

Certainly, a suggestion that Wolfe venture down into the subway would have been dismissed out of hand. And were he to see such a thing as the subway train rumbling into the Fifty-first Street station of the Lexington Avenue line he certainly would have uttered the most extreme word in the Wolfe lexicon: "Pfui!"

Four stops and twelve minutes later as Wiggins exited the subway at Twenty-third Street and Park Avenue South, he stood two blocks from the Gramercy Park Hotel and the culmination of the months of meticulous planning required to ensure that this year's Black Orchid affair surpassed all previous gatherings of the Wolfe Pack.

Parked along Lexington Avenue opposite the hotel, vans of four local television stations and a cable network made it clear that he had been right in telling Maggie Dane that her appearance with Theodore Janus would be controversial.

He had defended murderous radicals in the 1960s as patriots akin to Minutemen standing up for liberty at the Concord Bridge. Was it not Janus who had with a straight face painted a portrait of that newspaper heiress from California who had played footsie with black radicals as a victim and not a perpetrator? Who but Theodore Janus could have gotten off the beast who had strangled so many poor old women in Boston with an insanity plea? Janus's word stretching had succeeded in redefining federal wiretaps in the case against the godfather of organized crime as outrageous intrusion of a law-abiding citizen's privacy. The exhortation had resulted in freedom for the very man heard on the tapes ordering what amounted to wholesale murder, while the one who had gone to prison had been a low-level hood who cooperated with authorities in planting the wiretaps.

Could any other lawyer have managed the deft hedging that sent Morgan Griffith to federal prison instead of death row for the murders of Jonathan Dodge and two others, as well as his proven record as a traitorous assassin?

Who but Janus could carry off such a conceit as constantly wearing western-style outfits, even in the courtrooms of New York City? Yet the clothing served as a silent reminder that he bore the name of the ultimate easterner who went west, that famous coiner of a phrase that was the bedrock of American society, "the square deal," the old Rough Rider himself, Theodore Roosevelt. At least a dozen convicted felons across the country had reaped the benefit of Janus's impassioned pleas to parole boards for a grant of clemency that invariably concluded with the words of TR:

> Surely everyone of us who knows his own heart must know that he too may stumble, and should be anxious to help his brother who has stumbled. When the criminal has been punished, if he then shows a sincere desire to lead a decent and upright life, he should be given the chance, he should be helped and not hindered; and if he makes good, he should receive that respect from others which so often aids in creating self-respect—the most valuable of all possessions.

The foremost criminal defense attorney in the nation being a fan of Nero Wolfe had come as a surprise, for it was Wolfe who had said of the lawyers, "They are inveterate hedgers. They think everything has two sides, which is nonsense. They are insufferable word-stretchers."

Janus had proved to be exactly the sort of man who could read a compliment into Wolfe's condescension and live up to all the unflattering adjectives applied to him in the stern court of public opinion, as he recently had done in the sensational case in which the prosecution was led by his former protégé.

Entering the hotel lobby, Wiggins smiled gleefully at seeing them together for the first time since Janus had prevailed over her at trial. Side by side, each with an arm around the other, they beamed in the glare of floodlights.

Aglow with delight, he let his mind reel back to the tempest he had provoked in the steering committee meeting by his daring gambit in nominating Janus for the Nero Wolfe award.

Thrilled with both the outcome and himself, he also noted Janus alive, swaggering, grinning, and basking in the glories of his renown.

6

Booby Trap

"THE FIRST TIME I heard you make a speech," said Bogdanovic as he searched for a parking place a block from the Gramercy Park Hotel, "I was minutes away from being elevated from probationary cadet to police officer. You were a mere captain. I can quote almost verbatim what you said."

Goldstein shifted uneasily in the passenger seat. "I do hope this isn't going to be embarrassing."

"You said, 'Police work does not require genius. What is needed is common honesty, common sense, and common courage. Police work requires the practical virtues—the commonplace virtues that are absolutely essential if we are ever to make this force and this city what they should be. If these virtues are lacking, no amount of cleverness will save us.' I was impressed!"

"You ought to have been. I happened to be quoting Police Commissioner Theodore Roosevelt."

"You wound up your speech by telling us fledgling coppers that we could learn a lot about solving crimes if we were to read detective novels."

"Good advice that, in your case, appears to have gone in one ear and out the other."

"That's not true, Chief. I have *tried*. May I remind you that my study of the cases of Agatha Christie's little Belgian sleuth, Hercule Poirot, played a key role in ending the murder spree by Andrew Sloan and his girlfriend last year?"

"Proving my point about the importance of police reading mystery novels."

"What will I be hearing in your speech tonight?"

"It's not a speech. It's a toast. But I may take the opportunity to speak in long overdue defense of Inspector Cramer of the Homicide Squad and his day's version of Johnny Bogdanovic, Sgt. Purley Stebbins, as well as Lt. George Rowcliff. And I may even get around to praising Police Commissioner William Skinner and Deputy Commissioner O'Hara, who had the nicest office in the old headquarters building."

"Your office in One Police Plaza isn't what I'd describe as being uncomfortable."

"Good old Two hundred forty Centre Street." Goldstein sighed as Bogdanovic parked. "I miss that drafty old castle. It had real character!" Stepping from the car, he surveyed the venerable buildings around an iron-fenced, lightly snow-dusted square studded with old trees and laced with gravel footpaths. "Look at these fabulous houses. What a grand piece of real estate!"

"May I remind you, Chief, that just over there at number twelve once resided Gerald Chapman, America's first Public Enemy Number One? The late Jonathan Dodge's town house is a block from here."

"But he wasn't murdered there, was he? That deed took place in an apartment on the Upper West Side and the body was dumped in Stone County. And even if Dodge had been killed here, if I could afford it I'd love to live in one of these houses and I wouldn't care if my next-door neighbor was an ax murderer."

Standing on a curb as the traffic passed, Bogdanovic peered across Twenty-first Street at the hotel. "I stayed here once when I was in the academy. There'd been a blizzard and the whole damned city was shut down. I was living way out in Queens and drove in every day. I didn't even try digging that old heap of a car out. I think half my class was put up here. It's a very nice hotel. The place was full of Air France airline stewardesses that night, as I recall."

"*Vive la France,*" Goldstein said, stepping from the curb to the street. "*Vive la différence!*"

Dominating the northwest corner of Twenty-first and Lexington Avenue, the Gramercy Park Hotel rose seventeen floors. Pushing through a revolving door, they entered a lobby that seemed far too small for the crowd. Behind a tree of microphones in the middle of the throng stood Dane and Janus.

"Meet the press," Goldstein said grumpily. "The news media and celebrities, bees to the honeycomb."

"In Janus's case," grumbled Bogdanovic, "it's more like a swarm of flies on a pile of manure."

Frequently shouting over one another, the reporters acted as if the fame of those being questioned afforded those with press credentials hanging from cords around their necks the privilege of abandoning the courtesy of formality in addressing strangers for the familiarity of first names. She was neither Miss Dane nor the politically correct Ms. Dane, but Maggie. The man in fringed buckskin jacket, clutching an unlit long black cigar and towering over her, was not Mr. Janus, or even Theodore, but Theo.

"Maggie, how does it feel now that you're as famous as the man who used to be your boss?"

"Hopeful that it won't last."

"Theo, how did you feel about Maggie as your adversary?"

"Proud."

"How would you have felt if Maggie had won?"

"I never doubted for a moment that she'd lose. That's not a criticism of Maggie. She did the best she could with what she had to work with."

"Meaning?"

"A prosecutor plays the hand that's dealt. Maggie was given losing cards from the start. Evidence the police had was garbage. Their witnesses were ineptitude incarnate. It is a tribute to her skills that she almost turned a sow's ear into a silk purse."

"Speaking of purses, some observers say that it was only because your client had money to hire you that he got off."

"My client got off, to use your term, because the people's case was riddled from the beginning with reasonable doubt."

"Maggie, are you appealing?"

Janus blared, "Just look at her! That face! The flaming red hair! Those smiling green Irish eyes. Is she appealing? Why, the evidence speaks for itself."

"Maggie, are you appealing the *verdict?* Might there be a new trial somewhere down the road?"

Standing at the rear of the crowd, Goldstein grunted. "What an idiotic question."

"The people get no second bite of the apple," Dane replied. "Appeals can only be made by the defense. Unless there has been a mistrial, the constitutional provision against double jeopardy prohibits the state from holding a second trial."

"Even if new evidence turns up?"

"Mr. Janus's client could confess and it wouldn't matter. He cannot be tried again on the same charge."

"Isn't that unfair to the people?"

"We Irish have a saying. Life is unfair," Dane said as a TV news cameraman moved to capture her and Janus from behind with the crowd of reporters arrayed before them.

"There's a rumor out in L.A.," said a woman representing a supermarket tabloid, "that you're so disgusted with how the case ended that you are thinking about giving up on the law."

"I'll answer for Maggie," Janus said. "Irish never quit."

"How about a book, Maggie?"

She smiled broadly. "I recommend any novel by Rex Stout."

"Theo, what about you? Are you writing a book on the case?"

"I've got a lot of people still angry with me for the one I wrote five years ago, *Janus for the Defense*. There are so many clients who were upset with me that I vowed not to do a sequel. I am, however, planning a book."

A young man with a camera slung from a shoulder and grasping a traditional reporter's spiral-ring notebook pleased Goldstein by beginning his question politely with "Mr. Janus, . . ."

Janus stood on the tips of his boots to peer over the heads of the reporters. "Is my father here?" he joked, looking around as if searching for something. "Whenever someone says 'Mr. Janus' I think my old man must be around."

When the laughter subsided, the young man continued, "How do you sleep at night?"

Still basking in the joviality, Janus replied, "I sleep in the raw!"

The reporter shook his head violently. "What I meant was, how can you sleep at night knowing that you make it possible for so many guilty people to go free? Do you ever think about the feelings of the people who loved the victims of these criminals that you got off?"

Bogdanovic whispered to Goldstein, "There's a booby trap."

With frozen smile, Janus said softly, "I don't free anyone, young man. Juries do. And when they have rendered their verdict of not guilty, I sleep with the clear conscience of a baby."

Thrusting himself anxiously before the microphones, Wiggins declared, "Time for only one more question."

A young woman asked, "Theo, were you surprised to find out that you'd be getting this award from Maggie?"

"To paraphrase Nero Wolfe," Janus replied, tilting back his Stetson hat, "there are two ways for a man to ruin a friendship. One is to lend a pal a lot of money. The other is to question the purity of a woman's gesture."

As Goldstein and Bogdanovic stepped aside from departing reporters and camera crews, a mammoth figure rushed toward them.

"Welcome, welcome," bellowed Wiggins. "Chief, you're looking swell!" Black eyes barely visible in the fleshy folds of his face rolled toward Bogdanovic. "And, you, dear Sergeant B.," he said, patting a slight bulge of the detective's jacket, "Still packing the old reliable Glock! How goes the daily tussle against the criminal element of our fair city?"

Bogdanovic shrugged. "We keep on trying."

"You're too modest. The murder rate is down sharply."

"Tell that to the victims."

"Oh, Sergeant B., please don't be dour. Let yourself go. Have yourself some fun this evening. Chief, order him to."

"John doesn't approve of your choice of guest of honor."

"He's not the only one. One member has resigned over it."

"The only way I could get John to attend," Goldstein went on, "was to promise he'd get to meet Maggie Dane."

Wiggins squeezed the hard bicep of Bogdanovic's shooting arm. "You shall meet her right now, Sergeant B. I am delighted to declare that cocktails are now being served."

7

Archie Meets Lily

SURROUNDED BY ADMIRERS, she could barely be seen as Wiggins employed formidable girth and a bulldozing voice to clear a path across a room that seemed much too small for the crowd. Reaching her, he declared, "Maggie, this is Detective Sgt. John Bogdanovic of the New York Police Department. Is he not the spitting image of Archie Goodwin?"

"I hope I'm not under arrest, Sergeant," she said, extending a small, delicate hand.

Although no one noticed but him, his big hand trembled as he reached for hers.

"Now be a good lad, Sergeant B.," Wiggins ordered. "Go to the bar and fetch the lady a glass of something for the toasts. Make it champagne. Ever since she went Hollywood, it's her favorite."

A few moments later he presented the drink. "Here you go, Miss Dane. Champagne for one."

Taking it, she said, "I see you know your corpus, Sergeant."

"Beg pardon?"

" 'Champagne for One.' One of Wolfe's finest cases," answered Wiggins as he waddled away in the direction of a cluster of men crowding around Janus. Holding a martini, he stood like an oak.

"I'm sorry to disappoint you," said Bogdanovic, "but that 'champagne for one' remark was sheer coincidence. I had no idea it was a title. On the subject of Nero Wolfe, I'm an ignoramus."

"Are you also an abstainer? You're not drinking."

He looked at her smilingly. "Never on duty."

The ring of a spoon-struck glass cut through the din. Then

came Wiggins's commanding voice. "Ladies and gentlemen, it's time for the first toast of the evening by Judge Reginald Simmons."

Thin to the point of being skeletal, he moved to the front of the room with the practiced dignity of his calling. "Appreciating that we all came here tonight for the drinks and the food, not a lot of talk, I'll be brief. Archie Goodwin is sharp, inquisitive, impetuous, skeptical, pertinacious, and resourceful. With those traits, this paragon ought to have been a judge. To Archie Goodwin!"

As a hundred voices echoed the name, Dane said to Bogdanovic, "Wiggins was right, Sergeant. You are the spitting image of Archie Goodwin."

Bogdanovic laughed nervously. "Is that a compliment?"

"Oh definitely. Archie is very handsome. The brown hair and brown eyes. Broad shoulders. Narrow hips. How tall are you?"

"Six-two."

"A little off there. Archie is a trace under six feet. You have his nose. It's a fine one, but, like Archie's, not perfect."

"It was broken twice in the Marine Corps."

"Archie was in the army."

"I got slugged in the schnoz once more when I was in the uniformed ranks of the force. A perpetrator who did not care to come along quietly expressed that opinion by throwing a brick at me. Then he got himself a Civil Liberties Union lawyer and filed a complaint alleging police brutality. Never mind that it was my nose that got broken and my uniform with blood on it."

"When did you put away the blues for plain clothes?"

"It seems like a lifetime."

"Like Archie you are obviously very particular about your wardrobe. You pay a lot for your suits and you take care of them. You don't go around with your coat pocket flaps pushed in. What about smoking?"

"I never miss an opportunity to light up a good a cigar."

"See if you can wangle one out of Theo. He's always got a couple on him. Serve him martinis with two olives before dinner and a good cigar after and he's a happy man."

"There's nothing like a good cigar. But I'll buy my own."

"When you're off duty what do you drink?"

"Whiskey. All kinds."

"How about martinis?"

"Occasionally I'll have one," he said, watching a waiter deliver Janus a fresh martini on a silver tray. "Just one!"

"This is truly uncanny. Archie once had four martinis to be sociable but when he realized he'd missed an important point of a case as a result of them he limited himself to one during working hours. I'd like to meet you off duty sometime. As the young lady said to Archie in *Over My Dead Body,* I've never had a drink with such a darned good-looking detective."

A glass chimed again. The room quieted. Wiggins announced, "Toasting Inspector Cramer will be our beloved writer of a dozen best-selling thrillers, the inimitable Marian Pickering Henry."

Although the author of very thick books, she made her salute to the policeman brief. "There can be no finer tribute to Cramer than the words of Nero Wolfe. He undoutedly means well. And we must never forget that Archie said of Inspector Cramer that he never fiddle-faddles much and he is by no means a nitwit."

Over laughter, shouts of "Here here," and clapping, Bogdanovic said to Dane, "Tell me about Lily Rowan. Are you like her?"

"Not a bit. First of all, Lily is very rich. I live off the salary of a deputy district attorney. She's a blond. Blue eyes. Mine are green. My father preferred to say they were emerald. He was Irish, as was Lily's father, so that's one thing Lily and I have in common. Plus a passion for opera. What about you?"

"Do I like opera? I went to a performance of *Aida* years ago. But my knowledge of operatic music is pretty much confined to the well-known arias and what I hear of it on programs with Luciano Pavarotti on television. When I go out I take in a movie."

"Action pictures, I'll bet."

"Actually, I prefer little movies with real people in them. Ones with good stories. I see enough violence on the job."

"Books?"

"The chief is always after me to read more detective novels. I prefer biography and history. American. What do you read?"

"Legal briefs mostly. But when I have time, John Grisham. Marian Pickering Henry. Agatha Christie. Rex Stout, of course."

"Surely you've read all the Nero Wolfe there is by now."

"You can never get tired of rereading Nero Wolfe. Your boss is right about reading mysteries. You can learn a lot. When I was starting out in law, my boss insisted I read up on all the famous trials in American history. As usual, Theodore R. Janus's counsel was right on point. I learned so much from him. *Still* learning. He's the best there is."

"That's pretty darn forgiving of you, considering what he did to undermine your case against that wife killer," he said, his eyes on Janus draining his martini glass. "Watching that guy on television, I felt like putting a fist through the screen. I was stunned when I heard you were giving Janus an award."

"Why shouldn't I? We're old friends. And he deserves it."

Again, Wiggins's voice cut through the clamor. "The rest of the toasts will come during dinner, which is now being served."

8

Poison à la Carte

"As to seating arrangements," said Wiggins, taking Bogdanovic by the arm. "On Chief Goldstein's advice, I have fixed it so that you will be as far away from Theodore Janus and as close to Maggie Dane as possible. The geography wasn't easy. You will be at table three. That's adjacent to the head table, where Chief Goldstein will be seated beside Theo. Sharing your table will be Judge Reginald Simmons, retired, and Oscar Pendelton, whom you know from that recent unpleasantness regarding Morgan Griffith. Oscar's companion is Marian Pickering Henry. Such a charmer for someone who finds time to cultivate a prizewinning garden and grind out best-selling thrillers as if her word processor were a sausage machine! The other two will be Nicholas Stamos, of our steering committee, and his absolutely stunning missus, Ariadne."

Finding Dane seated alone, Bogdanovic looked around the room and let out a sigh. "Banquet halls I have known."

"I gather you attend a lot of these dinners."

"The chief attends," he said, sitting. "I go along. There are a lot of crazies around who might want to settle a score."

Leaning close, she whispered, "Hence, the pistol under your coat."

"Most of the events he goes to are given by civic groups who want to hear what the police are doing about the crime problem. But you can never know about crowds. This is the first time I've been to this event."

As he spoke they were joined at the table by Pendelton and Henry. With closely trimmed gray beard and horn-rimmed eyeglasses that gave him an owlish look, and a natty English-tweed shooting jacket, the publisher of Mysterious Doings Books said, "Let's hope tonight's festivities will not turn out like the Mystery Writers dinner two years ago, Sergeant, when the guy who received the Grand Master Award wound up being murdered that very evening." He turned to the woman at his side. "Have you met Marian Pickering Henry, Sergeant?"

"No, I haven't had the pleasure."

"Marian, this is Detective Sgt. John Bogdanovic. And the lady seated beside him is the incomparable Margaret Dane, scourge of criminals and defense lawyers alike."

"Having abandoned my garden and my computer to watch you on television every day during that trial," said Henry, "I feel I've known you all my life."

"And I you through your books. I've read them all. As to the Mystery Writers murder, Oscar, I followed it in the press."

"Oscar tried in vain to persuade me to write a book on the events of that incredible episode," Henry said.

"Alas," sighed Pendelton as they sat, "she felt the true story was so outrageous that if she were to present it as a novel, nobody in the world would believe it. But I am happy to say that I have finally persuaded her that the True Crime genre is coming close to outstripping fiction in popularity. I need only point to the drama in the courtroom that involved the man whom we chose to recognize with our highest award tonight."

All eyes turned in the direction of a knot of excited Wolfe Pack members surrounding Janus at the head table. A standout in his white hat, he alternately nibbled a wedge of bread slathered with salmon paste and sipped a martini with two olives in it.

"The same man," said Bogdanovic bitterly, "who managed to get the killer in the Mystery Writers murder off easy."

"Evidently, the case wasn't as open and shut as believed," Dane teased. "As I recall, John, Theo gave you a pretty rough time on cross-examination."

Bogdanovic fidgeted. "Sure it was spirited. But I'm a flesh-and-blood detective, not a words-on-paper one."

Carrying a glass of plain water, a concession to diabetes, Judge

Simmons appeared at the table. Tall, gaunt, and looking ill, he stated, "Nero Wolfe never did less than well at anything, but most of his tangles with prosecutors occurred before a case got to court."

"Sergeant, meet the distinguished jurist Reginald Simmons," said Pendelton. "He is known to his friend as Reggie."

"The one instance of Wolfe's testifying," Henry said as Simmons sat, "is found in the story titled 'The Next Witness.' He did not enjoy the experience. That's because Wolfe found very little enjoyable about leaving his house. With the exception of Rusterman's, he would not dine in a restaurant. To assure superb meals in his home he had a full-time Swiss chef, Fritz Brenner, complete with a cook's hat and apron."

"Naturally, he was a gourmet," Dane said, "as tonight's meal clearly proves."

Picking up a menu card, Bogdanovic read:

OYSTERS BAKED IN THE SHELL
TERRAPIN MARYLAND
BEATEN BISCUITS
PAN-BROILED YOUNG TURKEY
RICE CROQUETTES WITH QUINCE JELLY
LIMA BEANS IN CREAM
AVOCADO TODHUNTER
PINEAPPLE SHERBET
SPONGE CAKE
WISCONSIN DAIRY CHEESE
BLACK COFFEE

"It's the meal Wolfe ordered served at Kanawha Spa," Dane explained as waiters appeared from the kitchen with the first course. "The guests were fifteen master chefs."

"I think I saw the movie. Someone was killing all the great chefs of Europe."

"Not the same story. In *Too Many Cooks* only one master chef was murdered," Pendelton said.

"Wolfe nabbed him, of course?"

"Not without being wounded himself. He was rewarded with the recipe for *saucisse minuit*," said Pendelton.

"I was hoping it would be on the menu tonight," Henry said.

A movement next to her caused her to look up.

"Good evening, Nick! I swear, somehow you get handsomer and handsomer. What is it about you Greek men?"

"It's all that olive oil and fish," Pendelton said. "What have you done with your wife?"

"Ariadne is being Ariadne. She'll be along. You know how she is. She waits for *the* moment to make an entrance!" With a slight bow toward Bogdanovic, he said, "You must be the brilliant detective Wiggins told me about. I'm Nick Stamos! Don't get up on my account, Mr. Bogdanovic. I'm so glad you, unlike that movie director, haven't felt the need to add the *h* at the end of your name so that people would know to pronounce the *v-i-c* as *'vich.' "*

Bogdanovic shrugged. "To each his own."

"My wife is Hungarian," Stamos went on. "Her maiden name is Fotash. But she was raised in Zagreb. She is looking forward to speaking Croatian with you. You *do* speak it?"

"With my parents," Bogdanovic answered. "But English is my native tongue. I was born at Kings County Hospital in Brooklyn."

Stamos smiled and sat. "Very wise of you." Turning toward the entrance and a tall blond woman in a pale blue evening dress trimmed in gold, he said, "Ah! Here's Ariadne now."

As she proceeded slowly across the room, Bogdanovic said, "I notice there are quite a few women in attendance. When my boss took me to a Baker Street Irregulars dinner I was told that women were banned because Sherlock Holmes distrusted women. I gather Nero Wolfe didn't share Holmes's views on the opposite sex."

"He regarded them as astonishing and successful animals," Simmons replied, "that for reasons of convenience he chose to regard with indifference."

Maggie Dane lightly touched Bogdanovic's shoulder. "Archie was quite the opposite."

"The more I hear about Archie," Bogdanovic said, rising to greet Ariadne Stamos as she slipped as softly as a breeze into the chair next to her husband, "the more I like him."

Introduced to him, Ariadne Stamos greeted him flawlessly in his father's native language. *"Kokosi."*

He responded, *"Yasam dobro tebe."*

"Very cosmopolitan," said Pendelton. "Too bad no one else at the table knows what it means, Sergeant."

"She said, 'Hi,' and I basically said, 'How you doin'?' "

"English from now on, please. I hate feeling left out."

A waiter set a plate of oysters before Henry. "I've always speculated that the first person to eat one of these things at the dawn of history must have been very hungry," she said as she looked down. "They really are disgusting to look at. But I do love them. So I say thanks to that unsung, heroic man."

"Maybe it was a hungry woman," said Bogdanovic.

"More than likely." Dane laughed. "No matter how hungry my former husband was, it never occurred to him to open the fridge."

"Now I understand why the greatest poisoners in history were women. If the way to a man's heart is through his stomach, it was also an easy way to get rid of him."

"Only because the poor dears have always been the ones who were expected to do the cleaning," interjected Henry. "Knives and guns leave all those puddles of blood to mop up."

"If you wanted to bump me off at this banquet," said Bogdanovic, "how could you be sure that I'd be the one who got the poison? We're all eating the same dishes. How could you be certain the waiter delivered a particular plate?"

Henry smiled. "The poison would go into your food at the table. In your case, I'd have slipped it into your oysters while your attention was diverted by Ariadne's spectacular arrival."

"How could you count on her coming in after the rest of us?"

"Ariadne is famous for being late. Being a gentleman, you'd naturally stand to greet her."

"But how could you know in advance I'd be a gentleman?"

"If you proved not to be, the poison would go into some other dish. Sooner or later your attention would be diverted by someone or something. Not because you're a man. You are also a detective. Looking around you for anything suspicious or out of the ordinary is ingrained by nature and your training. I could never get close enough to shoot or stab you. Nor the man you are obviously here to guard. So you see, Sergeant Bogdanovic, you would be easy to poison. Child's play. Dare I say 'girl's' play?"

As the oyster plates were replaced with the terrapin soup, Bogdanovic turned to the waiter and held up a hand. "Excuse me, but you can take mine away. I'd feel guilty eating a turtle."

"It's mock, sir. Made from calf's liver."

Bogdanovic winced. "I still pass."

"I wouldn't give that soup to anyone else, waiter," Henry said with a devilish giggle. "There's poison in it."

Blushing, Bogdanovic muttered, "It's all right, waiter. The lady's making a joke. And her point."

When those who ate the soup were finished, Wiggins stood at the podium.

"Attention, please, the toast to Fritz Brenner will be given by Oscar Pendelton. Let's hope it will be in the form of one of the charming and witty limericks with which Oscar regales us year after year."

As a hush enveloped the room for the first time, Bogdanovic surmised that a treat lay in store.

Rising, Pendelton perched half-moon reading glasses on his nose then took his time in drawing a small sheet of paper from his shirt pocket. He read:

> "For a giant guzzler of malty brews
> Fritz cook'd up possum stews
> Or dished him up with equal pace
> Shish-ke-bab with thyme and mace.
>
> No turtle soup or oyster pie
> Beyond Wolfe's ken could lie;
> A shad roe dish was always fine
> Though a plate of eel was out of line.
>
> Roasted, baked, braised, or boiled
> Salted, peppered, or olive-oiled
> There was no dinner Wolfe wouldn't eat
> As long as it included meat.
>
> So here's to Fritz
> Who scorned the Ritz
> To get rich in

The West Side kitchen
Of Rex Stout's immortal hero
The hungry Wolfe named Nero."

"Bravo as usual, dear Oscar," exclaimed Henry as drinks were sipped around the room.

Dane sighed. "I'm afraid my toast will pale in comparison."

"You'll do fine," Bogdanovic said. "Just picture all these people as members of a jury."

"You overlook the fact that my last jury voted to acquit."

"Thanks to Janus's smoke and mirrors," said the judge as he put down his glass of water.

"Mind your manners, Reggie," whispered Pendelton. "The man of the hour is heading this way."

The mellifluous voice preceded him. "Oscar, Oscar! Very well done. What a charming bit of doggerel." Suddenly towering above them, he removed his hat in a broad, sweeping gesture with one hand and with the other set his martini on the table. "I just had to come over here and visit awhile with the three most beautiful ladies in the room. And the handsomest men."

"You're looking fine, Theo," said Marian Pickering Henry.

"Marian, darling. I missed you while you were in London. I assume your little hothouse and all your devoted fans are glad that you're back among them."

"Hello, Theo," said Stamos. "How's the three-million-dollar man this evening?

"Long time no see, Nicky. Ariadne, you are stunning."

"And you know Judge Simmons, of course," said Pendelton.

When the jurist did not rise, Janus said, "I'm afraid His Honor is not one of my fans."

"Oh, everyone loves you, Theo," exclaimed Dane.

Janus bent and planted a kiss on her forehead. "Isn't this just a swell evening, Maggie? I'm thrilled that you are part of it. And I see you have been taken under the protective wing of Sgt. John Bogdanovic of the New York Police Department. Did you know that this is the man whose testimony nearly won it for the district attorney in the Morgan Griffith murder trial? I hope, Sergeant, that you are not a man to nurse hard feelings."

"I'm only upset by injustice, Mr. Janus."

"Where was the injustice? You did your duty on the witness stand and I did mine cross-examining you. How would you have it, Detective? Shall you be old Fury in *Alice in Wonderland?* I'll be judge and jury and try the case and condemn you to death?"

Retrieving his drink, he turned and strode away so fast that he ran into a waiter and dropped the delicate martini glass. "I'm sorry, sir," gasped the faultless waiter. "I'll get you another."

"Hell yes, boy. With two olives."

As Janus returned to the head table, Bogdanovic regarded the guests at his table. "Sorry. I just don't like that guy."

"Don't apologize, Sergeant," said Simmons as he waved off a waiter who tried to pour a glass of wine for him.

9

The Next Witness

"CHIEF GOLDSTEIN," said Janus, clasping his fresh drink as he resumed his place at the head table, "your able sergeant is a man with forceful opinions forthrightly expressed."

"John's Croatian."

"Yes, that would account for it. The Balkan temperament can be fiery. I could use a man with his passion working for me."

"Johnny Bogdanovic as a private investigator for a defense attorney? I don't think that's in the cards. He's committed to sending murderers to prison."

"Too bad. I like him." He reached for the martini. "I toast to murderers, Chief Harvey Goldstein, Sergeant Johnny Bogdanovic, all others who pursue them, and people like me who do our duty by defending them!"

Goldstein lifted a bottle of beer. "I prefer to drink to the cause of justice."

When they set down their drinks Janus asked, "Is making a deal for Paulie Mancuso's testimony justice?"

Goldstein smiled. "The district attorney's office turned him into a witness. He's in protective custody. My office has never been invited into the loop."

"Be glad you're not being dragged into that quagmire," said Janus as a scoop of rice with a dollop of quince jelly went into his mouth.

"Will you be jumping in on Mancuso's side? Or have you been hired by the people he'll be testifying against?"

"Neither, thank God. Merely curious."

With delicate movements he took up knife and fork and cut a small piece of turkey only to be interrupted by a book's appearance before him. "Sorry to bother you, Mr. Janus," said a young woman, holding the book between him and his dinner plate, "but will you please autograph this for me?"

Taking a pen from his breast pocket and opening *Janus for the Defense* to the title page, he looked up at her smilingly and asked, "What's your name?"

"It's not for me. I bought this for my father. He's a great admirer. Could you make it 'To Sidney' and then write something personal?"

After thinking a moment, he wrote in green ink, "To Sidney, Nothing corrupts a man as deeply as writing a book," and signed "Theo Janus" with a flourish.

When the young woman was too far away to hear he said, "Very rude of her. But at least it was the hardcover edition, not the paperback."

"If you are not getting involved in the Mancuso thing," said Goldstein, "why did you bring it up?"

"I represented the scoundrel once. For about fifteen minutes. We parted company when he asked how much money it would take to bribe a couple of jurors. Maggie Dane was with me at the time. It was all I could do to keep her from leaping across the table and strangling the jerk. We've all come a long way since that day. I can't get out of my thoughts what a splendid career Maggie could have had if she had stayed on my side of the courtroom."

Goldstein's eyes settled on her. "I guess she preferred to stand on the side of the angels."

Cracking a smile, Janus turned his attention to the turkey. "Sergeant Bogdanovic may have inherited his passion, but it's too bad he hasn't your gift for quiet self-righteousness."

Goldstein looked admiringly and with welling affection toward Bogdanovic. "John's a good man. If I could get him reading more detective novels, he'd be even better. He's yet to grasp the truth that being a homicide cop isn't just a job. It's an art."

"To quote the scripture according to Wolfe, 'Competence is so rare that it is a temptation to cling to it when we find it.' "

10

Help Wanted, Male

As a waiter served sherbet and sponge cake and Bogdanovic's intense brown eyes were directed not at the dessert but toward the head table, Maggie Dane leaned close. "Relax, Sergeant. No one is going to attack your boss."

"Famous last words. Mrs. Lincoln: 'Come on, Abe, a night at the theater will do you good.' President Kennedy to the Secret Service: 'They love me in Dallas. Take the bubbletop off the limo.' Dr. Martin Luther King in Memphis: 'Let's step out on the balcony for a little fresh air.' John Lennon to Yoko Ono outside the Dakota: 'The kid only wants my autograph.' "

With a little laugh that was a gust of warmth on his cheek, she startled him with a feathery kiss. "You are a gem. How did Harvey find you?"

Picking up a dessert spoon, he replied, "It was through the police department magazine *Spring 3100,* named after what used to be the department phone number. It had an article saying that the chief of detectives was looking for a man to be his assistant. I tossed my name in the hopper. Weeks went by. I assumed he'd found his man. Then I was called in for an interview. This consisted primarily of a lecture on the value of reading detective stories for real-life police. He never actually came right out and said I'd gotten the job. I found out after I'd left the office when his executive assistant asked me if I'd be needing anything special in the way of furnishings for my office. How did Wolfe find Archie Goodwin?"

"Unlike Dr. Watson, who wrote about how he and Sherlock Holmes came to meet, Archie never said, except to indicate that he'd been working for someone else and Wolfe was impressed with the work. Like you, Archie's duties included bodyguard."

"Did he ever save Wolfe's life?"

"Many times. This included smacking a Cuban woman who had revenge on her mind. She'd smuggled a dagger into Wolfe's office in a sock."

"How sweet of her. Good for Archie."

"Exactly what would you do were someone to attempt such a thing this evening?"

"Whatever I had to."

"Even at the risk of injuring an innocent bystander?"

"Absolutely."

"Have you ever had to jump in to save his life?"

"Thankfully, no," he said, looking toward the head table as Wiggins left it to stand at the podium.

Holding a glass of white wine, Wiggins said, "It's my pleasure to introduce the distinguished Wolfie who is to offer the toast to the genius whose life and legacy we salute this evening. The next toast will be given by none other than someone who is so much like both the author and the character he created. Namely, *myself.*"

With a grin of delight he basked in a chorus of groans, boos, and catcalls.

"No, my friends, it's quite true. Like Nero Wolfe, I am—"

Goldstein blared, "Fat."

With feigned indignation, Wiggins turned and wagged a thick finger at him. "I heard that, Chief!"

Goldstein winked. "I intended you to."

"As I was about to say before being so rudely interrupted," Wiggins continued, "like Nero Wolfe, I am a genius."

The room hissed.

"As to my commonalites with the venerated author," he went on undaunted, "I am mad about books, food, music, people who work, and heated arguments. I dislike politicians, preachers, genteel persons, closed minds, loud noises, and oily people."

Bogdanovic whispered to Dane, "Then what the hell is Janus doing here?"

"That's why I have taken unto myself," Wiggins proceeded,

57

"the honor of standing here and asking you to rise and join with me in lifting a glass of cheer in grateful tribute to the creator of Nero Wolfe, et al., the one and only Rex Todhunter Stout."

As one voice, the audience invoked the hallowed name.

Putting aside his drink, Wiggins began his introduction of Goldstein by talking rapturously of how the proprietor of the Usual Suspects bookstore himself had been considered a suspect in two recent sensational murder investigations. He continued, "That I immediately ranked high on the list of possible murderers and found myself eliminated much too quickly was due entirely to the efforts of a brilliant homicide investigator. He is a man I am certain Nero Wolfe would have hired in an instant and thoroughly enjoyed working with. And I am thrilled that Detective Sgt. John Bogdanovic is with us this evening!"

Lowering his head and trying to sink from view, Bogdanovic let out a throaty groan.

With hands clapping like flippers of a trained seal, Wiggins scolded, "Don't be shy, Sergeant B. Stand up and take a bow!"

11

The Silent Speaker

STILL SAVORING THE amusement of Bogdanovic's embarrassed look at being forced by Wiggins to stand up and accept public acclaim, Goldstein realized with a start that Wiggins now spoke of him.

"In Chief of Detectives Harvey Goldstein," he said, "this grand and beloved city of ours has for nearly twenty years had in its service a man with utmost dedication to leading such stalwart sleuths as Detective Bogdanovic in a relentless struggle against crime, especially the most fascinating one of all—murder. But he and his intrepid assistant have not come here tonight to solve a case, unless one of you has homicide on the mind. If you do have a plan, I caution you against acting it out. The chief is not here to solve a crime, but to lead us in a toast to the woman who has graciously accepted our invitation to represent Miss Lily Rowan and to present the Nero Wolfe Award. Therefore, with great pleasure and without further ado, I give you Chief Goldstein."

With balding head barely visible above the podium, he said, "Except in the category of beauty, I detect nothing of Lily Rowan in the woman who represents her here this evening. Lily is lazy. Very lazy. She is, to use Nero Wolfe's adjectives, 'rich, intemperate, and notorious.' She once lived at the Ritz and now owns a posh penthouse on an exclusive block of East Sixty-third Street with a Kashan carpet that set her back fourteen thousand dollars. She spends summers at her place near Katonah and owns a ranch in Montana. But she doesn't have a clue as to how to get somebody indicted nor how to try capital cases, whereas in that department the woman I am honored to toast in her role of Lily Rowan is without par."

Beaming as he stood beside Dane with a glass of club soda in his hand, Bogdanovic said softly, "Here's to *you,* Maggie."

When the toasters resumed seats, she rose. "As Lily Rowan, I thank you from the bottom of my lazy, rich, intemperate, and notorious heart. As myself, I simply can't avoid comparing this evening to one in the Wolfe case entitled 'The Silent Speaker.' "

Her eyes turned down to Bogdanovic.

"For benefit of Chief Goldstein's aide-de-camp," she said, lightly touching his shoulder, "who informed me during the meal that regarding Nero Wolfe he is an ignoramus . . ."

Titters of amusement rippled around the room.

"For Sergeant Bogdanovic's enlightenment, then," she went on, looking round the room, "in 'The Silent Speaker' Cheney Boone had been invited to make the main speech at a dinner in the Grand Ballroom of the Waldorf-Astoria. Of the fourteen hundred guests, a hundred were invited to a private reception. To go over notes for the speech, Boone left the group to shut himself up in a small room off the stage. It was there that Alger Kates would discover him dead on the floor. Murdered."

With a sidelong look, she saw Janus clutch his throat as if he were straining for breath, then pitch forward so that his head struck the table with a thud. Amid gasps of alarm, he jerked upright with a broadening grin and bellowed in a feigned western drawl. "I'se here to git my award and no damn murderer's gonna keep me from it. So git on with it, darlin'. Time's a wastin'."

"Theo, I can't imagine who'd wish to kill you," she replied with a little laugh. "Except everyone who saw you at work on TV in a certain recent murder trial."

Shoulders twitching with laughter, Janus grumbled, "The verdict's in, Maggie, and you cannot try the case over. Or file an appeal. Dem's da *rules.*"

"Indeed they are, Theo. And nobody wants to change them. I thank God that ours is a system that believes it is better that a thousand guilty men go free than an innocent one go off to prison."

12

Before Midnight

A THUNDERCLAP OF applause and a rain of cheers left no doubt that the Wolfe Pack wholeheartedly agreed with Maggie Dane and that nothing Theodore Janus might say during his speech could change their minds. They had not gathered to honor him for his work as America's most famous defense lawyer. It was because he had compiled an encyclopedia that he clutched their Nero Wolfe Award, in the form of a small bust of the immense detective they so revered and who in their minds and hearts existed not in the imagination of Rex Stout and his readers but *actually*, along with Archie Goodwin and the others, in an elegant brownstone somewhere on West Thirty-fifth Street.

Taking Dane's arm as they followed Goldstein and Wiggins into a more intimate room for a private reception arranged by Janus for members of the steering committee, Bogdanovic said, "I don't want to disillusion you, Maggie, but I worked for a time in the Tenth Precinct, which covers West Thirty-fifth Street. There are no residences. It's all industrial property."

"Just because you stayed awake on Christmas Eve and never saw a bearded fat man in a red suit doesn't mean there's no Santa Claus, Detective."

"Right. And if I staked out Baker Street in London and didn't see a tall guy in a cape and fore-and-aft hat would not mean Sherlock Holmes isn't living there."

She let go of his hand and came to an abrupt halt. "Well of course he's not! He's old, retired, and keeping bees in Sussex."

"What about Nero Wolfe? He must be pretty long in the tooth by now, too. What has he retired to keep?"

"Same as he kept when he was working cases," she answered as she walked on. "Orchids!"

Catching up with her, Bogdanovic slowly shook his head. "Do any of the detectives in all those books you and Goldstein never cease reading ever die?"

"Hercule Poirot passed away in 1975. His obituary ran on the front page of the *New York Times*. Since no obit has appeared for Holmes or Wolfe, they are obviously alive and well."

Entering the room, its atmosphere already suffused with the pungent aroma of cigars, Bogdanovic found Janus standing at the bar in the center. Holding a box of them open for all takers as Bogdanovic approached, he said, "I know Cuban cigars are banned in America, Detective, but have one anyway."

"Thanks, but no thanks."

"What a stalwart defender of the law you are! Well, if I am to be arrested for possession of contraband, so be it. If a genuine Cohiba isn't worth going to jail for, what is?" Offering the box to Dane, he said with a smile, "How about you? More and more women are smoking them nowadays, especially in Hollywood. They call it 'cigar chic.' "

"You know me, Theo. I've never been interested in keeping up with the latest vogue."

"And you never objected to my smoking cigars, either. Thank God you weren't like the Maggie in Rudyard Kipling's poem. As I recall, it's called 'The Betrothed' and is about a man who's having second thoughts about marrying a gal named Maggie who's given him an ultimatum to choose between herself and his cigars. Part of it goes:

> Open the old cigar box,—let me consider anew,—
> Old friends, and who is Maggie that I should
> abandon *you?*
>
> A million surplus Maggies are willing to bear the
> yoke;
> And a woman is only a woman, but a good cigar is a
> Smoke."

Bogdanovic grunted and said, "Maggie, if you'd care to kill him right now, I'd be delighted to testify on your behalf that it was justifiable homicide."

"Don't worry, John," she said, lightly kissing Janus on the cheek. "If I wanted Theo dead, he'd have been pushing up daisies long ago."

"Since you won't take my cigars," said Janus, "I hope you'll enjoy the fine cognac I'm providing. It's not everyday that I'm given the Nero Wolfe Award, made all the sweeter because it came from the hands of the second-best lawyer in the country."

A moment later as she sipped brandy, Bogdanovic stared at Janus as he distributed more cigars. "Look at him," he said. "How can you put up with that condescending snob? *Second-best.* Meaning he's the top."

"If he isn't, please tell me who is."

"Maybe I *should* arrest him for possession of contraband."

"If you do so," she said, surprising him by giggling like a schoolgirl, "you'll be made to look the fool."

"Really? How so? Cuban cigars have been banned in the United States since the 1960s."

"They're not Cuban. It's an old scam of Theo's. Only the box and the bands are Cuban. The real Havanas are kept in a special humidor in a locked room at his ranch upstate and when he travels in a box in the glove compartment of his Rolls-Royce, from which he takes what he needs and transfers them to a leather pocket case."

"What a shyster! No wonder he gets along so well with the top mugs in the mob. Birds of a feather."

"Mark Twain didn't hang around with gangsters, but he did the same thing once. He had friends who constantly accused him of smoking the worst cigars in the world. One of them was notorious for smoking only costly and elegant cigars. So one day Twain went to his house when no one was looking and took some of the man's choicest. He removed the labels and put the cigars into a box of his own stogies, then passed them out to those friends at dinner. After they'd gone he found the cigars on the lawn, only partially smoked, where the snobs had tossed them away. The next day the person he'd stolen them from told him that someday he was likely to get shot for giving people such awful cigars."

"But Janus isn't making a point, is he? He's perpetrating a fraud on people who just gave him an award, and in my book that makes him as low as a snake's bellybutton. Well, snakes have been known to get their heads bashed in. Or swallowed by bigger ones."

"They can also be murder weapons, as in *Fer-de-Lance,* Nero Wolfe's first recorded case."

"I haven't read it."

"A fer-de-lance is a snake."

"There was also a deadly snake in the Sherlock Holmes case that Dr. Watson called 'The Speckled Band.' "

Goldstein's voice intruded. "It was a swamp adder, trained to climb a bell rope."

Turning to Goldstein, Bogdanovic blurted, "A *trained* snake?"

"It answered to a whistle," said Dane, grinning.

"Unfortunately for Dr. Grimesby Roylott of Stoke Moran," said Goldstein, holding a half-smoked Janus cigar, "it ignored common wisdom about never biting the hand that feeds you and sank its fangs into its owner and trainer. Dare I ask you what's prompted this discussion of snakes?"

Dane answered, "Your assistant thinks Theo Janus is one."

"You're holding the evidence in your hand," Bogdanovic said. "The band on your cigar says it's Cuban, but it isn't."

"Is that so?" Goldstein said, studying the black and gold band. "Is an arrest for consumer fraud imminent?"

Bogdanovic glared at Janus. "No, but I wouldn't slap the cuffs on anybody who gave Janus a poke in the eye, either."

Goldstein puffed the bogus cigar, took it from his mouth, and declared, "Fake Havana or not, it's a pretty good smoke. All this talk about Havana cigars being the best in the world is, in my opinion, a bunch of baloney. Many fine cigars are being made in the Dominican Republic, Honduras, and Jamaica."

As he spoke, he heard the chirping of Bogdanovic's beeper.

"Of course," he continued while Bogdanovic read the message in the window of the device, "the best cigar is the one you don't have to pay for. There is no such thing as a bad free cigar, no matter who gave it to you."

With a worried expression, Bogdanovic interrupted. "Excuse me, Chief. The message was from Red Reiter. He wants a callback as soon as possible."

"Did he say where he is?"

"No. And I don't recognize the phone number he listed," said Bogdanovic, reaching into his inside coat pocket for his cellular phone. "I think it's an uptown one."

Looking around the room, Goldstein said quietly, "Discretion is the thing, Johnny. Members of the press might still be around. Use a phone booth in the lobby."

Watching Bogdanovic impatiently threading through the happy throng that stood between him and the exit, Dane smiled a little, then turned to Goldstein. "You can always tell a detective!"

"Yes," he replied through a puff of smoke, "but not much."

"May I deduce that Red Reiter is another of the breed?"

"He and his partner are what you might call a first-response team," he said, looking anxiously toward the exit. "It's their job to check out situations that might require my attention."

"As in situations that might require the personal appearance at the scene of the crime by the chief of detectives and what our dear friends in the news media like to call high-profile cases?"

"That's it exactly."

"Well, let's hope this very pleasant evening isn't going to turn out to be one of them."

As they both looked toward the door, Theodore Janus arrived at Goldstein's side. "Pardon this old bloodhound for butting in, Chief," he whispered, tapping a finger to the side of his nose, "but the hurried departure of your sterling aide-de-camp after being beeped and your rapt attention on the door through which he departed so hastily suggest to my keen olfactory sense that the game may be afoot. Dare I hope it's a juicy case of murder?"

"What's the matter, Theo?" demanded Dane, playfully poking him in the ribs. "Is that beat-up briefcase of yours empty?"

"Have you forgotten the first lesson I taught you in law school, my darling? There's *always* room for one more opportunity to hold the prosecution's feet to the fire known as proof beyond a reasonable doubt."

"What was the title of that course?" asked Goldstein. "Was it by any chance 'How to Get Rich by Chasing Ambulances'?"

With a thin smile as he walked away, Janus answered, "Very droll response, Chief. I am certain that when I repeat it to my accountant he will be most amused. I hope you enjoyed the cigar."

"I know he's a friend of yours, Maggie," Goldstein said as he removed the half-smoked fake Havana from his mouth, "but that guy is a bigger horse's ass than any you'll find on that ranch of his upstate."

As the cigar went into an ashtray, Bogdanovic appeared in the doorway to beckon him with upraised hand and a wiggling of fingers. "Evidently Theo's acute sense of smell was right," Dane said. "It seems the game *is* afoot. Good sleuthing, Mr. Holmes."

"Oh no you don't. You're coming, too," Goldstein said, gripping her hand. "As Sherlock advised, 'A trusty comrade is always of use.' Especially if that comrade is one of the best district attorneys in the country."

When they reached the doorway Bogdanovic blurted, "There's big trouble at the hotel where the DA stashed Paulie Mancuso. He seems to have changed his mind about testifying. Half an hour ago he took a nosedive out a ninth-floor window."

PART THREE

A Window for Death

13

Home to Roost

EXCEPT FOR THE curvy eastern boundary shaped by the East River, the Nineteenth Precinct formed a perfect rectangle with Fifth Avenue and Central Park on the west, East Fifty-ninth Street at the bottom and East Ninety-sixth Street at the top. More expensive land and more privileges of wealth could not be found in the city of New York. Politicians called it the Silk Stocking District. For more than half a century the most ambitious of their breed had done their best, and sometimes their worst, to reside within its most prestigious address. Located in Carl Schurz Park, a stately house built in 1799 by the Scottish shipping magnate Archibald Gracie became the official residence of the mayor in 1942.

Gazing past its surrounding trees as Bogdanovic turned the car onto East End Avenue, Goldstein said to Dane, "The first of New York's mayors to move into Gracie Mansion did so reluctantly. Fiorello La Guardia didn't think the people of New York should be footing his rental bill. He left his small apartment in Spanish Harlem only because of personal security considerations growing out of the fact that the country was in the midst of the Second World War. Plus the fact that he realized the taxpayers would be paying for the mansion's upkeep whether he lived in it or not."

One of the best-policed areas in the city, with its elegant town homes, high-rise co-op and condominium apartment houses, and a handful of residential hotels, the Gracie Mansion neighborhood qualified in terms of criminal activity as the quietest in the Nineteenth Precinct. Consequently, a report of a man found dead on the sidewalk across the street would have promoted a far more urgent response by the police than, say, the same scenario on a street in Harlem.

In this case, the bloodied, pulpy corpse had brought such a flood of blue-and-white patrol cars with flashing lights and men in plain clothes and unmarked cars that a passerby might assume an attempt had been made against the life of the person who lived in the large house in the park.

"Save for periodic eruptions from groups of protesters and picketers venting views on a variety of causes, from the cost of living to the Vietnam War," Goldstein continued as Bogdanovic stopped the car behind a radio patrol unit, "the only arrest we made in the mansion was in 1987."

Bogdanovic snorted a laugh. "I remember that one. A burglar was caught red-handed. When he found out the house he was burglarizing was the home of the mayor he asked, 'Can't I just put the stuff back and leave?' "

Stepping from the car, he turned up the collar of a heavy gray overcoat and peered up at a white curtain flapping through a ninth-floor window of the Hotel Radcliffe.

"The guy was a rat," he said, shaking his head as Goldstein and Dane came around the front of the car, "but that is a really nasty way for anybody to check out."

Goldstein looked up at the window. "Fifty years ago at the Half Moon Hotel out at Coney Island a hit man for the Murder, Incorporated gang, by the name of Kid Twist Reles, also went out on a flyer while in protective custody as a material witness. The newspapers had a field day writing about a canary who could sing but couldn't fly. What Kid Twist did not know was that the cops who were supposed to guard him were on the mob payroll."

As he spoke, they were joined by a rangy and rugged young man wearing an open brown suede duster coat and snakeskin western boots. "Evening, Chief. Sorry to have interrupted your night out to bring you to this mess." Recognizing the woman beside him, he asked, "Are you working for the New York DA now, Miss Dane?"

"Maggie, meet Red Reiter," said Goldstein.

"I'm merely an interested spectator," she said, lifting her eyes from the body. "A busman's holiday!"

Goldstein asked Reiter, "Where's your partner in crime, the indomitable Detective Leibholz?"

"Al's upstairs taking statements from the three blind mice."

"Three blind mice?"

"The district attorney assigned a trio of assistant DAs to watch the store while the investigators who had been assigned to guard Mancuso got the weekend off. According to the mice, Mancuso said he was going to bed early to do some reading."

Goldstein grunted. "Who'd have thought Paulie Mancuso was a bookworm?"

"After about an hour watching TV," Reiter went on, "the mice heard a commotion from down on the street and when they looked out the window they saw what was left of Paulie splattered all over the pavement."

"Has District Attorney Vanderhoff been notified?"

"Yes. He's on his way into the city from his place in the Hamptons. Meantime, two of his deputies—Jeffrey Marx and Tommy Farley—are reportedly on their way. They ought to be showing up at any minute."

"What about the press? Do the newsies know about this yet?"

"This is also their weekend. The newsrooms are geared down. They've got their second-stringers working. It's also on the late side. The Sunday newspapers are already out and the TV news shows won't be cranking up until morning. I don't picture any of them creating a problem for us before then."

"Okay. But tell the uniforms that should any members of the Fourth Estate show up, they are to be kept at a distance. Now, let's go up and see what these three blind mice have to say for themselves before Marx and Farley get here and tell them to clam up. Marx and Farley! Sounds like a vaudeville act."

Dane turned away. "I'm going to be in your way. I'll wait in the car."

"Nonsense," exclaimed Bogdanovic, grabbing her coat sleeve. "You're coming with us."

She looked quizzically at Goldstein. "Only if your boss says it's okay."

Goldstein smiled. "Fur coat notwithstanding," he said, "only a cad would leave a lady outside on a night like this."

Entering the large lobby, they stepped into a green and red wonderland of seasonal decorations. Gleaming white marble walls were festooned with evergreen garlands. Giant wreaths were dotted with pinecones and striped candy canes, and a towering Christmas tree in a corner was decorated with angels. Two small trees atop the reception desk achoed the motif. Flanked by a pair of jolly Santa Clauses on the mantle of a going fireplace stood a menorah with yellow electric bulbs signifying the next to the last day of Hanukkah. Two police officers flanking a waiting elevator added a dash of navy blue as they snapped salutes as Goldstein strode past them.

When he stepped out of the elevator on the ninth floor he found Detective Sgt. Al Leibholz in the hallway. Clutched in his left hand was a small notebook.

According to the New York Police Department's Investigator's Guide, chapter 1, page six, the notebook used had to be small enough to be carried in a pocket. A bound one was preferrable: The notes remained intact and because the pages were not normally removed or easily lost, it was more acceptable in court.

Leibholz's was a left-sided spiral-ring with a blue cover and eighty blue-lined five-by-three pages. By the time Goldstein arrived he had used a ballpoint pen with black ink to fill almost half of them, as regulations demanded, with only that information relative to the investigator's case, without including extraneous information and personal opinions.

Yet a dozen years of experience as a homicide investigator had taught him it was the latter Goldstein would want. He did not disappoint. Barely out of the elevator, Goldstein asked, "What the devil happened here, Al?"

"Everything points to Mancuso committing suicide by the old tried and true method, when all other means are not available, of defenestration. Otherwise, you'd have to believe that three guys on the staff of the district attorney colluded in giving him the heave-ho for some reason known but to them."

"What are are their names?"

"Tyson, Dearborn, and Davis. Assistant district attorneys."

"Not after Cornelius Vanderhoff gets done with them. They'll be lucky if they're not disbarred. Which room are they in?"

"End of the hall," Leibholz answered, using the notebook to point. "Suite nine-twelve."

"Well, let's have at them again before the reinforcements from downtown get here to circle the wagons."

14

Prisoner's Base

SEATED SIDE BY side on a couch, the three coatless young men appeared to Maggie Dane like first-year law school students holding an all-night cram session before an exam. Worried, tense, on the edge of their seats—literally—and quite possibly at the end of their wits, they looked up nervously as the door opened.

"This is Chief of Detectives Harvey Goldstein," Leibholz declared as they gaped with startled expressions. "He'll be asking you a few questions."

Rising abruptly and violently shaking his head, the middle youth was tall and slender with long coal black hair. "We've been advised to say nothing further about this incident until District Attorney Vanderhoff gets here."

Goldstein advanced briskly across the room. "Is that so? Who gave you that advice? And how did you get it?"

"By phone from Deputy District Attorney Jeffrey Marx."

"When did you talk to him?"

"A few moments ago."

"What's your name?"

"Anthony Dearborn."

"Are you the senior man here?"

"Yes."

"How long have you been in the DA's office?"

"Three years."

"How long with the criminal division?"

"Since my second year."

"Then you surely ought to have learned by this time that the investigation of a suspicious death such as this is the province of the police."

"I see nothing suspicious about it at all," Dearborn said as he smoothed his hair with a neatly manicured hand. "Mancuso leapt out the window. He committed suicide. End of story."

"When the state's star witness has been sequestered at great expense to the taxpayer in a posh Upper East Side hotel room with three bodyguards," Goldstein said sternly, "and he winds up with his guts all over a sidewalk right across the street from Gracie Mansion, I seriously doubt that the news media will think of this as the end of the story. I'd say that you and your two associates will be reading and hearing about yourselves in the papers and on the airwaves for quite a few days. Maybe weeks. End of the story? Hell, this is just the beginning. Now, have a seat and answer my questions. Unless you'd care to make things a whole lot worse by invoking your right to remain silent."

A fair-haired youth lurched up from the couch. Short and with an athletic build, he protested, "We're not criminals, sir."

"Your name, please?"

"James Tyson."

Goldstein looked to the third man. "And you are?"

Standing, he was as tall as Dearborn, though not as slender. A lush brown mustache seemed to be intended to divert attention from severely premature baldness. "I'm Spencer Davis."

Goldstein said, "I have not accused any of you of being criminals. But you are material witnesses in, to use Mr. Dearborn's term, an *incident* to which the police department has been called and whose duty it is to investigate. It may very well be that Mancuso killed himself. I'd even go so far as to say that his death evidently seems to be a suicide. But until I know for sure, this will remain a police matter. Now, I need to hear for myself what happened, and I don't give a damn which one of you tells me."

The three exchanged anxious glances but remained silent.

"Very well," Goldstein said, sliding into a large armchair opposite them. "Because he's senior man, I pick Mr. Dearborn."

With a shrug of resignation and a sigh he asked, "Where do you want me to start?"

"How long has the DA's office had Mancuso stashed here?"

"About three weeks."

"Did he in those three weeks ever attempt to kill himself?"

"Not that I know of. We were with him only on weekends."

"On those three weekends were you all assigned to him?"

"Just two of us. Davis joined the team Friday a week ago."

"Why was that? Why did two suddenly become three?"

Davis interjected, "It's a training assignment."

"How long have you been with the criminal division?"

"About eight months. Before that I handled civil cases."

"I know how the system works, Mr. Davis. Now, Mr. Dearborn, on the weekends what was the routine you followed?"

"What do you mean by routine?"

"The question seems clear to me, young man. I want to know what went on from Mancuso's getting up in the morning to his going to bed at night."

"He had breakfast, lunch, and dinner and between them he was either watching television, playing cards with us, or reading."

"What about questioning him or going over his testimony?"

"All that was handled during the week."

"About the meals. Where did they come from?"

"Room service, mostly."

"And when they didn't come from room service?"

"Sometimes we'd call out for pizza or Chinese."

"We'll need to know from which pizza and Chinese places."

"What for? He wasn't poisoned. He jumped out a window."

"According to my information, Mancuso had been in protective custody someplace else for several months before settling down in this hotel three weeks ago. Suddenly, he decides to kill himself. Is it not reasonable to assume that something happened after the move to prompt him to make the big leap into eternity? I doubt it was displeasure with the accommodations."

"Nothing . . . happened."

"Besides members of the DA staff, who had contact with him?"

"No one."

"Hotel staff? Maids? Cleaning women?"

"We did all that ourselves."

"Food delivery people?"

"The food was usually delivered to the desk in the lobby and Davis went down to get it and bring it up."

Goldstein smiled at Davis. "The wages of being at the bottom of the pecking order, eh, son?"

"I welcomed the chance to get out of this damned room."

"Back up a minute. Mr. Dearborn said the take-out food was *usually* delivered to the desk. Were there times when it wasn't?"

"Last Saturday for lunch I walked over to Third Avenue to a deli. Paulie had a craving for a corned beef sandwich."

"What about today's?" He looked at his wrist watch. "That is, yesterday's meals?"

Dearborn answered, "Breakfast and lunch came up from room service. Dinner was Italian, from a *ristorante* Paulie knew about on First Avenue. It was delivered to the lobby."

Bogdanovic blurted, "Are you telling us you let Paulie pick the take-out places?"

"Why the hell not?"

"I could give you lots of reasons not to. Especially if he recommended Italian. What did he order?"

"I believe it was spaghetti and meatballs."

Goldstein asked, "What did you do with the container?"

"What do you think? We threw it out with a lot of other garbage that accumulated during the day. It went into a big plastic bag. Davis shoved it in a trash chute at the end of the hall."

"How soon after dinner did Mancuso go to his room?"

"We ate around seven o'clock. We watched a little TV until eleven or so. He went to bed to read."

"Where did he get the book?"

"His wife sent him a bunch."

"Excuse me? His wife sent him books?"

"Well, she didn't send them directly. She didn't know where he was. She sent them to him by way of our office."

"Did she ever write to him?"

"There were a few letters. But they were read by someone in the office before he got them."

"Did he ever talk to her on the phone?"

"Are you nuts? Phone calls can be tapped and traced."

"What about the books?"

"What about them?"

"Were they examined before he got them?"

"Certainly."

"How were they examined?"

"The pages were looked through and then they were turned upside down and shaken. If there'd been anything stuck between the pages it would have fallen out."

"What mood was he in before he went to his bedroom to read?"

"He was fine. For a lowlife and thug he was an amusing guy, always making jokes. I assure you there was nothing about him to suggest he was thinking about taking a swan dive."

Goldstein sat silent a moment, gave a nod, and stood. "Where is Mancuso's room?"

15

Might As Well Be Dead

STANDING BESIDE DANE in the doorway at the end of a short corridor as Goldstein went into the room, Bogdanovic peered into a space that seemed barely larger than the state prison cell that certainly would have been in Mancuso's future if he had not cut a deal with the district attorney to testify as the star witness in a series of major trials against his former associates in crime.

Motionless in the middle of the room, Goldstein stood with hands loosely clasped behind his back in a stance that brought to Dane's mind the image of another short, balding, and middle-aged detective. But her glance at the reflection in a mirror above a bureau of the clean-shaven face dispelled comparison to Hercule Poirot. Nor did she find any resemblance to the other sleuths in whom Harvey Goldstein found much that was admirable and eminently quotable for the instruction of his detectives.

As she watched him opening and closing the bureau's drawers, she saw nothing about him physically that came close to the tall, thin, hawk-nosed automaton that Dr. Watson had described as the deductive reasoner of 221B Baker Street. Nor did Goldstein as he poked around in the single closet of the spartan but comfortable hotel room invoke a picture of a corpulent but sedentary deducer in a house on West Thirty-fifth Street.

Should she take up the writing of the mystery novels which Goldstein extolled as valuable textbooks for his true-to-life detectives, she decided as she and Bogdanovic observed him from the doorway, she would have to invent something distinctive for him. Holmes had his pipe, Inverness cloak, deerstalker cap, and ever present magnifying glass. Agatha Christie had bestowed upon

Poirot a ridiculous waxed mustache and required him to wear spats long after they had gone the way of gentlemen's walking sticks. Rex Stout made Nero Wolfe an expert on orchids and beers. And in countless other mysteries other authors had created hallmarks to set their detectives apart from the growing pack. The little old lady from the quaint but illuminating English village of St. Mary Mead. A dapper Nick and chic Nora Charles belting down martinis. Suave and erudite Chief Inspector Roderick Alleyn. Mozart-loving, lonely, and tormented Inspector Morse. Hard-boiled, trench-coated Samuel Spade, Philip Marlowe, and Mickey Spillane's Mike Hammer. Early-years Ellery Queen, the supercilious aristocrat before he got a sense of humor. Pigeon-English, aphorism-quoting Charlie Chan. Columbo with his battered French car, rumpled raincoat, and cigar. Kojack sucking a lollipop and asking "Who loves ya, baby?" Jane Tennison with her fierce feminism. The streetwise New Yorker cops of *Law and Order,* the fouled-mouthed detectives of *NYPD Blue,* and the partner-teams working the murder beat in the City of Baltimore on *Homicide, Life on the Streets,* so far removed in time and place, as well as reality, from monosyllabic Sgt. Joe Friday of *Dragnet.*

Yet here in this room with unexceptional hotel furnishings and a wide-open window of death was Harvey Goldstein, chief of detectives of the greatest police force in the world, looking at Mancuo's unslept-in bed as if he were the traveling shoe salesman Willy Loman about to unpack a suitcase filled with samples of products that customers no longer wished to order.

Standing beside the bed, Goldstein directed his attention to the nightstand next to it, and to a stack of six books atop it.

Picking up the one on top, he turned a few pages and broke into a smile. "Well, well, well, what a small world we live in," he said. "Come in and check this out, John. You, too, Maggie."

Bogdanovic crossed the room, took the book, and exclaimed, "A small world indeed. *Janus for the Defense!*"

"Look inside at the title page," Goldstein said.

Scrawled across it in handwriting in black ink was:

To Paulie Mancuso, a man of honor who
loves his wife and children and will always

do the right thing for them.
Theodore R. Janus

Bogdanovic passed the book to Dane and with a contemptuous sneer said, "This was obviously intended as a carefully crafted warning to Mancuso. It's a threat. If you want to protect your wife and kids, do the right thing. No wonder he took a header." He thrust the book to Dane. "No wonder your friend and colleague Janus is called the mouthpiece for the mob."

"How very interesting," Dane said, studying the inscription. "The trouble with that theory, John, is that Theodore Janus did not write this."

Goldstein grabbed the book. "What's that?"

"It's a forgery."

"Cite your evidence, please."

"This is not Janus's handwriting. He always signs his books in green ink. And he invariably autographs them Theo Janus, not Theodore R. Janus. He is scrupulous about never using the exact signature that he puts on legal documents and checks."

Goldstein frowned. "You're certain about this, Maggie?"

"I am, but you don't have to take my word for it. Take that book to Janus and he'll tell it's not his hand."

"Of course he'll deny it," Bogdanovic retorted.

"If you don't want to believe him," Dane snapped, "then get examplars of his writing. Then have your lab check the damn book for his fingerprints."

"All right, folks, cool down." Goldstein pleaded. "We're on the same side in this unfortunate fiasco. From here on we'll be treating the demise of Paulie Mancuso as a homicide."

Bogdanovic shook his head. "That's going to make a certain district attorney look pretty foolish."

"If Vanderhoff's people had been on their toes, this mess wouldn't have happened. John, get the ball rolling by having Red and Al take formal statements from the three blind mice. Then I want a complete background check on them. Get a crime scene unit up here. I want prints lifted from all these books. Come morning Leibholz and Reiter are to find Mrs. Mancuso and inquire into the circumstances around the sending of the books, specifically where she got Janus's. My hunch is she never laid eyes on it, or any of the books for that matter. Also in the morning, or as soon as you can arrange it, Johnny, have a chat with Janus. Maggie, if you're not otherwise engaged, you're invited to go along as a referee. Okay with you, Johnny?"

"Absolutely okay!"

"Maggie, do you know where Janus is likely to be found on a Sunday morning?"

"He'll probably be at his ranch. It's about three miles west of Newtown."

"Ah, that's in Stone County," Goldstein exclaimed. "John and I have a good friend up there. Her name's Arlene Flynn. She's the top gun on the investigating staff of DA Aaron Benson. John and she worked a murder case a couple of years ago."

"Then Janus jumped in and kept the killer from landing in a cell on death row," Bogdanovic said in disgust as excited voices coming down the hallway drew his attention toward to the door.

A moment later the familiar figure of the district attorney burst into the small room.

Customarily pictured in newspapers in double-breasted pin-striped suit and glowingly described in articles as taciturn and stoic, he was wearing a navy blue blazer, pale blue polo shirt with open collar, and gray slacks. Looking around the room with ice blue eyes and an expression of unrestrained anger, he demanded, "What's going on here?"

Turning with a smile, Goldstein exclaimed, "Cornelius!" His hand extended in greeting. "I'm glad you got here so quickly."

Fists on hips, Vanderhoff said, "Harvey, an explanation is in order."

"It certainly is," Goldstein said quietly. "I'm afraid we've got a rather sticky mess on our hands. Shall we find someplace where we can talk about it privately?"

As the men left the room, Bogdanovic chuckled and whispered to Dane, "How would you like to be a fly on the wall of the room during that clash of the titans!"

16

If Death Ever Slept

DURING THE NEXT hour and a half, Dane sat in a surprisingly comfortable overstuffed armchair in the parlor of the suite. Observing the activities of the New York City police in action at a crime scene and appreciating the opportunity for comparisons to the work of the Los Angeles police, she found herself recalling a debate with Janus on television years ago in which she had been required to defend the fact that while district attorneys were routinely on scene when an investigation was beginning in order to provide legal advice, supervise the collection of evidence, and authorize the detention of witnesses or approve the arrest of a suspect, defense lawyers were not.

A defender was called in only after evidence was in hand and somebody was expecting to be, or had been, charged with a crime.

Janus had been forceful in insisting that for many hapless and bewildered individuals it was often far too late. Their fates had been sealed, he argued, because they soon discovered that the scales of justice had already been heavily weighted in favor of the prosecution—unless they had the ability to hire a Johnnie Cochran, Robert Shapiro, or F. Lee Bailey, as O. J. Simpson had done. He also cited Roy Black, who had been called in by William Kennedy Smith to fight a rape case. After initial representation by Robert Shapiro, Lyle and Eric Menendez engaged Leslie Abramson and avoided the death penalty.

Others had hired Theodore Janus with an equally satisfying effect, he had pointed out. But, he asked, how many prison cells held hapless, luckless men and women who could not afford such defenders?

"I say that even if it's only one," he thundered in conclusion, "it is one too many."

Now, silently observing the police as they followed the directions of Sgt. John Bogdanovic while he carried out the orders of Chief of Detectives Harvey Goldstein to treat the death of Paulie Mancuso as a homicide, she wondered what the presence of Janus might make of their efforts in a court of law. Would the police find themselves on trial? Might John Bogdanovic again find himself subjected to a withering Janus cross-examination?

For a time she stood at the window and looked down to the sidewalk while the corpse was inserted in a green body bag, then lifted by a pair of husky white-gloved men in blue coveralls into a white van belonging to the medical examiner. In due course the verdict on the cause of Mancuso's death would state the obvious. He died because his plummeting body had slammed into the cement after a nine-story fall.

Turning away from the window, she remembered Leibholz's word for what had happened in the adjoining room and muttered, "Death by defenestration."

Summoned one by one by Detectives Leibholz and Reiter out to the corridor, the three blind mice had gone, tails between their legs, for questioning as to how such a thing could have occurred.

A young woman wearing a blue jacket with "Crime Scene Unit" in yellow across the back had gone into Mancuso's room and come out carrying a plastic evidence bag containing Janus's book.

In another room of the suite, she supposed, Goldstein was explaining to the district attorney that the inscription on the title page of the book raised the tantalizing possibility that Mancuso had been driven by a concern for the well-being of wife and children when he had followed the implicit suggestion in the words that he do the honorable thing and take his own life.

If this could be proved, she mused as she waited patiently, the death of Paulie Mancuso was not suicide. It was murder, as surely as if someone had pushed him through the window.

Pondering this, she was startled to find Bogdanovic standing before her. "We're done here," he said. "The chief's waiting for us in the lobby."

"I didn't see him go out."

"That's why he's chief of detectives," he said, grinning. "He prides himself on being the unseen force. He had his heart to heart with Vanderhoff in a room across the hall. I'll drive him home and then I am to escort you to your hotel. Which one is it?"

"The Waldorf."

"Well, I'm impressed."

"It's courtesy of the Wolfe Pack."

"That's only fair."

They found Goldstein settled into the rear seat of the car. "I'm glad I don't have the day ahead of me that Vanderhoff has in store," he said. "Sooner or later the poor guy is going to have the press all over him demanding to know how his star witness, who was in *protective* custody, ended up dead."

"It's a good question," Bogdanovic said as he and Dane got in the car. "Suicide or murder, it happened under the noses of three of his own men. That's pretty embarrassing."

"You're a prosecuter, Maggie," Goldstein said. "If you were in Vanderhoff's shoes how would you handle it?"

"There's a very simple solution, really. I'd say that it was under police investigation and refer the baying news hounds to the office of the chief of detectives."

Goldstein grunted. "Thank you very much."

As the car edged past a parked patrol car, Bogdanovic asked, "What did Vanderhoff say when you told him about that inscription in Janus's book?"

"He looked at me as if I'd told him Mancuso was accidentally dropped by some little gray beings from outer space while loading him into a flying saucer in an attempted alien abduction."

"So what *is* he going to say to the press?"

"The official line will be that for a reason known only to the deity, Mancuso decided to kill himself. He will also say that his death will have no effect on prosecutions of his former pals in organized crime because Mancuso had already provided evidence in writing and on video tape sufficient to convict all of them."

Dane shook her head slowly. "The man is whistling past the graveyard. Without Mancuso on the witness stand to verify those statements, any second-year law student could get a judge to toss them out as hearsay. And even if they were admitted before a jury, a good lawyer can argue that the statements were coerced. Given the attitude of the public in the wake of the Simpson case with its aspersions on police tactics, there is likely to be at least one juror willing to believe it. As you well know, one is all you need. I do not envy the task that confronts Vanderhoff."

"Don't underestimate Cornelius," Goldstein said as the car turned a corner and moved westward. "He's cut from the same cloth as Fletcher M. Anderson. Vanderhoff is a man with professional ambitions, and no fool."

Glancing at Goldstein's reflection in the rearview mirror, Bogdanovic asked, "Who the hell is Fletcher M. Anderson?"

"You tell him, Maggie."

"In the Nero Wolfe novels he was at first an assistant DA in New York City. For a time he was the bane of Nero's existence. Then he married rich and moved up to White Plains, where he became DA of Westchester County."

"To quote Wolfe," Goldstein interjected, " 'Nothing is more admirable than the fortitude with which millionaires tolerate the disadvantages of their wealth.' "

Suddenly braking the car to avoid slamming into a cluster of giggling, boisterous, and obviously inebriated young men surging out of a corner bar and into the street against the light, Bogdanovic growled, "Look at those damn fools. They should watch out where they're going. They could've been killed."

"You're right, John," Goldstein said, reaching forward and clapping him on the shoulder as the young men zigzagged to the opposite corner. "They are certainly drunk and disorderly. Will our youth never learn to behave properly?"

"Jaywalking, too! And on the morning of the Sabbath," Dane added. "What is this old world coming to? Somebody should call the police."

"You're absolutely right, Maggie," Goldstein exclaimed as he sat back. "But we all know that you can never find a cop when you really need one."

"And even if they were arrested," said Dane, "some smart-assed lawyer and a bleeding-heart judge would have them out on bail. Before the arresting officer finished filling out the report those kids would be hitting the bars again."

"Gilbert and Sullivan were right on the money," Goldstein said. "A policeman's lot is not a happy one."

Dane turned slightly. "Name a cop in a Nero Wolfe story who claimed to have once arrested a man who turned out to be guilty."

"Too easy, Maggie. It was L. T. Cramer. That's how he got to be an inspector."

With hands tightly gripping the steering wheel and eyes on a red light he could have avoided if the drunks had not forced him to brake, Bogdanovic let out a forlorn sigh. As he waited for the light to go green again, he resigned himself to the inevitable as Goldstein and his amenable passenger engaged in Goldstein's favorite pastime of detective story trivia.

For thirty-two blocks heading downtown to Goldstein's apartment on Fifty-sixth Street just east of Second Avenue, he listened in silence while they traded rapid-fire questions and answers, each drawn from a seemingly bottomless well of Nero Wolfe minutiae.

By Eighty-second Street he had learned that any spoke will lead an ant to the hub, frogs can't fly, a hole in the ice was a peril only to those who go skating, you can not pick plums in a desert, and Nero Wolfe did not like being pestered, bullied, riled, badgered, or hounded.

Were any of these to occur, he heard from Dane as the car dashed across Seventy-ninth Street, Wolfe was likely to protest with expletives from a quaint thesaurus: "Egad!" "Pfui" "Confound it!" "Great hounds and Cerebus!" And the occasional "Bah."

The great detective had resolved cases recorded under the names "Bullet for One," "Omit Flowers," "Black Orchids," "Booby Trap," "The Father Hunt," and "Death of a Doxy," whatever the hell a doxy was.

Brought to a halt at Sixty-fifth Street by a traffic light he was regaled by domestic arrangements of the house on Thirty-fifth Street. An orchid nursery on the roof watched over by a man named Horstmann. A basement with a pool table and a cubbyhole with a couch, as well as the quarters of a majordomo called Fritz and an insulated room for storage of bottled beer. The ground floor had an office for Wolfe, a front room, a dining room, a kitchen, and an amply stocked pantry.

Finally, as he turned the car into East Fifty-sixth Street, he learned that there was an unresolved question concerning where Wolfe had been born. Although he claimed to have come into the world in the United States, he was on record saying he had been born on the border of Montenegro and Albania in the shadow of the Black Mountain, from which he claimed the name Nero was taken.

"All in all, it's been an interesting evening," Goldstein said as he left the car. "A fine dinner, the camaraderie of the Wolfe Pack, two extremely pleasant companions, the stimulation of literary conversation, and a challenging case of murder. Could we ask for anything more? Good night to you both."

Bogdanovic smiled fondly. "G'night, Chief."

"Pleasant dreams," said Dane.

With a wave of hand, Goldstein went up two steps, unlocked the door, and entered the building.

A moment later as a light turned on in a front window on the first floor, Bogdanovic turned to Dane and said, "Okay. Next stop, the Waldorf-Astoria."

"Do you always wait around until he's in his apartment?"

"There are lots of people that he sent to prison through the years who might be out walking the streets and decide that now is the time to finally settle their accounts."

"That's very touching, John."

"It's pretty selfish of me, actually. I have no desire to spend a lot of time breaking in a new boss."

"Yes, I can see why you'd feel that way, especially when there are so many bad guys that need to be brought to justice in a city that never sleeps."

"Do you ever miss New York?"

"Sometimes."

"What times?"

"When I'm looking at a television show about cops, or at a movie that was made here, and there's a shot of the skyline at night, all lit up and sparkling like a million jewels. Sometimes a courtroom drama will gave me a nostalgic tug by reminding me of the years I spent jousting for justice for the people of New York in the down-at-the-heels chambers in that foreboding, ugly gray monstrosity known as the Criminal Courts Building at One hundred Centre Street."

"Then why did you leave all that?"

"That's a very long story," she said as the car moved along deserted streets. "No, it's more like a Joan Collins novel. Woman falls in love with a dashing and handsome guy, follows her heart instead of her head, then realizes too late that the heart is not a very reliable compass. By then she has the responsibility of a child and before she knows what's happening she finds herself the lead prosecutor in what should have been a slam-dunk case. But it becomes the trial of the century with the whole country watching her and justice go into the sewer on Court TV."

"Janus took it into the sewer."

"He did what he believed he had to do for his client," she said looking through the window and realizing they had arrived at the hotel. "Wiggins raided the Wolfe Pack treasury to put me up in this palace and now I'm too damn excited by all that happened at that uptown hotel to sleep."

"Murder has a way of doing that."

"You're quite right, Sergeant Bogdanovic," she said, opening the car door. "But if death ever slept, you and I would be out of a job, wouldn't we?"

"What time shall I pick you up for our visit to Janus?"

"Suppose I give him a call around ten to see what hour he'll be ready to receive us at his ranch. Since the subject under discussion will be himself, I'm sure he'll be eager to do so."

HALF AN HOUR later, after circling the block several times and failing to find a legal place to park, Bogdanovic gave up looking and put the car in a bus stop. Trusting the blue police department parking permit in the front window would be noticed, should a traffic enforcement cop pass by looking to meet a daily quota for writing tickets, he turned up his coat collar against a cold wind biting from behind and walked the two blocks to his apartment house.

On the south side of Eighty-ninth Street just east of Riverside Drive with its pretty park dominated by the majestic rotunda of the tomb that had been built for the repose of the remains of Ulysses S. Grant, the stately limestone-front, five-story nineteenth-century mansion had been converted in the 1980s to one-per-floor apartments. Standing in its wood-paneled lobby and peering up four flights of stairs, he thought back eight years to the day he had rented the one on the top floor in anticipation of sharing it with a woman he had hoped to marry.

Wiser than he, she had discerned in that prospect the seeds of disaster in the form of the demands of conflicting careers and had left him to move, brokenhearted, into the apartment alone. Bigger than one person needed, it poved too much of a prize to give up.

It had two large bedrooms, one of which became an office. A spacious bathroom had a huge tub with a Jacuzzi. Closet space was more than ample. The kitchen had a cozy breakfast nook. The huge living room offered a fireplace. A skylighted loft proved perfect for workout equipment.

Then, he had welcomed the prospect of a daily steep climb as an adjunct to keeping physically fit. Scaling the steps two at a time, he reasoned, would save the cost of joining a health club. He also looked forward to not having to waste time waiting to use workout equipment at the persistently crowded departmental gym at One Police Plaza.

Now, he regarded the stairs and wondered not only if he could summon the energy to make the climb, but if he ought to look elsewhere for a smaller apartment closer to police headquarters. And in a building with elevators and a garage.

Only slightly out of breath after the ascent, he opened the door and paused a moment to reflect upon Chief Goldstein's first visit to the apartment. Invited up for drinks a few weeks after the move in, and having been given a tour of the apartment, he'd plopped into a corner of a long couch and declared, "You've got a lot of space for a single guy, John, but don't worry about that. Soon you will discover the truth of what I call Goldstein's Maxim Number One Regarding Living Accommodations. I quote: The rate of acquisition of things that are of absolutely no practical use but absolutely essential to a civilized lifestyle is in direct ratio to the space available to be filled. Unquote."

"If there is a Goldstein first maxim, I deduce there must be a second,"

Goldstein sipped from a glass of single-malt scotch. "You deduce correctly. It goes thusly: A man can never have too much room for books." Looking round, he added, "On that score I find you woefully remiss." He raised the hand holding the glass and pointed across the living room. "I observe *a single* bookcase. And from this distance I perceive not one volume in it that belongs to the mystery novel genre. We'll have to take steps to correct this glaring deficiency."

Intervening years had brought further visits marked by Goldstein's presentation of books drawn from the stock of the Usual Suspects bookstore, resulting in one bookcase devoted entirely to mysteries given to him by Goldstein. Assuming its place beside the first and two more that accommodated a wide range of other titles and subjects, it joined a steadily increasing accumulation of possessions that made moving into a new apartment a daunting prospect.

Deciding to go directly to bed, he paused in the doorway of the adjoining bedroom that had been made into an office. A green light on his answering machine signified that no one had called.

When the ringing of the phone beside his bed jolted him awake, a crisp male voice greeted him with, "I'm sorry to disturb you, Sergeant Bogdanovic. This is Officer Jim Trainer in communications. We've just got a report from the One-three Precinct of a man shot in the head in a car across the street from Thirty-six Gramercy Park East. Captain Tinney ordered me to inform you right away that according to the name on the victim's driver's license, the victim is Theodore R. Janus."

PART FOUR

Death of a Dude

17

Bullet for One

"FIRST, WE HAVE a mob informant who has flung himself out a ninth-floor window," said Goldstein as Bogdanovic's car sped down Second Avenue. "Number two: In Mancuso's room we found the book written by Theodore Janus, who has a reputation as the mouthpiece for the mob. Third, at one time he represented Mancuso. Fourth, Janus might or might not have inscribed a message in that book to his former client. Fifth, the words used could be interpreted as a threat, namely, that if Mancuso were to sing he could expect to see his wife and kids no more."

"Thereby providing the impetus for Mancuso's leap into the arms of Abraham," Bogdanovic said.

"Sixth and last," Goldstein continued, "a few hours later Janus apparently has been found shot to death. Do you find that all this as fascinating as I do, John?"

"It could be coincidence."

"I happen to be a graduate of the Sherlock Holmes college of criminology," Goldstein said as the car hurtled past Forty-second Street. "When everybody else sees the simple explanation, I find myself looking for a more complex one. I am prompted to do so in this instance because of what Janus said to me at the Wolfe Pack dinner when we talked about Mancuso's decision to turn state's evidence. Janus asked if I was involved in that matter. When I told him I wasn't he expressed the opinion I was lucky I had not been dragged into what he called *that quagmire*. The words went in one ear and out the other at the time. In retrospect and in view of all that's happened since that dinner I have to wonder what he meant by it."

"Quagmire," said Bogdanovic. "The last time I heard anybody use that word was in reference to the Vietnam War."

"That was boggy ground, indeed. But what comes to my mind is the fearsome Grimpen Mire in *The Hound of the Baskervilles*. Not even Sherlock Holmes was able to rescue Stapleton once he'd blundered into it in a desperate effort to escape."

Bogdanovic smiled. "Will there ever be a situation in which you won't come up with a parallel in some mystery story?"

"Impossible," Goldstein answered as the car raced past the funnel of approach lanes to the entrance to the Midtown Tunnel at Thirty-sixth Street. "I know only two literary sources that offer more insight into the human condition than the mystery story. They are the Holy Bible and the plays of Shakespeare."

Five minutes later, as Bogdanovic slowed the car to execute a right turn from Second Avenue, he found long, blue-painted wooden police barriers blocking entry into the first of three blocks of East Twenty-first Street known as Gramercy Park North, despite the fact that only one of the blocks actually adjoined the park. Beyond the barriers, revolving lights on the roofs of a line of patrol cars flashed streaks of red and blue on the facades of the surrounding buildings.

"Scene of the crime," Bogdanovic muttered, wedging the car between a barrier and the last of the patrol units. "Two in the same night."

"Not for the first time," Goldstein said, getting out.

After walking a short block, they turned into Gramercy Park East. Ahead on the right in front towered a white apartment house with elaborate Gothic motifs, bay windows, and balustrades. Two silver-painted stone figures of knights in armor flanked the entrance court of number Thirty-six. Their hands in mailed gauntlets grasped long poles that looked like lances but were topped with unlit lamps.

As residents of buildings surrounding the park leaned from windows to see what had happened to disturb the serenity of their park and their sleep, the two statues with their helmeted heads seemed to watch impassively as across the narrow street police officers in navy blue uniforms and detectives in plain clothes milled around the silver Rolls-Royce.

Seated at the steering wheel, the body of the dead man was upright with the head slumped slightly to the right. From a small hole in the left temple a trickle of blood had run down the left side of the face. Slanting from the right corner of the mouth was a half-smoked cigar with a black and gold band.

If the statues had eyes behind the narrow openings of the visors of the helmets, and if their maker had given them brains, mouths, and tongues, Bogdanovic mused as he and Goldstein strode toward the car and the men, there would have been no mystery as to what had happened during the night to Theodore R. Janus. But the task and challenge of resolving that question had fallen to a collection of human beings with police shields pinned to coats or carried in wallets in suit pockets.

Captain Walter Tinney stepped forward to greet Goldstein with a handshake, Bogdanovic with a nod and a smile, and no amenities. "The single shot to the left temple appears to have been from small-caliber gun, probably a twenty-two."

Bending down a little and peering into the car, Goldstein asked, "Who found him?"

"It was one of our own. Officer George Wieser of the One-three was on his way to work and thought the occupant might have had a heart attack. When he stopped to have a look he saw that the window was down. But it doesn't appear to be a robbery. I've got officers canvassing the neighborhood to find out if anybody saw or heard anything."

Bogdanovic asked, "Any idea when it happened?"

"Wieser found him just before four o'clock."

"I think you may assume that he took that bullet a little after midnight," Goldstein asserted, stepping away from the car. "Do you agree, John?"

"Makes sense to me," Bogdanovic said. "Unless he hung around the hotel awhile after the dinner."

"Excuse me, fellas," exclaimed Tinney. "You two sound as if you were with him last night."

"Right over there," Bogdanovic replied, pointing toward the Gramercy Park Hotel. "Janus was the honored guest at a banquet of the Wolfe Pack. Unfortunately, the chief and I were called away from the festivities a little early."

"Ah yes," interjected Tinney. "The Mancuso thing uptown."

"Yes. So we have no way of knowing exactly what time Janus may have left the Gramercy Park Hotel."

"I think it's safe to assume he didn't linger long," Goldstein said. "Janus wasn't a man to stick around after the spotlight was turned off. He would have tucked his Nero Wolfe Award under his arm and headed for the ranch."

"Even when the traffic is light that's almost an hour's drive from the city," said Bogdanovic."

"There's also a clue to the time of death in the cigar he's got in his mouth," Goldstein continued. "It's thick, and I'd say it was originally seven inches long. He smoked about half of it by the time he was shot, which would take him about half an hour. More than likely, he lit it at the hotel and was still smoking it when he reached this car. He may have decided to finish it before he drove away."

"Then somebody walked up to him," Bogdanovic said.

"Somebody he'd felt safe enough to talk to by winding down the window," suggested Tinney.

"That's why this isn't likely to have been a random act," Goldstein said. "In this era of car hijackings Janus would never sit still, much less roll down a window, for some stranger, even in Gramercy Park. Not to mention the fact that Theodore Janus was a lawyer who managed to accumulate more enemies in one year than other attorneys have been able to do in their entire careers."

"Including a few who had dinner with him last night, barely a stone's throw from this very spot," Bogdanovic said. Smiling at Goldstein, he added, "Maybe at the dinner last night there was a wolf in Wolfe's clothing."

Slowly shaking his head, Tinney said, "Would you two care to save me lot of time by naming the shooter?"

"Nothing would please us more, Walt," said Goldstein. "Alas, the suspects appear to be legion. There may also be a connection between Janus's murder and the one uptown."

"Mancuso wasn't a suicide?"

"I'm reasonably sure he went out the window of his own volition, but there are indications he was coerced into it. Now we're faced with a killing that may be related to what happened uptown. That's why, Walt, as of now my office will be running both the Mancuso investigation and this one, with Johnny coordinating."

Tinney smiled. "That's just fine with me, Chief."

"I know it is, Walt. But let no one else doubt, no matter what his rank, that if Sergeant Bogdanovic gives an order it will be the same as though it came directly from me. There is, as of now, no case on the books with any higher priority."

The captain's smile stretched into a broad grin. "I know the drill, Chief. Whatever Johnny wants, Johnny gets!"

With a little bow, Bogdanovic said, "At the moment, Johnny wants the assistance of Leibholz and Reiter."

"I'll flash the Bat Signal for the dynamic duo immediately."

"Now, if you'll excuse me," said Goldstein, "I need a Batmobile to take me down to headquarters. I've got some phone calls to make that are going to mess up the rest of this weekend for a certain district attorney, not to mention His Honor the mayor."

18

When a Man Murders

THE NEXT HALF hour brought the arrival at the crime scene of the tall, slender figure of red-haired Detective Joseph Reiter and his partner, Detective Albert Leibholz, whose appearance had been altered by more than a year and a half of strict dieting as demanded and enforced by his wife from bearlike to nearly as thin as Reiter's.

With them came all the men, women, and equipment required to carry out all the procedures developed over more than a century and a half of criminal investigating. Using the techniques that forensic sciences had devised, they would work to answer all the questions raised by the act of murder.

First into action, a photographer spent fifteen minutes documenting the scene in general and the body in particular on color film from every possible angle.

An earnest young woman in the white coveralls of the crime scene unit used a small brush to apply a gray powder to the door of the car in hopes of discerning fingerprints, only to announce a disappointing outcome. "Lots of prints," she said. "None of them is more than a smudge."

"It's a small entrance wound," declared medical examiner Hassan Awini, leaning into the car. "This is interesting. I note that there has been a surprisingly minor effusion of blood from the wound."

"I want the body removed as soon as possible," Bogdanovic said. "I expect the press to start showing up at any minute. I'll have an area set up for them as far from here as possible until after the body's gone. The last thing we need is a bunch of pain-in-the-ass reporters getting in our way and news photogs elbowing one another aside to grab a shot of that cigar in Janus's mouth as they did a few years ago when mobster Paul Gigante was gunned down after he lit up a stogie in the garden of Umberto's Clam House."

He turned to Leibholz. "Round up some uniforms to set up a corral in front of the hotel. If they start screaming about the trampling of their First Amendment rights to sensationalize, tell them somebody will brief them on all the gruesome details."

As Bogdanovic spoke, Captain Tinney arrived at his side. "All we've gotten so far from canvassing the residents is that a few heard what they thought was a car backfiring. Saturday nights there's always a heavy flow of traffic on the north side of the park where Lexington Avenue dead-ends and the cars have to make a right turn either to get over to Park Avenue South or to go around the park to Irving Place. We also turned up an elderly gentleman who lives on the west side of the park who said he also heard a loud bang and that when he took a look out his window he saw a flash of light on this side of the park. It could have been the muzzle flash."

"Not if it came *after* the bang." He turned to Reiter. "Red, I want you to interview that gentleman again about the timing. Then meet Leibholz at the hotel and between the two of you find out if anybody recalls what time Janus left the hotel. Also ask if anyone saw him leave and if so whether Janus left with anyone. Or if it appeared he might have been followed."

As Reiter departed, Tinney added, "To locate late-night dog walkers, joggers, anyone who was out for a walk or anyone else who might have been passing by, we'll be posting notices on doors, poles, trees, and park fences that will have a phone number for possible witnesses to call."

WITH THE BODY removed, a criminalist entered the car to dictate his findings to a second criminalist, who jotted them into a notebook. "All doors locked. Driver's side window down. Key in the ignition. Nothing remarkable about the rest of the interior. Glove compartment closed. Contents of same: a New York state road map, a New York Police Department parking permit, a leather travel humidor with capacity for a dozen cigars. I count only ten. Same gold and black bands as the one in his mouth."

"I'll stick to Phillies," said the criminalist as his partner passed him a box of plastic evidence bags. Inserting the humidor into one of them, he added, "You had better post a guard on this, Sergeant, or somebody in the property room will burn up your evidence one at a time."

Presently, Leibholz and Reiter returned.

"The old gentleman says he's positive the bang had to come first," Reiter reported. "He says it was the sound that made him look through the window. He says he saw the flash a few seconds later."

"Did he tell you what sort of flash it was?"

Nodding, Reiter answered, "He said it was like somebody was using a flash camera."

"Didn't that strike him as a little odd? Who snaps a picture in Gramercy Park at night on Saturday?"

"I asked him that. Apparently, it's not that unusual. A lot of fashion photographers use the park and the surrounding houses as backgrounds. Quite a few movies are made here, as well."

Bogdanovic looked to Leibholz. "Any luck with the people at the hotel, Al?"

"There were a lot of people leaving the hotel, on account of a big banquet of some kind that was held there last night."

"That was the Wolfe Pack dinner. They are devotees of Nero Wolfe, the famed fictional crime solver. I was there myself with Chief Goldstein."

"If I recall correctly," said Leibholz, "you and the chief were also present at another of those mystery fan shindigs. I also recall that someone who'd attended that affair turned up murdered not long after."

"What is your point, Detective?"

"It occurs to me," Leibholz said, chuckling, "that the rate of murders in this town might go down appreciably if you and the chief were to stop accepting invitations to banquets."

"Very droll, Detective. May we now get on to the business of the murder at hand? What else did you learn at the hotel?"

"One of the bellman *thinks* Janus left with a young woman."

"*Thinks* is not helpful."

"There's a lot of press over there," Reiter said.

Bogdanovic turned his head in the direction of the hotel and said, bitterly, "The ubiquitous Fourth Estate, voracious as ever to bite into and chew on the latest atrocity in the naked city of eight million stories."

"Somehow they learned whose body was in that car."

Bogdanovic's eyes narrowed. "Nobody but our own people have been near this scene since the moment Officer Wieser discovered the body. Who the hell could have tipped them off so quickly?"

"Maybe one of those reporters killed him," Leibholz joked. "I wouldn't put anything beyond them if it meant getting a byline on a juicy story."

"As tempting as that notion may be," Bogdanovic said, "we're going to have more than enough work to go around in getting to the bottom of this case without adding the entire membership of the New York Press Club to our list of suspects."

"Maybe a news photographer did it," declared Reiter with an impish grin. "That would explain the mysterious flash."

"I see. A guy with a camera in one hand and a pistol in the other just happened to be hanging around Gramercy Park awaiting a chance to kill the most famous defense lawyer since the days of Clarence Darrow."

"Someone obviously was hanging around waiting for him," said Leibholz. "From all I've seen, this was not a spur-of-the-moment killing. It was an assassination."

"As usual you've got it exactly right, Al," Bogdanovic said, jamming his hands into the pockets of his overcoat. "But if you'd care to accompany me as I meet with the press you will hear that it is the settled decision of the police that this was a matter of Janus's having been in the wrong place at the wrong time. After all, murder by a stranger is hardly unheard of on the streets of li'l ol' New Yawk, is it?"

19

Invitation to Murder

WHEN THE RINGING of the telephone startled Maggie Dane awake she shared the unnerving experience of all those who travel long distances across several time zones. For a moment she had no idea where she was, nor the time. But in the seconds required to lift the bedside phone and answer it with a sleepy "Hello," she remembered where she was, why, and everything that had happened in the hours before she had tumbled wearily into a Waldorf-Astoria bed.

"Sorry to wake you up so early," said Bogdanovic, thereby resolving the question of whether it was morning or evening. "I have some terrible news that I wanted you to hear from me before it gets in the newspapers or on radio and TV."

Sitting up, she blurted, "Has something happened at home?"

"Don't worry. It's not about your kid or anything bad out in California. It's your friend Theodore Janus. He's been murdered."

"But we were with him just a few hours ago," she said, realizing immediately the senselessness of what she had said, as though Janus's having been in their company somehow had rendered him immune to murder. Her next words were the logical questions expected by a homicide detective when making an official notification, as well as by a prosecutor for whom a report of a murder was a familiar cause for a phone to ring early in the morning. "When? Where? Do you have a suspect in custody?"

"He was found shot to death in his car around four o'clock, not far from where the Wolfe Pack dinner was held. We are fairly certain it was not a robbery attempt. All the signs point to the shooters having followed him, or laid in wait. It also looks as if they were engaged in a conversation. The car window was lowered. That suggests he either knew the shooter or felt no reason to be concerned about whoever it was that walked up to the car. He was obviously feeling safe enough to be looking straight ahead when he was shot. He was also smoking. He still had one of his Cuban cigars in his mouth."

"The smoking explains the open window. Theo always rolled it down when he smoked in the car."

"As I said, I wanted to let you know about this, rather than have you find out through a news account. The vultures known as reporters, photographers, and TV news crews showed up in droves."

"That will have Theo smiling, wherever he is. Nothing ever pleased him more than seeing that leathery face of his spread all over the front pages or on the TV screen."

"Maggie, I know this has to be a shock to you, but because you knew him so well, and because it's possible that he was shot by someone he knew, and because you two were so close—"

"You want my help in compiling a list of possible suspects."

"Whenever you feel up to it, of course."

"Tell me where you want me to be and when."

"What about ten o'clock this morning in my office? That's at One Police Plaza, sixteenth floor. I'll send a car to fetch you."

"Save taxpayers money, John. I'll get there on the subway."

"Right! I keep thinking of you as a Californian, even though I know you were born and bred a New *Yawk-uh*."

"I'm looking forward to renewing my acquaintanceship with the good old downtown number six."

AT NINE O'CLOCK, with the practiced indifference of untold hours spent behind the bulletproof glass of a subway token booth at Grand Central Terminal, a middle-aged female clerk ignored Maggie's "Good Morning" and wordlessly exchanged three dollars for two small brass discs. Fifteen minutes later, she waited on the platform with a small group of Sunday-morning travelers who gazed impatiently toward the black mouth of a tunnel as though by looking they could will the arrival of a train. When it came they heard a screeching of steel wheels rubbing against curving tracks well before its blunt nose emerged from the dark.

Unimpeded by the teeming throngs that on workday mornings surged into the already packed downtown local, slowing its pace, the nearly empty train carried her with what seemed breathtaking speed to the City Hall–Brooklyn Bridge station. There, as if all the years since she had left the city for California had been erased, habit led her through familiar passages and up a flight of stone stairs into a thicket of sturdy columns and soaring arches opposite City Hall.

Built in 1914, the twenty-five-story Municipal Building, the architectural masterpiece of the renowned firm of McKim, Mead & White, had been hailed at the time as the solution to the problem of how to house all the agencies of a mushrooming city government. Now, it was but one of many city office buildings built or rented in a seemingly futile effort to keep up with the demand for even more space.

Emerging out of the shadowy, cathedral-like underpinnings of the towering Municipal Building, she faced another manifestation of that expansion. In the shape of a huge block of red brick with a honeycomb of square windows, police headquarters was known as One Police Plaza. But rather than crossing the broad plaza itself, she walked toward St. Andrew's Church. A neo-Georgian structure, it was a graceful remnant of the 1920s. Entering it in the middle of the Mass, she thought there was no more fitting place to contemplate and give thanks for the life, work, and inspiration of her friend, mentor, and adversary, Theodore R. Janus.

He had labored long and hard in the cause of equal justice under law that was the solemn promise of the state and federal courthouses of nearby Foley Square and along Centre Street, and the sacred duty of those who argued cases in them.

Now, he was dead.

God willing, she prayed, his murderer would stand in one of the hallowed chambers to answer for his crime and, reap the punishment prescribed by law.

First, however, he had to be caught.

Leaving the old church's assurances that good shall always triumph over evil, she stepped into December sunlight that shone brilliantly but without warmth on the red brick plaza and walked boldly toward police headquarters with a determination to provide as much assistance as possible in that cause.

To her surprise as she stopped at the security desk just inside the lobby and reached into her handbag for identification, she was greeted by the portly middle-aged police officer behind the desk with, "Good morning, Miss Dane. Glad to see you again."

Embarrassed at not remembering him, she said, "Thanks. It's nice to be back. I've got an appointment with—"

"I know. Sergeant Bogdanovic. Go right up. Sixteenth floor. His office is straight ahead and down the hallway, last door on the right, next to Chief Goldstein's office."

DISCOVERING BOGDANOVIC'S DOOR wide open, Dane peered into an office that seemed overwhelmed by computers and their associated equipment. Behind a gray government-issued steel desk, his head bent down as he read Officer Wieser's report on the discovery of Janus's body, Bogdanovic was coatless. A patterned tie was loose, revealing the undone top button of a pale blue cotton shirt with sleeves neatly folded back to the elbows.

Giving a single rap on the door with a knuckle, she said, "Excuse me, mister. Do you know where a lady might find a cop in this half-assed town?"

He looked up with a scowl. "The police department is closed on Sundays. Come back tomorrow."

"Oh, that's too bad. In that case, do you know the way to the Statue of Liberty?"

"Why? You don't look to me like you're one of the tired, the poor, or the homeless refuse of a teeming shore. Wait. On second thought I could be wrong about that. You do look like someone who might have come from that burg out on the other coast. Give me a second and I'll think of the name of the place. You know the one. The sleepy little town where they make movies about car crashes, exploding buildings, and cops filled with angst and snappy one-liners like 'Go ahead, make my day.' You look as if you might be a movie star."

"Actually, I'm known for my television appearances."

"Take my advice. Shoot for the big screen."

"Speaking of shooting," she said, coming into the office, "I suppose it's too early for there to have been developments."

"All I've got so far is a report by the officer who found the body and summaries of the canvass of the neighborhood and the hotel employees. A few people may have heard the shot, but nobody saw anything. The only exception is a man who lives on the west side of the park who said he heard a bang and then saw what he called a light, as if somebody used a flash camera."

"May I read the reports?"

"Of course. That's why you're here," he said, gathering them from his desk and handing them to her. "Then we'll go next door and hash 'em over with the chief."

She looked surprised. "Harvey's in his office?"

"He's been here all night. He's convinced there's a link between Janus's being shot and Paulie Mancuso's fatal attempt at flying. He doesn't believe in coincidences."

"What about you?"

"I believe in facts. But at this point I don't have enough of them to know which way to go in either investigation."

"To paraphrase another detective, if you want to make bricks you need clay."

"Don't tell me who said it, let me guess. Nero Wolfe!"

"No cigar for you, Sergeant. Sherlock Holmes."

20

Homicide Trinity

LEAVING BOGDANOVIC'S SMALL, sparely furnished office with its overcrowding computers, Dane entered a space as commodious as she had expected the New York Police Department to provide for its chief of detectives. But as Goldstein stood to greet her from behind an expansive desk of highly polished wood, she saw in the contrast of the spaces a definition of the men working in them.

A corner bookcase attested to Goldstein's unbridled passion for reading and learning from fictional mysteries. Each met the romantic requirement that all crimes be solved through intuition and ratiocination, followed by a confession. In bringing villains to justice, an observant detective's intellect would set aright a world whose morality, equanimity, and peace had been upset. Chief of Detectives Harvey Goldstein was, she decided, the very embodiment of a breed of detectives who would have been known and grudgingly respected by Nero Wolfe.

Bogdanovic's office represented a latter-day kind of sleuthing. His world was microprocessors, computer chips, screens, keyboards, printouts, and modems connecting him to law enforcers around the globe, if need be. It was an electronic universe in which the criminals *might* be tracked down and arrests sustained, not only because of a smart detective employing time-tested ways but also on the basis of scientific analysis of data. Bogdanovic was, she mused, the detective Sherlock Holmes might have been if Sir Arthur Conan Doyle had lived into the age of computers.

But in real life Bogdanovic's detective work under the supervision of Harvey Goldstein was followed all too frequently by a bargain struck between a prosecutor and a lawyer for the defendant that restored neither morality, equanimity, nor peace. Sometimes, if the attorney happened to be Theodore Janus, there might not even be a conviction.

"Condolences on the loss of your friend," Goldstein said as Dane sat before his massive desk.

"Thank you very much. But Theo was more than a friend."

"In that regard you certainly are in a unique position to assist John in following the first rule of murder investigation: Know the victim."

"I doubt that there's anything I can add to what you already know. His life was literally an open book. The man I knew is the one in *Janus for the Defense*. He was the Theodore Janus you both saw when he jousted with those reporters prior to the Wolfe Pack Banquet and later during the dinner. I thought Theo was amusing, self-deprecating, and thoroughly charming."

"What I saw," said Bogdanovic, "was conceit, arrogance, and an amazing capacity for duplicity. I saw nothing admirable in him."

With eyes flashing anger, she answered, "Could that have been because you went to the Black Orchid dinner prepared to find nothing admirable in him?"

Bogdanovic blinked in surprise. "That's not it at all."

"Oh I think it is," she retorted. "I believe you are still smarting because Theo got the better of you in the Griffith trial."

"That is ridiculous."

"You're like that young reporter who asked Theo how he could sleep at night knowing that he'd gotten so many guilty people off."

"It was an excellent question, the point of which, I remind you, Janus managed to avoid answering by shifting the blame onto the jury."

"Blame? Where is the blame in an attorney's zealously carrying out his duty to defend a client whose very life is at stake?"

"Excuse me, folks," Goldstein said, drumming fingertips on the top of his desk. "As much I'm enjoying this bantering, it is not the purpose of this meeting, is it? We are here in order to benefit from Maggie's special relationship with Janus. I think we can agree he was a controversial individual. The question I have for you, Maggie, is whether you know of anyone who resented him deeply enough to want to see him dead?"

"He's got a file drawer in his office at his ranch crammed with threatening letters and notes that date back to his earliest cases. As a matter of fact, I started that file while I clerked for him when I was in law school. He had me label it the 'Thou Art Only a Man' file. He told me he got the idea when reading a book about the triumphal processions of ancient Rome. Riding in the chariot with the hero was a slave who held the laurel wreath above the hero's head while constantly saying, 'Remember thou art only a man.' In spite of the flamboyant style Theo affected, he was always aware that he was only a man."

"After the trial," said Goldstein, "did he get threats?"

"Sure he was threatened. So was I."

Gently touching her right hand, Bogdanovic said, "You were not the one shot to death in your Rolls-Royce parked on Gramercy Park East."

Goldstein asked, "Why did it happen there? Why should the killer pick that location, John?"

"I thought that was pretty obvious. He was stalking him. He simply followed him from the hotel to the car."

"That hypothesis requires the killer to have known Janus was at the hotel."

"If he was stalking Janus, he didn't need to know. He just followed Janus from his ranch."

"Why bother? It seems to me if he intended to murder Janus he would have seen that he would have a better chance of getting away with it at some secluded spot up in Stone County rather than on a street in Manhattan on a Saturday night. I think the more likely scenario is that the killer was lying in wait for Janus to leave the dinner."

"That theory rests on the presumption the killer knew Janus would be at the dinner and when and where the Black Orchid dinner was being held."

"There's no mystery in that," Maggie said. "Wiggins sent out announcements to the news media that Janus and I would be there."

Goldstein grinned. "Why am I not surprised that Wiggins saw the publicity value in bringing together the lawyers who had held the country spellbound in the trial of the century? Good old Wiggins simply acted on the maxim stated by none other than Sherlock Holmes in 'The Six Napoleons.' 'The press is a most valuable institution, if only you know how to use it.' "

Dane smiled knowingly. "In fairness to Wiggins, he did warn me that if I accepted the invitation to present Theo the Wolfe award I could expect a lot of press to show up. He told me he'd understand if I chose to opt out."

"Of course he did. He knew you wouldn't."

"This is just great," Bogdanovic said. "Thanks to Wiggins and his damn press release, any nut with a score to settle with Janus could have found out where he would be and when simply by reading a newspaper."

"So, Sgt. John Bogdanovic," Goldstein said, "how do you propose to proceed in this very fascinating investigation?"

"There's not much I can do until I've reviewed the written reports on the canvass of the neighborhood for possible witnesses. Plus the reports from the medical examiner and the ballistics unit regarding the gun that was used. The Rolls has been impounded for a thorough going-over. The fingerprint section is going to see if lasers can find anything useful in the smudges that were found on the door at the scene."

"Have you given any thought to motive?"

"We've ruled out robbery. That leaves three ways to go. One is the mob angle. We can't dismiss as coincidence the fact that Janus was murdered on the same night that Paulie Mancuso went out a window. Next is the possibility someone had a personal score to settle. Who knows how many of the guys Janus defended still did time? One of them could have blamed Janus for not getting him off. And I see no reason why we shouldn't consider the possibility that a member of the Wolfe Pack did it. I never saw so many eyes with daggers in them as I did last night."

"The mob, a vengeance-minded former client, and the Wolfies at the banquet," said Goldstein. "You've got your work cut out for you, John. Where will you begin?"

"I was hoping I might continue to enlist the assistance of a person who knew Janus better than anyone," he said as he turned toward Dane. "That is, if Maggie's got the time."

As the men looked at her expectantly, she said, "I happen to be on a well-deserved vacation. Nothing would please me more than helping John bring Theo's killer to account."

Goldstein beamed. "Good. As of now, Maggie, you may consider yourself an official consultant to this office."

PART FIVE

Omit Flowers

21

The Doorbell Rang

"I'M PROBABLY WAY out of line," Boganovic said, clearing a chair for Dane by removing a stack of computer discs and piling them on the floor, "but I do feel, since we're going to be working closely on this case, that I should know what you meant when you told Goldstein that you and Janus were more than friends."

"Are you asking if Janus and I were lovers?"

Sitting at his desk, he took a deep breath. "Yes."

"You're not out of line. It's a fair question. The answer is that we were not. What I meant when I said Theo was more than my friend is that I feel I owe him for my career in law. Whatever successes I have achieved could not have occurred without his constant encouragement and frequent counsel."

"Was he upset when you became a prosecutor?"

"As far as Theo was concerned, we were opposite sides of the same coin. I'll never forget his saying to me on the day he arrived in L.A. to lead the defense in what the press persists in calling the trial of the century that with me prosecuting and him defending there could be no question the defendant and the people would get a fair trial."

"Yet most observers believe the people didn't get one. They blame the outcome of that trial on Janus's slick lawyering in the way he maneuvered the judge into excluding crucial evidence that would have let you win the case."

"That is utter nonsense. Theo won the case by accepting the rules that both sides had agreed on at the start of the trial and then using them to his advantage. In short, he outlawyered me."

"If you say so. But at least you've had the satisfaction of winning the case in the court of public opinion."

"That's exactly what Theo said to me."

"He wasn't upset by the beating he took in the press and on all the TV talk shows?"

"Theo was a realist and a fatalist. You have to be if you're a defense attorney and the public's decided before the trial even begins that your client is guilty. He used to say that losing in the court of public opinion was as inescapable for a defense lawyer as the inevitability of one's death. He liked to joke that at times he envied prosecutors because they faced only two things in life that they could not avoid—death and taxes, whereas every defense lawyer had been cursed with a third: losing a case. He hated the fact that the prosecution had so much at its command. In a criminal trial the district attorney has money, police, crime labs, the FBI, and every kind of expert to testify in every branch of science. And public opinion on his side. What does the defendant have? Most of the time it's a single defense attorney who is likely to be a public defender with a hundred or more other cases to handle at the same time."

"How did you feel about the gangsters he defended?"

"The last time I checked it, the Constitution of the United States did not bar a gangster from claiming the right to have the services of a lawyer."

"Neither does it require a lawyer to represent everyone who rings his doorbell."

"The only thing Theo cared about when the doorbell rang was that the person pushing the button was cloaked in the presumption of innocence."

"Even when he knew the guy at the door was guilty?"

"It's the guilty guy who most needs a defense attorney. The glory of our system of justice is that there are men and women who are prepared to defend the rights of the guilty in order to safeguard the rights of the innocent who are wrongly accused."

"Which rarely happens."

"If it occurs once, that's too often."

"I'm certain if you asked everyone who's now in prison, and that person told you the truth, you'd learn they're all guilty of what they were convicted of."

"But I would also hope they would tell me that because they'd had a competent lawyer, they'd gotten the fair trial they were entitled to."

"Isn't that also the responsibility of the prosecution?"

"Of course it is. But thanks to the wisdom of the founders of this country, anyone who stands accused of a crime will have a defense attorney to make sure the prosecutor does not shirk that responsibility. Unfortunately, although the Constitution grants an accused person the right to have an attorney, very few get the benefit of being defended by a Theodore Janus. His death is a terrible loss for the cause of justice. And I've lost a beloved old friend."

"When's the last time you saw him prior to last night?"

"After the trial he took me to dinner at my favorite restaurant up in the Hollywood hills."

"What was his mood?"

"He was very happy, except for the fact that he was down to his last Havana cigar until he returned home. He was eager to get back to New York to work on what he said might be a breakthrough in the correction of a great miscarriage of justice."

"Did he provide any details?"

"No. He said he was flying to Watertown to interview a man in prison."

"Janus didn't even hint what great miscarriage of justice he was hoping to correct?"

"Naturally, I tried to wangle it out of him. But he told me that the case was so potentially dangerous—"

"Potentially dangerous?"

"His exact phrase. He said it was so potentially dangerous that he could not go beyond what he'd told me. He said I would have to wait and find out along with everyone else when he was ready to go public."

"Did he indicate how long that might be?"

"No, but I sensed that he expected to make the breakthrough when he talked with the man in Watertown. Since he did not go public with anything, I assumed that his trip turned out to be nothing but a chance to take up his Mooney."

"His what?"

"Theo has—had—his own plane. It's a single-engine four-seater. He parks it at the Stone County Airport. He welcomed any opportunity to fly that plane, so I suppose the flight to Watertown was a pleasant time for him, even though it apparently did not result in the big breakthrough he was hoping for. That is, if he actually made the visit."

"We can find that out easily enough," he said, reaching for his phone. "The prison will have a record of his visiting in its computer."

Easing back in her chair to observe him at work, she again felt she was in the presence of an incarnation of Archie Goodwin. Handsome, impeccable in attire, direct, impatient, and assertive, he was the man of action conveying a restless urgency even when seated at a desk.

Connected, he switched on a speakerphone.

"Watertown Correctional Facility, Officer Mike King."

"This is the office of the Chief of Detectives, NYPD, Sergeant Bogdanovic. Shield number eleven, twenty-six, seventy."

"How can I help you, Sergeant?"

"I'm checking on whether there was a visit to an inmate of your facility."

"Inmate's name and number?"

"I'm sorry, I don't have that information. But the visitor's name was Janus. Theodore R. Janus."

"The big-shot laywer?"

"Yes."

"Do you know the date of the visit?"

"No I don't."

"Hang on a sec while I bring it up on the computer."

"Thanks."

"Yeah, here it is. Janus, Theodore R. He was here on several dates starting in July. On all occasions the inmate refused to see him."

"What's the inmate's name?"

"Let's see. Elwell, John. Nickname of Jake. Oh holy hell."

"Holy hell *what?*"

"I'm sorry to tell you, Sergeant, but the day after Janus was here, Elwell was stabbed to death."

"Stabbed to death? By whom?"

"I'm afraid we've not determined that. No one's talking."

"Do you know the circumstances?"

"Again, no one's saying. It happened in the showers. We have to assume somebody had some kind of beef to settle with him."

22

Where There's a Will

"I GUESS THAT explains why Theo never made an announcement of a big breakthrough," Dane said, her face grim as Bog-danovic hung up the telephone and switched off the speakerphone. "Theo never talked with Elwell."

"But someone found out he'd been there. Then it became the old, old story of the dead man telling no tales. An inmate beef my foot. Elwell was murdered because Janus had been there to see him. There's more here than a coincidence in the killing of a prisoner a day after Janus went all the way to Watertown to interview him. When Janus told you he was working on something potentially dangerous, he wasn't simply engaging in a bit of his famous lawyerly hyperbole."

"The immediate question is what was there about Jake Elwell that made him so important?"

"The name does not ring a bell for you, Maggie?"

She shook her head slowly. "If Jake Elwell was a client, it was after my time in Theo's office."

Swinging around in his chair, Bogdanovic faced a device that she supposed would have been welcomed by Archie Goodwin and viewed with suspicion by his employer, had the creator of Archie and his curmudgeonly employer lived longer.

Bogdanovic gleefully turned on the computer. "Let's have a gander at what the late Mr. Elwell's rap sheet can tell us."

Prompted by a few keystrokes and a decisive punching of the Enter button, the monitor screen flashed: ACCESSING DATA. PLEASE STAND BY.

With a smile and wink at Dane, Bogdanovic said, "Good old data bank!"

A split second later as the screen provided the file Dane saw his expression turn to disbelief as the screen produced only a few lines of information.

"What the hell is going on here?" he demanded of the screen. "This is . . . *it?*"

Insistent fingers seemed to assault the keyboard, commanding the system to provide more, only to produce the same file.

"This can't be right," he said, angrily. "According to this, the son of a bitch had only one arrest. One charge of grand larceny in the second degree. He pleaded no contest."

"If it was grand larceny in the second degree," Dane said, thoughtfully, "it was theft of more than fifty thousand dollars, or larceny by extortion. The no contest smacks of plea bargain."

"Which suggests he was in it with somebody else," Bogdanovic said. "He cut a deal to testify against whoever that was. What's the normal sentence for larceny two?"

"It depends on the type of larceny. If it's embezzlement, for example, and it's a first offense, the judge would have wide discretion. He could even give probation with the stipulation of restitution. But that offense also covers, as I said, larceny by extortion. If the extortion was accompanied by the instilling of fear of physical harm, you're talking about serious prison time. But the criminal procedure law covering second-degree grand larceny also includes the use or abuse by a public servant of his official duties, such as failing or refusing to perform duties, thereby affecting some other person adversely."

"So what could Janus's interest have been in what looks to me like small potatoes?"

"It's small potatoes if Elwell was *charged* with a second-degree larceny. But I'd bet he wasn't. If he bargained to get off with second degree, he was probably looking at first degree."

"I'm listening, counselor."

"Grand larceny in the first degree involves property exceeding one million dollars."

"Therefore, if Elwell testified against someone charged with first degree, his testimony probably put whoever it was in prison for a lot more than five to ten. Such a person or persons might go a long way to take out revenge on Elwell, such as have him hit in the shower room."

"Why hadn't the revenge been taken sooner? Why now?"

"Because he was getting visits from a lawyer?"

"I think we may safely assume that Theo was not there in the role of Elwell's lawyer. Guys in prison don't refuse to see their lawyers. At the very least, they'd welcome an opportunity to get out of their cells. No, Theo was not representing Jake Elwell."

"Then who was he representing? The person or persons Elwell had testified against? Perhaps to try to persuade him to recant, thereby getting the case reopened?"

"That's possible. But in my conversation with Theo I had the impression that whatever he was pursing and regarded as potentially dangerous was not in the interest of a client. I may be wrong, but I can't help believing Theo was acting on his own."

"I could also be wrong about there being a link between the murder of Elwell and Janus's visit, but I don't think so," said Bogdanovic, pressing a button labeled Print Scrn. "Whether the chief of detectives agrees with me is another question. Come with me while I put it to him."

Looking startled to see them, Goldstein barked, "Are you two here to tell me you've cracked the case already?"

"It gets curiouser and curiouser," Bogdanovic answered as he placed the printout on Goldstein's desk.

Tilted back in his chair, Goldstein read it while fingers of his left hand twisted a few long strands of lank brown hair atop his balding head. "What could have been so important about a guy serving time for a five-year-old second-degree grand larceny that got Janus excited?"

"There are two ways of finding that out," Bogdanovic said. "We can ask ask the district attorney's office to root out the case file from the archives, which will probably take forever, or we get our hands on the files in Janus's law office."

Goldstein stopped the hair twisting and laid down the paper. "What is there to keep you from doing the latter?"

"Not a blessed thing, Chief," Bogdanovic said, smiling. "I'm just covering my ass."

"If you don't clear this case quickly and it turns into one more media three-ring circus with the mayor, police commissioner, and district attorney in the center ring, your ass will be in for a boot from my size-ten brogans whether it's covered or not. As to some lawyer in Janus's office giving you a problem in looking at the files, I'm sure I can rely on you to remind that person in your inimitable and charming manner that impeding the police in a murder investigation is a sure way to lose his law license."

"Excuse me, fellas," said Dane. "If Theo had a file on Jake Elwell it won't be found at his law offices. That's the sort of case he'd handle without involving his law firm. If a file exists, it's probably in his private files in the office at his ranch."

"That's where?" asked Goldstein.

"It's a few miles north of Larkville in Stone County. I've been there many times."

"That's good, because a certain Brooklyn-born detective who shall go nameless grew up believing that spending an afternoon in the country was walking his dog in Prospect Park. With you along he won't end up getting his city-boy butt lost in the woods and I won't have to call up my friend District Attorney Aaron Benson to send out a search and rescue party. Now, about getting entry to Janus's house. Is a member of his family likely to be there to let you in?"

"Theo had no family. A young man named Kolker lives on the ranch. He takes care of the horses and looks after the place when Theo is away. He knows me, so I'm sure he will cooperate."

"Good. I like people who cooperate with the police. More of them should do so. You two have a nice trip."

A FEW MOMENTS later as they waited in the sixteenth-floor lobby for an elevator, Bogdanovic said, "For the record, Maggie, that crack of Goldstein's about me getting lost in the woods is a bunch of baloney. Before that city boy he talked about became a cop he taught wilderness survival in the Marine Corps."

"Yes, sir. Duly noted, sir. *Semper fi,* SIR," she snapped.

As her hand jerked to her forehead, he looked at the curving fingers with the thumb tucked beneath with disgust. Scowling, he said, "That is the sorriest excuse for a salute I have ever seen. If you were in boot camp I'd order you to do two hundred push-ups in full pack."

"You can take the boy out of Brooklyn," she said as the door of the elevator slid open, "but you can never take the pride out of a marine. Theo was in the corps, you know."

"No I didn't," he said, pressing the button for the garage floor. "I figured him to be army. Judge Advocate General staff."

"He fought in Korea and got wounded in the retreat from the Chosin Reservoir."

"That was *not* a retreat. It was a strategic withdrawal."

"I'm sorry you never got to know the real Theodore Janus. He was so much more than the tough defense lawyer who gave you such a hard time as a witness, or the man who got under your skin at the Wolfe Pack dinner. He could be kind, generous, and caring. I'm sure that in his way he admired you. And I'm sure that wherever he is now, he's delighted that you are the one who will bring his murderer to justice."

When the elevator door opened to ranks of parked blue-and-white patrol units, police vans, and unmarked detective cars, Maggie smelled the acrid garage odor of countless drops of leaked motor oil and numberless years of automobile exhaust fumes. This was a world that was and always would be, she supposed, primarily a place for men like the one striding beside her toward the plain black sedan that would convey them to the sun and fresh air of Theo Janus's ranch. No matter how many women were already in the ranks of the police, nor the number that might choose to follow them, as she hoped they would, this was a realm of hard men in steel vehicles. All sinew and muscle as hard as the rubber of the squealing tires that left black scars on the floor, they sprang into these modern chariots to speed away with their Glock pistols, as the knights of old in glinting armor carried broadswords in defense of a civilization that could not survive without them.

Gripping the steering wheel, the modern knight errant beside her was not one of the characters of detective fiction, certainly not Archie Goodwin on yet another mission for Nero Wolfe, but the real Sgt. John Bogdanovic of the New York Police Department with an actual murder case to be solved. That he had regarded the victim with little, if any, esteem was immaterial. Someone's life had been taken unlawfully and his solemnly sworn oath as a knight in a sports jacket and slacks was to see that the person or persons who committed that crime were brought to account.

As he drove out of the police department's garage, she saw him beginning a quest as sacred as any venture by a knight in the Middle Ages riding away on horseback toward the Holy Land to find the Holy Grail.

Aware of her eyes on him, he gave her a quizzical, sidelong glance and a quick, self-consciously boyish smile. "What is it?"

Embarrassed at being caught looking at him, she asked, "What is what?"

"Why were you looking at me like that?"

"Was I looking at you?"

"Yes."

"I'm sorry. I wasn't aware of it. I was just thinking. When I think about things, I look without seeing."

"What were you thinking about?"

"A man on a horse, actually."

"Janus? I've heard he was quite a horseman. Or was that one more part of the Janus mystique, like that cowboy hat, boots, and fringed buckskin jacket he always wore?"

"Oh dear," she gasped. "I wonder what will become of all his beloved horses? The last time I was at the ranch he had seven or eight of them. I've never seen such magnificent animals. Now, I suppose, they'll be sold when the estate is liquidated. How sad."

"Maybe he bequeathed them to someone in his will. This man Kolker, for instance." He smiled at her impishly. "Since you're a westerner, maybe he left them to you."

"No, the terms of the will provide that I get his all of his personal papers, the leather-bound collection of the opening and closing statements he delivered in his celebrated cases, plus all future royalties and subsidiary rights for his books."

"I don't mean to sound ghoulish, but does that mean you'll be as rich as Lily Rowan?"

"The potential for a lot of money is enormous. When he told me, I was flabbergasted."

"Did he happen to let you in on who else might stand to benefit from his death?"

"Enough to kill him for? You do have a policeman's mind! I'm glad I have an airtight alibi."

"You know what they say. Where there's a will—"

"For an ignoramus you have an amazing ability to inadvertently refer to a Nero Wolfe title. In this instance it's *Where There's A Will*. At the Black Orchid dinner you gave me a glass of champagne and said—"

He smiled. "Champagne for one."

She fell silent a moment, thinking, then sighed deeply and declared, "Nero Wolfe was correct about wills. They are noxious things. It's astonishing the mischief they can provoke."

"I return to the question you have so skillfully avoided answering. Did Janus happen let you in on who else might stand to benefit from his death?"

"He did not, but I can try to satisfy your policeman's mind by reminding you that Theo had no family. His wife died a few years ago of cancer. They were childless. The bulk of his estate in the form of cash, stocks, bonds, and a valuable collection of Americana and American art will go to museums and colleges, as well as to the cancer society and several charities. I know all this because I worked with him on the conveyance instruments. Believe me, whatever residue there might be of Theo's estate would not be worth killing him for. In this case, where there's will there is no motive for murder."

"I had to ask. My job would be a lot simpler if the motive were good old greed. I'm a cop. I look for the obvious."

"If you read Nero Wolfe, you would know that nothing is obvious in itself. Obviousness is subjective. It was obvious to you that Theo was overbearing and arrogant. What was obvious to me about him was that he was—"

"I know. Generous, caring, loving, fighter for justice, and all-round good dude who loved horses. But somebody *killed him*."

23

Too Many Clients

THE CAR CRESTED a hill to reveal a shallow valley of gently undulating, snow-blanketed, sun-glistening pastures.

"In the summer," Dane said, "you'd see Theo's thoroughbred horses romping around or grazing in those fields."

"Very picturesque, I'm sure," Bogdanovic replied as the road became a long, curving descent toward a stretch of unleafed trees on both sides, their wall-like trunks and overarching limbs forming a tunnel. "How much farther?"

"The driveway is about a half a mile beyond the woods," Dane said as the car plunged into a darkness that enveloped them as totally as if someone had switched off a lamp. "You'll find white fencing with a gate on the left. The house is another mile or so up the driveway, tucked into a copse."

"Tucked into a *cops?*"

"C-o-p-s-e. A copse is a cluster of trees."

"Pardon me! I'm just a kid from Brooklyn where a tree was a tree, a bunch of trees was a forest, and cops—c-o-p-s—were guys with nightsticks who felt free to use them on your backside when you didn't move along after they told you to."

"There is more law at the end of a policeman's nightstick than in any ruling of the Supreme Court," she said, reciting as if she were a schoolgirl. "Thus endeth the reading of the gospel of law and order according to a nineteenth-century police captain by the name of Alexander 'Clubber' Williams."

"Well, old Clubber knew what he was talking about," Bogdanovic said as the tunnel ended, the light went on again, and a white slatted fence came into view.

Easing up on the accelerator, he slowed the car, wheeling it left between a pair of tall white poles supporting a curved wooden board into which had been burned: LITTLE MISERY

Peering up at the sign as the car passed beneath, Bogdanovic said, "I'm afraid I don't get the point of the name."

"When Theo's namesake, Theodore Roosevelt, went west in the 1880s he settled in the Little Missouri area of the Dakotas. The people out there pronounced it 'Little Misery.' Theo adopted the name for his ranch because, he said, the name also summed up his mission as a defense attorney, which was to bring a little misery into the lives of prosecutors and certain judges he considered to be pro-prosecution."

"Maybe we're on the wrong track. Maybe we should be taking a look at judges whose lives Janus made miserable."

"If you look to the bench for suspects, John, you'll have to investigate virtually the entire judiciary, including two sitting associate justices of the Supreme Court, as well as the criminal and civil courts of New York and several other states. Then there is His Honor Reginald Simmons, retired."

"What makes him stand out?"

"Theo handled the appeal of a case that Simmons regarded as his springboard to a seat on the U.S. Supreme Court. I'm sure you recall the case. A gang of long-in-the-tooth 1960s radicals suddenly surfaced in a botched robbery at a Stone County shopping mall."

"Hell yes I remember. They ambushed a van that was picking up cash from a branch bank. One of the guards was gunned down."

"Lawrence Newport was his name. The news media made him into a symbol of the times. The hardworking, middle-class family man with a loving wife, a two-year old son, and a baby on the way."

"The leader of the gang was a woman."

"Victoria Davis was *the* woman. She'd been on the FBI's most-wanted list for more than twenty years, ever since she ran away naked and screaming after a radicals' bomb factory blew up on a quiet street in Greenwich Village."

"So how did Janus get involved?"

"Because of so-called inflammatory pretrial publicity, the trial was moved out of Stone County to Judge Simmons's courtroom in Queens. Davis was defended by the clown prince of all radical causes, Richard Hardon. As usual, he turned the proceedings into a carnival. As usual, he lost but claimed a moral victory. It was at that point that Davis's wealthy father asked Theo to handle an appeal. Because of his brilliant brief and his personal argument before the appeals court, which will be studied for years to come in law schools, the verdict was overturned by unanimous vote. Theo negotiated a deal that let Victoria walk out of jail with time served and probation. To make matters even worse, Simmons was excoriated for judicial errors. It was so humiliating, he had to retire from the bench and kiss his dream of a seat on the nation's highest court good-bye. I believe that's why Simmons, as a member of the steering committee of the Wolfe Pack, vehemently objected to giving Theo the Nero Wolfe Award. Frankly, I was surprised to see him at the dinner."

"That's all very interesting. It gives Simmons a motive, and his being at the dinner provided the opportunity. But what about means? Was Simmons one of those judges who pack guns under their black robes?"

"The only weapon Judge Simmons ever wielded was the blunt instrument known as a gavel."

As the car reached the house, a short, sinewy, suntanned black-haired young man in faded jeans, open shearling jacket, brown cowboy boots, and battered tan western hat ambled over to them from the direction of the stables.

"Good morning, Miss Dane," he said, tipping the hat as she and Bogdanovic left the car. "It's good to see you again."

"I'm sorry it's not a happier occasion."

"I'm glad you're here to take charge. It's been a madhouse. Reporters and cameramen have been showing up all morning." He looked down at his boots. "I can't believe somebody murdered Mr. Janus." The eyes turned up to Bogdanovic. "Were you also a friend of his, sir?"

"This is Sergeant Bogdanovic of the New York City police," Dane said. "He's in charge of the investigation and wants to have a look around Theo's office."

"Pleased to meet you, Sergeant," he said, extending a hand. "I'm Dave Kolker. Help yourself to the house."

"Before we go inside," Bogdanovic said, "I have a couple of questions for you, if I may."

"Of course. Anything I can do to help."

"When was the last time you saw Mr. Janus?"

"Early Saturday evening. He looked in at the stables on his way out to attend a dinner in the city."

"How did he seem to you?"

"He was his usual self, except that he was excited because he was getting an award of some kind."

"Did he have any visitors that day?"

"Not that I know of. He was working in his office most of the day."

"Did he ever tell you to keep an eye out for strangers?"

Hooking thumbs into the loops of a wide black belt, Kolker slowly shook his head. "No, sir, he didn't."

"Did you ever see anyone in the vicinity who might have been watching the ranch? Did you ever notice a car driving past this place several times? Or one that might have been parked awhile?"

"People driving by sometimes and stop to look at the horses in the pastures. Once in a while someone will drive up the road to look at the house because they know who it belongs to. One day I had to ask the sheriff's department to send out some deputies because there was a bunch of people down by the gate. They were yelling a lot and carrying signs that accused Mr. Janus of letting a killer go scot-free. But they never got anywhere close to the house."

"Did Mr. Janus express any worries to you about his safety?"

"The only safety worry he ever expressed to me was about the horses," he said, looking toward the stables. "He was concerned that some nut might try to harm them as a way of getting at him. But nothing like that ever happened."

"Were there any threats made against him by phone or mail?"

The big hands became fists on hips. "Plenty of those came in during and after the trial, but Mr. Janus was used to that sort of thing. He's got drawers full of them. He said he was going to publish them someday."

"Who else works at the ranch?"

"There's a housekeeper, Mrs. Fulmer, who comes in twice a week to clean and do the cooking, which she leaves in the fridge."

"Thank you, Mr. Kolker. We won't detain you further. If you have any more problems with the press bothering you, I'm sure the sheriff's department would be happy to send someone out to chase them away. If that doesn't do it, give a call to the district attorney's office. Ask for Arlene Flynn and tell her I said I'd appreciate anything she might do to help out."

"Thanks, Sergeant, but I can handle the press," he said as he strode away. "If I can do anything to help you and Miss Dane, give me a shout. I'll be at the stables."

With a smile as the young man walked away, Bogdanovic said, "Where did Janus find him, Maggie? He looks as if he came right from Central Casting's bronco-buster department."

"Theo actually discovered him at the Fishkill Correctional Facility. He was doing time for armed robbery and working in the prison law library, preparing appeals and writs of habeas corpus for inmates. One of them somehow found its way to Theo's desk and was so impressive that when Dave was up for parole Theo went to bat for him and offered him a job as a paralegal. Then he discovered that Dave's ability to handle horses exceeded his skills as a jailhouse lawyer. The result is a life rescued from the revolving door of crime, prison, parole, and recidivisim."

"You've made your point, Maggie," Bogdanovic said as they entered the house. "I was wrong about Janus. He wasn't the tricky Philadelphia lawyer I took him to be. He was a saint."

"He was hardly that, John," she said, leading him toward the office. "He was a decent human being with a law license. And if you dare to make a crack about that being an oxymoron, I'll give you a swift kick in the ass."

Pausing in the doorway of the office and regarding the walls festooned with the artifacts and memorabilia of the career of the man who had been named in honor of the twenty-sixth president of the United States, Bogdanovic let out a low whistle and muttered, *"Si monumentum requiris circumspice."*

With eyes blinking in astonishment, Dane gasped, " 'If you

would see the man's monument look around.' I am impressed, John!"

"By my Latin, or by Janus's monument to himself?"

She stepped into the room as softly as she might enter the tomb of a great man. "Theo did not believe in sticking memories in a drawer. He told me once that there are three things to do with a wall. Leave it empty, hang a single supreme work of art, or cover it with everything meaningful in your life."

"I don't know about walls," he said, advancing across the room, "but I do know that if you want to find what's really important in someone's life, start by looking in the desk drawers, then move on to closets."

As he sat behind the massive desk, she stood before a set of glass-front cabinets containing morocco-bound volumes, each with the name of a Theodore R. Janus case embossed in gold. "These are his collection of openings and closings I told you about."

"Fascinating, I'm sure," he said. "But ancient history."

She opened a case, withdrew a slender volume, and opened it. "Here's the appeal he filed on behalf of Victoria Davis, along with a transcript of his amazing oral argument."

In a triumphant tone Bogdanovic declared, "And here is his appointment book. If you would see the man, look up who he made dates with."

"Happiness for the detective is finding a paper trail," she replied, gently replacing the Davis volume. "What do you hope to find in his date book?"

"I'll know it when I find it."

"Pity the murdered," she said, moving from the glass-front cases to a shelf of books Janus had written. "They are allowed no secrets. Everything about them must be ferreted out and revealed. If the murderer is to be caught, you must first get to know the victim. All the secrets, the dirty linen, lovers, if he cheated on his taxes, all the human things that might point to a motive. Does it ever bother you, John?"

"Looking through a victim's effects? Not really."

"*Effects.* What we call effects, someone called possessions. A watch, a wallet, clothing. An appointment book."

"According to this one, he hasn't had many clients lately."

"Theo never had a lot of clients. He was highly selective and always pragmatic. His genius was not, as everyone believed, in taking on every seemingly impossible case that came his way and winning them, but in analyzing the likelihood of success before leaping in. He was never the modern Don Quixote tilting at windmills the press made him out to be. If he chose to fight, it was because he was certain he had the weapons that would give him a *chance* to win. He liked to say that David defeated Goliath not because David was brave, or because he appreciated he was expert with a slingshot, but because he had analyzed the vulnerability of the foreheads of giants to rocks."

"Ah! Here's Mr. Elwell," Bogdanovic said excitedly. "It's a note on his last attempt at seeing Elwell. Quote: I have no hope whatsoever of breaking case without Elwell's cooperation. Time to move on. Have informed all those concerned with it that the matter is closed. Unquote. What do you make of that, Maggie?"

"If he decided to drop the Elwell matter and he'd informed all those concerned with it, I think you have to look elsewhere for a motive."

"But how would you explain Elwell's being murdered after Janus tried to see him?"

With a shrug, she replied, "Coincidence."

"Oh, come on, Maggie," he retorted. "Elwell's being stabbed to death one day after Janus tried to talk to him was *coincidence*?"

"Elwell was killed after Theo's *last* attempt to visit him," she said as Bogdanovic flipped open the lid of a humidor at the right side of the desk. "It seems to me that if someone had been worried about Elwell talking to Theo, he would have been killed after Theo's *first* visit."

"Someone might have been afraid that Elwell might change his mind about talking to Janus," Bogdanovic said, fishing out a long black cigar from the humidor. Sniffing it, he grunted, "Strong!"

"Assuming that someone wanted to kill Elwell in order to prevent Elwell from changing his mind," she continued, "and assuming that purpose had been achieved the day after Theo's latest visit, why was it necessary to also kill Theo?"

"To keep Janus from revealing what he learned from Elwell," he answered, replacing the cigar and closing the humidor.

"But Theo had learned nothing," Dane protested.

"The killer didn't know that," he said, looking around the room. "There must be a file on Elwell somewhere in this room."

"With Elwell dead, it wouldn't matter what Theo knew," Dane said. "Without Elwell's testimony there could be no case. Theo recognized that himself. If he felt that it was time to move on, I think we should, too."

"You're probably right, but just to be certain, I'm going to get someone up here to go through Janus's files."

"If it turns out that the Elwell case was not the motive for Theo's murder," Dane said, "where does that leave us?"

"It leaves us smack dab in the middle of the dreaded Paulie Mancuso quagmire. Or have you come up with a logical explanation for the *triple* coincidence of Paulie's going out the window of that hotel room, a copy of Janus's autobiography on the table next to Mancuso's bed, and Janus's being found shot to death a couple of hours later?"

"I must admit it's a puzzle worthy of the pen of Rex Stout, who seems to have had a fixation on the numeral three."

"Being ignorant on the topic, I wouldn't know."

"I didn't make the connection myself until I read Theo's wonderful Nero Wolfe encyclopedia. There were six collections of short stories with the word *three* in the title, one with the word *triple,* one with *triplicate,* one *trio,* and one *trinity.*"

"Well three cheers for Mr. Stout."

"You ought to have a copy of Theo's book. Yes. I shall drop by Wiggins's bookstore and get you one as a Christmas gift."

"Thank you, but I'm still trying to get through the complete adventures of Sherlock Holmes that Goldstein thrust upon me a few years ago. I find it impossible to get excited about a man who's always running around in a cape and a ridiculous hat in Victorian London, yelling, 'The game's afoot' at Dr. Watson."

"Of course you can't. You're the two-fisted New Yorker, just like Archie Goodwin."

Looking again at Janus's appointment book, Bogdanovic said, "Janus had some visitors in the past few months. Stamos, Henry,

Pendelton." He gave a little bark of a laugh. "Speaking of people who run around in a cape, here's an odd entry. The Sunday after Janus's last trip to Watertown, he was expecting a visit from our mutual friend Wiggins. He wrote, 'Send Dave in Rolls to pick up Wiggins.' That is very odd indeed."

"What's so odd about Wiggins making an excursion into the country on a Sunday?"

"What is odd about it," he said, closing the book, "is that Wiggins is notorious for hating to leave his store. Suddenly, he's making a trip into the country."

"He probably wanted to go over arrangements for the Black Orchid dinner."

"I've known Wiggins a long time. He would have done that by telephone. If Janus sent his car to bring him here, the visit was Janus's doing. He wanted to see Wiggins about something he didn't want to discuss on the phone, or by dropping in on Wiggins at his bookstore."

"It's an easy matter to clear up. Ask Wiggins."

"I intend to do just that. I'll drop in at his store first thing tomorrow."

"Oh how thoughtless of me," she exclaimed. "I ought to have called him and told him about Theo. Do you think he's found out by now?"

"If he hasn't heard it from the radio or TV, it will be all over the Monday morning papers."

"What a horrible way for him to find out. As his friend, I really should call him, John."

"I appreciate your feelings, Maggie, but I prefer that you not talk to him before I do. He could be a material witness. You are, of course, welcome to come along with me when I talk to him in the morning."

"Very well," she said dejectedly. "It is your case."

"Besides, having been delighted to have been regarded very briefly as a prime suspect in the Griffith case a few years ago, I'm certain Wiggins will be thrilled to find himself smack in the middle of this one. And while you and I are visiting with him to inquire about his singular departure from the city, Leibholz and Reiter will be sifting through the files in this office with the proverbial fine-tooth comb. As the detective's handy guide to how to solve a murder, Latin edition, says, '*Si motivum homicidum requiris circumspice filum.*' Now, how about lunch? I happen to know a terrific seafood place overlooking the Hudson River in a delightfully quaint section of Newtown called the Cove."

24

Three Doors to Death

"ON A CLEAR DAY," said Bogdanovic as a hostess seated them at a table overlooking the river, "you can see Sing Sing prison on the opposite shore."

The window next to the table reflected the warming glow of a fireplace and a sea of flickering flames of stubby candles that reminded Dane of votive tapers in a church. Through the window she saw scattered across the broad, placid surface of the gray, slowly flowing river an expanse of flat, thin shards of drift ice that looked like pieces of a giant jigsaw puzzle.

"It's a charming spot," Dane said. "How did a city boy ever find it?"

"The way all good restaurants are discovered. I was brought here by a friend."

"Am I correct in deducing that the friend was a woman?"

"You tell me the basis of that deduction, and I'll tell you whether you're right."

"It's elementary. You said a friend brought you here. Only a woman takes a man to a place as romantic as this."

"It was strictly a business lunch."

"For you, perhaps," she said, smiling. "But not for her."

"You're wrong there. The business was murder. The Griffith case. The woman was also a detective. The murder had been done in the city, but the victim's body was found in a boathouse several miles from here, so it was a matter of interjurisdictional cooperation that brought us together. Romantic ambiance had nothing to do with Arlene Flynn's bringing me here."

"Before I concede the point, I would have to question her, woman to woman. Perhaps you'll introduce me to her someday."

"You'd like her. She's the chief investigator for District Attorney Benson. And a hell of a detective. Since her outstanding work on the Griffith case, Goldstein has been trying to lure her away to work for him."

"Why hasn't he succeeded?"

"Arlene prefers living and working in Stone County the way someone else I know chooses to live and work in California, when she belongs in New York."

"Chauvinism, thy name is Bogdanovic."

A waiter in a snug white jacket appeared with menus. "Would you care to order from the bar?"

"A glass of white wine, I think," Dane replied. "A chablis, if you have it."

The waiter bowed slightly. "Of course."

Bogdanovic asked, "New York or California?"

"We have both, sir."

Grinning, Bogdanovic looked at Dane. "Your call, Maggie."

"Oh, the California," she said emphatically.

"Scotch for me," said Bogdanovic, grumpily. "Single malt. Do you have Dalwhinnie?"

"We certainly do, sir. How would you like it?"

"Neat, of course," Bogdanovic said, sharply. "It's the only acceptable way."

As the waiter withdrew, Dane laughed. "Now I appreciate how Sherlock Holmes felt when he called Watson the one fixed point in a changing universe. For Sgt. John Bogdanovic, it's single malt neat or none at all. It's New York chablis over California. And the only crimes that matter are committed in New York City."

"Not all of them," he said, frowning as he picked up a menu. "Just most."

"Obviously, Arlene Flynn doesn't agree with you."

"That is her mistake. And probably her tragedy."

"Did you two work well together on the Griffith case?"

"Why wouldn't we? If you are supposing there was a male-female problem, there wasn't. She's an excellent detective, a true professional in every way. So am I."

"I have no doubt. I'm confident that you will solve Theo's murder in short order. It will be fascinating to see how you go about doing it."

"I see the solving of a murder in terms of a room that has three doors," he said, putting down the menu. "Each door has a sign. One says Love, which is to say hate or betrayal. The second is labeled Money. And the third is Revenge. But only one door is real. The others open to a brick wall. The job of the detective is to know which of the doors will get him into that room. At the moment, in view of Janus's background and all of those who might have had a reason to hold a grudge against him, I'm concentrating on door number three." He laughed. "I sound like one of those emcees on a TV game show! 'Well, Monty, I choose door number three.'"

"Explain for me why you're so positive it's door three."

"As to the first door, nothing has turned up so far pointing to Janus's being romantically engaged. Agreed?"

"I believe I can vouch for Theo's not having been involved in a love affair."

"Murder in the name of love—the *crime passionnel*—is most likely to be a spur-of-the-moment event. The scene of the crime is usually in a domestic setting. An irate husband or wife bursts into the bedroom and catches the loved one in flagrante in the love nest, a gun blazing. I have difficulty picturing a jealous or jilted lover shooting Janus sitting alone in his Rolls-Royce in the heart of Manhattan. As to door two, murder for profit, you have to look for someone who stands to benefit from a will or an insurance policy. According to you, the beneficiaries of Janus's estate are charities and other entities, not someone unwilling to let time and nature run their course. This is one case in which I won't have to stake out a funeral to check out the mourners for possible suspects."

"There won't be a funeral as such," Dane said, peering out the window. "Theo didn't want one. He was not what you would call a religious man. But at some point, I presume, there may be some sort of a memorial. A strictly secular one."

"I see. One of those events where a Mark Antony in a pin-striped suit gets up not to bury Caesar, but to praise him."

Dane turned from the window angrily. "There is a great deal to praise him for."

"His numerous virtues aside," Bogdanovic said sarcastically, "I remind you that *somebody* murdered Caesar."

"And you believe that that *somebody* was lurking behind door three with revenge in his heart."

"Revenge is a category that includes several possibilities. It might have been the need to settle a grudge or some grievance arising from something Janus did, either recently or a long time ago. On the other hand, he might have been killed preemptively. He could have been eliminated to prevent him from doing something, or to stop him from continuing a case he was working on."

The waiter arrived with their drinks.

Scooping up his glass of scotch, Bogdanovic said, "A toast to murder."

Startled, the waiter wheeled round and hurried away.

"It's an interesting coincidence that you mentioned Caesar's being murdered," Dane said as Bogdanovic sipped the scotch. "In a case called 'Some Buried Caesar,' Nero Wolfe also made a journey out of New York City, reluctantly, of course. Some of the world's most renowned orchid growers were competing for the top prizes at the North American Exposition. Wolfe ended up claiming the gold medal and three ribbons."

Bogdanovic lowered his glass. "The number three again."

"Wolfe also found himself investigating three murders, one of which was that of a prizewinning bull. He was the Caesar whom some wanted to bury, by the way."

"A bull?" Bogdanovic exclaimed. He shook his head. "That's not a murder. It's a *moo*-der. And who did Wolfe find responsible for this *horn*-icide? Was it someone like the guy who killed Jake Elwell because he had a *beef* with him? Or was there an *udderly* different motive?"

Dane groaned and rolled her eyes. "Sergeant, if Arlene Flynn was subjected to your brand of barnyard humor in the Griffith case, I can hardly fault the woman for turning down Goldstein's repeated offers of a job."

"Arlene happens to have a keen sense of humor."

"She must have," Dane said, smiling as she lifted her wineglass, "to have put up with you."

"It's not my barnyard humor that's got you riled up."

"No? Then what has?"

"You don't like me making jokes at the expense of the sacrosanct Nero Wolfe."

With eyes as icy as the river, she said, "Of whom you have admitted knowing nothing."

The waiter reappeared, smiling solicitously. "Are you ready to order? May I recommend the blackened swordfish?"

"Just a salad for me," Dane said. "Considering the occasion, make it a Caesar."

"Also considering the occasion, and in memory of a murdered bull by that name," said Bogdanovic, "I'll have a sirloin steak and a baked potato."

With an uncertain look, the waiter asked, "How do you prefer your steak, sir?"

"Rare as possible," Bogdanovic said, eyes crinkling and lips twitching with an incipient smile, "but without actually mooing."

As the puzzled waiter strode toward the kitchen, Dane said, "He must think we're crazy. First he heard us talking murder and then we ignored the fact that this is a seafood restaurant."

Looking round the crowded room, Bogdanovic said, "I wonder if Janus was ever a customer here."

"Theo was like you. A meat-and-potatoes man. It's sad that his last meal had to be turkey."

"If a dose of cyanide or arsenic had been sprinkled on it, solving his murder would be a lot easier. Instead, I have on one hand the possibility that he was murdered and Paulie Mancuso driven to suicide as part of a scheme by some mastermind of the underworld, and on the other the prospect of rummaging around in Janus's history for someone whose dislike of him could date back decades. Either way, the likelihood of an arrest is bleak. A bit of poison in his turkey would have limited the suspects to those at the dinner."

"Assume for the moment that Theo was not murdered by someone with an old grievance nor by a real-life Professor Moriarty, but by a member of the Wolfe Pack," Dane said excitedly, "which of them would be a suspect?"

"I could start with Marian Pickering Henry. She had a lot of fun explaining how easily she could have poisoned *me*."

"Marian would be thrilled," said Dane gleefully. "Not since Agatha Christie gave up the ghost has a woman sent so many souls to meet their maker as a result of a little extra spice added to a meal. Or a drink. Oscar Pendelton calls his best-selling author the poison pen."

"Since we're talking about Wolfe Packers as suspects, did everyone at our table dislike Janus?"

"Not everyone," Dane said as the waiter brought their food.

"With the exception of you, of course," Bogdanovic said with a smile at what appeared to be perfectly cooked steak. "You think Janus was the cat's pajamas. But, alas, he wasn't poisoned at the dinner. He was killed with a gun in a manner that tomorrow morning's newspapers will undoubtedly describe in gory detail in the headlines as a gangland-style execution befitting the mouthpiece for the mob."

"That was uncalled for, John," she snapped, spearing a leaf of lettuce as though her fork were a dagger. "He wasn't a demon. Theo earned and deserves a better obituary. But as Mark Antony said at the funeral for Julius Caesar, 'The evil that men do lives after them. The good is oft interred with their bones.' "

"Let's make a deal, Maggie. No more talking about the case. We'll pretend we're not a couple of sleuths. We are an ordinary couple having Sunday lunch out. How's your salad?"

"It's fine. How's your steak?"

"Perfect!"

"I'm glad. Now what shall we talk about?"

He thought a moment, then said, brightly, "I could discuss the nuances of differences between single-malt scotches."

She sighed in dismay. "That's pretty boring."

"How about the weather?" He gazed through the window at the glowering gray sky above the icy river. "It looks as if we might be in for a little snow. That ought to please the skiers."

"On the other hand, it would be bad for anyone who has to drive into the city in it."

"I suppose that's one of the things you like about living in California. There's no snow to scrape off your car. No need to worry about antifreeze. No steaming up of the car windows while you're dashing merrily along the freeways. Of course, you do have to be worried about all those drive-by shootings we easterners hear about from time to time on the news."

"In New York it's much more personal. You get shot while you are *parked* in your car."

He winced. "Touché, Maggie. But Janus wasn't a victim chosen at random. He was killed because he was targeted. If it had been anyone else in that car we might be at a loss to know where to start looking for the killer. As it is, we're fortunate in that we appear to have several ways to go in the investigation. Unfortunately, I don't expect the killer to suffer a sudden pang of conscience that will compel him to walk in and confess. Nor is he likely to blab about it to anyone. Barring any such break, we're left with old-fashioned legwork and the hope that it may provide the clue that will clinch a case we said we weren't going to talk about anymore while we're eating. How the devil did we manage to get back on the subject?"

"The weather. You were talking about snow. I suppose that as you talked about Californians' not having to be concerned about their car windows steaming up, we both thought subconsciously of the shot through the open window of Theo's car." She fell silent a moment, thinking, then said, "I guess we could lay the blame for what happened on that blasted cigar. If Theo hadn't lit it up, he wouldn't have rolled down the damn window."

"He would have been shot," he said, turning attention to his steak, "even if the window had been up."

"Perhaps he would have been," she said, ignoring her salad and gazing at the river.

Jerking up his head, he demanded, "What do you mean?"

Her eyes came back to him. "It would have been difficult to take aim at a target behind a tinted window, and quite impossible through bulletproof glass."

Bogdanovic slapped his knife on the table. "What was that?"

"Theo's car was equipped with tinted bulletproof glass. I thought your crime lab people would have reported it to you. But I suppose they haven't had time yet to examine the car."

"How do you know Janus's windows were bulletproof?"

"He told me he'd had the original windows replaced when he returned from California."

"Did he explain why?"

"No. I assumed it was because of the death threats that came in during, and especially after, the trial."

"What car did he use in California?"

"He usually hired a limousine service to take him to and from court."

"Do you know if the limos had bulletproof windows?"

"I'm sorry, I don't."

"Did he use hired limos the entire time he was in L.A.?"

"I assume so. No, wait! When he took me to dinner after the trial ended he picked me up in a convertible."

"That's odd. If he was worried enough about threats to have all the windows of his Rolls bulletproofed in New York, why was he tooling around L.A. in a convertible? I'll tell you why. The danger was not in California. It was at home. Whatever danger he was guarding against did not arise from the trial. The danger was here. That he knew about it raises a couple of questions. Who was he protecting himself against, and how did he come to know he was in danger?"

Dane thought a moment, then said, "He was warned."

Bogdanovic pushed aside his plate. "Maggie, if you intended to kill somebody, would you alert your intended victim? I don't think so. You would go ahead and do it."

"John, that's it! Theo knew that someone wanted to kill him because that person had tried. It's obvious he didn't know who it was. He would have gone to the police. Yet he didn't do so."

"We don't know that, Maggie."

"If somebody was charged with attempting to murder Theodore Janus, it certainly would have made headlines coast to coast. Did you see any?"

He shook his head slowly. "Not that I can recall."

"Of course you can't. There were no such headlines because Theo hadn't a clue as to who had tried to kill him. Hence, the bulletproof windows for the Rolls."

25

Immune to Murder

ON MONDAY MORNING Bogdanovic double-parked his car at the corner of Broadway and Eighty-sixth Street, bounded out, and picked up the first edition of the Monday morning *New York Graphic*. Feeling vindicated in his prediction of how the press would treat Janus's murder, he read the headline:

MIDNIGHT HORROR AT GRAMERCY PARK:
SATURDAY SLAYING OF MOB MOUTHPIECE
THEODORE JANUS WAS GANGLAND-STYLE
EXECUTION; FOUND SHOT ONCE IN HEAD

To the right of the headline a photo showed Janus slumped on the front seat of his car with a half-smoked cigar in his mouth.

The caption read, "Legal legend shot to death in Rolls-Royce as he puffed on cigar after receiving top award at literary society's banquet."

Below this was "Photo: A *Graphic* Exclusive. Other pictures of Janus's last news conference on page 3."

A FEW MINUTES past seven, as Bogdanovic searched for a gap in traffic that would allow him onto the East River Drive, the chief of detectives sat in the rear seat with the newspaper on his lap. "If the press was kept away from the crime scene until after the body was removed by the medical examiner," he demanded, "how did the *Graphic* manage to get its slimy hands on this picture?"

"That's an excellent question," Bogdanovic replied, finding an opening in the traffic. "Because there was no way it could have been taken by one of the paper's photographers, it has to have come from someone at the crime scene with a camera."

"Meaning one of our own people! That's just great! First we have three assistant district attorneys watching television while in the other room Paulie Mancuso is leaping out a window. Now we apparently have someone from the crime scene unit or the medical examiner's office peddling a crime scene picture to a newspaper. And not just any newspaper. The *New York Graphic*. No wonder the public has nothing but contempt for government."

"There is another explanation."

"Really! If the *Graphic*'s man didn't take it, and it didn't come from one of our people, who snapped the damned thing?"

"The murderer."

Goldstein bolted forward. "Did you say the *murderer?*"

"At the time of the killing," Bogdanovic answered as he negotiated from the center lane into the faster far left, "a man who lives across Gramercy Park saw a bright light that came from the direction of Janus's car."

Goldstein sank back in the seat. "He saw muzzle flash."

"It couldn't have been. The man heard a bang. The noise is what got his attention. *Then* he saw the light. He said it looked as if someone took a picture using a flash camera."

"That's a first! Somebody brings a gun *and* a camera, shoots someone, snaps a picture of the body, develops and prints it, and then sends it to a newspaper. Why would he do that?"

"I can't say for sure until we arrest him," Bogdanovic said, turning slightly toward Goldstein. "But I have a theory."

"I'm sure you do. But while you expound it, do me the favor of keeping your eyes on the road. And while you're at it, ease up on that lead foot of yours so that you and I will live to see if your theory proves right."

Facing forward, Bogdanovic said, "I think the killer snapped the picture to guarantee that the shooting of Janus would be recognized for what it was. He used the picture to send us the very clear message that this was not a chance murder."

Goldstein let out an exasperated sigh. "Then why didn't he just send the picture directly to us?"

"Evidently, we were not the only ones he felt he had to send his message to. Either he wanted the general public to know it, or he expected the picture to be seen by someone who, like him, wanted to see Janus dead."

"Your theory is highly imaginative, Johnny, but I think it's also highly improbable."

"Improbable, maybe. But not impossible."

"Anything is possible, such as your slowing down this car and our making it to One Police Plaza alive, well, and ready to fight crime."

"When you have eliminated the impossible, according to your favorite sleuth, Sherlock Holmes of Baker Street," Bogdanovic said with a smirk, "whatever is left, no matter how improbable, must be the truth."

"Presuming Janus's killer was the same individual who took the picture of him," Goldstein said, "you should be looking for a psychopath with a fetish for necromancy, not to mention a flair for publicity. If cameras had been available to Jack the Ripper when he was hacking up prostitutes, London newspapers would have been flooded with snapshots, instead of a chunk of human liver."

"It was a piece of kidney, actually," Bogdanovic said as he edged the car into the exit lane for the government center. "As to Janus's killer being a psychopath, I don't think so. I believe Janus was being stalked, and I have evidence that indicates that Janus knew it."

As the car turned from the highway with police headquarters looming directly ahead, Goldstein again leaned forward urgently. "What evidence?"

"The windows of Janus's car were tinted black."

"He was a famous person. Celebrities sometimes want to enjoy a bit of privacy."

"The windows were also bulletproofed. *Recently.*"

TWO HOURS AFTER Bogdanovic drove his car into the garage of police headquarters and accompanied Goldstein in an elevator to the sixteenth floor, a houseboy rapped twice on the white door of Wiggins's bedroom, entered, and found the proprietor of the Usual Suspects bookstore wrapped in a yellow silk oriental robe with dragons embroidered in red. Propped like a pasha on purple satin pillows, he lounged on a massive Victorian four-poster bed.

"Ah, good," he exclaimed with delight. "My breakfast!"

Carrying a silver tray bearing an eight-ounce glass of hand-squeezed orange juice, a white porcelain mug of freshly ground coffee with cream and three lumps of sugar, a stack of raisin scones slathered with clotted butter, and the *New York Graphic,* the youth said, "There's a headline that should be of interest to you on the front page of the paper."

Reading it, Wiggins slapped his chest with a meaty hand and gasped, "Oh, my soul, no."

Leaving the bedroom, the young man looked back and said in a singsong voice, "I told you you would be interested."

With stunned disbelief as he looked at the gruesome photo of Janus, Wiggins bellowed, "Timothy, you'll have to tend the store this morning." He flung the paper to the floor. "Maybe all day."

The boy spun round in a sullen manner that was half of his charm. "Oh yeah? How come?"

"I have business at police headquarters," Wiggins roared as he rolled from the bed. "I must speak to the chief of detectives and Sgt. John Bogdanovic. Go out front and hail me a cab!"

Half an hour later, with the mangled bullet given to him by Janus tucked into a vest pocket and the newspaper jammed into a pocket of his Inverness cape, which was flapping like the wings of a huge brown bird, he crossed police plaza with the agility and grace of a ballet dancer one-third his weight. Pausing at a metal detector in the lobby, he placed into the tray a cluster of keys, coins, the mashed bullet, and a pinky ring with an enormous diamond.

"That's an interesting trinket," said the officer in charge of the detector, reaching into the tray.

With pounding heart and expecting the officer to pick up the slug, Wiggins blurted, "That's nothing. A friend gave it to me."

"That's quite a gift," the officer said, picking up the ring. "I recommend you not wear this openly out on the streets. People have been murdered for a lot less."

With a long, relieved breath Wiggins retorted, "You needn't advise me on the subject of murder, Officer. I am expert on the subject. Indeed, I have come here about a murder."

The cop blurted, "You have a murder to report?"

"Nothing to trouble you, Officer," Wiggins said blithely as he went through the metal detector. "I am taking up the matter with the chief of detectives himself." Scooping up the ring, the coins, the keys, and the mercifully overlooked slug, he added, "I know the way to his office. I have been there many times. We are old friends, you see. You might even say the chief and I are comrades in fighting crime."

As the elevator lifted him toward Goldstein's office, each floor was noted by the ding of a bell and a lighted numeral. At the sixth, two uniformed police officers got on wordlessly, but scanned him suspiciously until the bell and the light signaled the thirteenth floor. Exiting, one quipped, "Inspector Lestrade's office is on sixteen, Sherlock."

When the door opened, a sign on the opposite wall declared: Chief of Detectives. An arrow pointed to a corridor on the left.

Seated behind a desk at the end of the hallway, a woman in police uniform whom he knew only as Officer Sweeney greeted him with a surprised smile. "Mr. Wiggins. How nice to see you. Was Chief Goldstein expecting you?"

"No, but I must see him without delay."

"I'm sorry. The chief is in a conference at the moment."

"Then I'll see Sergeant Bogdanovic."

The officer smiled. "That's who the chief is meeting with."

Jerking the *Graphic* from the pocket of the Inverness and unfurling it, he demanded, "Inform them I have come with vital information concerning this."

A stubby thumb and pudgy forefinger dipped into the pocket of the vest and brought out the slug.

"And *this* may be the clue that will solve the murder."

PART SIX

Eeny, Meeny, Murder, Mo

26

A Family Affair

BOGDANOVIC SLOUCHED IN a bulky, encompassing red leather armchair with his long legs straight out and crossed at the ankles.

"I doubt that this bullet came from the gun that was used to kill Janus," he said, studying the slug as he rolled it between thumb and forefinger. "This looks like a thirty-eight caliber. A bullet this size fired at the close range at which Janus was shot would have blown his head off."

Resembling a giant jack-o'-lantern with slits for its eyes, Wiggins turned his massive head toward Bogdanovic. "Sergeant B., I do not claim that this bullet came from the same gun. What I do say is that it came from a weapon that was fired at Janus from a passing car and that Janus gave it to me as evidence to take to the police in the event of his death to prove that somebody was determined to kill him."

"Why didn't he go to the police at the time?"

Wiggins turned to Goldstein. "Chief, with all due respect to Sergeant B., may I be permitted to tell you the story behind this bullet without interruption?"

"You know me, my friend," Goldstein answered with a glance at Bogdanovic that conveyed a command to remain silent. "I love a good mystery, well told."

Speaking with the spellbinding skills of a storyteller long before the advent of mysteries in books, Wiggins conducted the detectives to the Sunday afternoon of summer sun and hot air of a countryside, Janus's horses frolicking behind white fences, and green pastures.

There was every reason to believe, Janus had told him, that

there would soon be an attempt to kill him. Indeed, someone had already tried. He had been exercising one of his horses when a shot was fired from a passing car. He heard the bullet's zing as it went past his ear.

"When he gave me what remained of it—the very slug you hold in your hand, Sergeant B.—Janus said that in the event he was murdered I could take it to my friends on the police. In answer to your question, Sergeant B., as to why he did not report the incident to the police, he said he preferred to handle the matter by himself. I replied that an attorney who hired himself as a detective had a fool for a client. Janus told me that in order to catch the individual, he had to be given the chance to try again. He thought there might be an attempt to do so on the occasion of the Black Orchid dinner."

"That certainly proved prescient," blurted Bogdanovic.

"I think fatalistic is a better way to put it," Wiggins replied. "He said, he could only hope that before he died there'd be time to smoke one more good cigar."

"Well he certainly got what he hoped for," Bogdanovic said.

"When he was alive and well at the Black Orchid dinner," Wiggins continued, with a scolding look at Bogdanovic, "I assumed he no longer considered himself to be in jeopardy. You both were there. I think you will agree that he did not appear to be worried about his safety. Quite the contrary, in fact. You'll both recall how he put that scare into everyone by pretending his food had been poisoned. When he pitched forward so convincingly, my heart skipped a beat."

Goldstein chuckled. "So did mine."

"I had never seen him as relaxed as he was Saturday night," Wiggins exclaimed. "He appeared to be delighted that everyone treated him like a cherished member of their family."

With a grunt Bogdanovic shifted in his chair. "Not the people at my table."

The slits of pumpkin eyes widened. "What do you mean?"

"If opinions could kill," Bogdanovic said, unlimbering his body and stretching as he stood up, "Janus would have been dead long before dessert was served."

"Surely, Sergeant B., you do not suspect that he was killed by a member of the Wolfe Pack!"

"To borrow a cliché from the detectives in all those mystery books you sell in your store," Bogdanovic said as he stood at the window and looked beyond the East River toward the flat, dreary expanse of Brooklyn, "I suspect no one, I suspect everyone."

"I hope you are jesting, Sergeant B. If not, I am prepared to vouch for the integrity of everyone who attended the dinner."

Bogdanovic turned from the window. "What about the ones who didn't attend?"

"The only member I know to have specifically stayed away because of Janus was a member of the steering committee, James Hamilton. He was one of the three who voted against presenting the Nero Wolfe Award to Janus. The other two, Nicholas Stamos and Judge Reginald Simmons, attended the dinner. But talking about a murderer being a member of the Wolfe Pack is ridiculous. It is clear to me that he was killed by the person who shot at him."

Bogdanovic held up the slug. "I wonder why that attempt was made with a thirty-eight and the murder carried out with a smaller caliber pistol?"

Wiggins sighed in exasperation. "Good heavens, Sergeant B., do you expect me to have the answer to *everything?*"

"Of course we don't, Wiggins," declared Goldstein. "But by bringing us the bullet that Janus claimed was fired at him you've certainly cast this case in a new light, for which Johnny and I are in your debt."

"Thank you, Chief. Now may I ask you a question?"

"Certainly."

"I'm afraid it will smack of criticism."

"What are friends for, if not to offer criticism?"

"It's that ghastly photo in the *Graphic.* How could you have permitted it to be released to that disgraceful rag?"

Goldstein shrugged. "All I can say about the picture is that it was one of those inexplicable things that sometimes happen in the hurly-burly of a murder investigation. I am deeply sorry that it's upset you. And I assure you that I intend to send someone to the *Graphic* to have a chat with the editor on the subject of the responsibilities of journalism."

"Excuse me for saying so, Chief," Wiggins said, rising ponderously from his chair, "but using the term 'responsibilities of journalism' in the same sentence as the *Graphic* is an oxymoron, and chatting with Jerry Abelman on the topic is a fool's errand."

"On the other hand, my friend," Goldstein said, accompanying Wiggins to the door, "remember what Sherlock Holmes said on the subject of newspapers in 'The Six Napoleons.' "

"Yes, yes, I know. The press can be a valuable institution if you know how to use it. It's true. I find my daily copy of the *Graphic* quite useful as a liner for the box where my cat shits."

With a little laugh and a pat to Wiggins's shoulder, Goldstein said, "Again, my friend, thanks for telling us about the attempt on Janus's life, and for bringing us the evidence of it."

"As always, I stand ready to render whatever assistance you might require of me in future."

"And, as always, Johnny and I appreciate the offer."

"There's something you can do to help now," said Bogdanovic from his chair. "I'll be needing a list of guests at the Black Orchid Banquet."

The slit eyes glared angrily. "You are wasting your time."

"I'll also need the names of members who were invited but didn't show up, possibly because they were protesting Janus's presence and his getting the award."

"As I said, there were some cancellations," Wiggins said as his pumpkin face turned an angry pink. "But other than Hamilton's boycott, I have no way of knowing whether anybody else chose to stay away in protest. There are always cancellations. The Black Orchid is held in December. People catch colds. Others have babysitters who don't report for work. Some can't get their cars to start. Take my word for it, Sergeant B., if you set out to find a murderer among the Wolfe Pack, you will be off on the proverbial wild goose chase."

Bogdanovic flashed a boyish grin. "Humor me."

In Wiggins's eyes, the smile constituted a misleading weapon in Bogdanovic's personal crusade against crime, for in Wiggins's experience in observing him at work in two murder cases, Bogdanovic had proved that beneath the veneer of the disarmingly winning charm, the casual, college-boy attire and manner, and the fashion-model good looks worked a brain as keen as any creation of the master writers of detective fiction, past and present, on the shelves of his bookstore.

Defeated, Wiggins said, "Very well, I'll give you the lists. But I know you are wrong."

With that, and a flurrying of the Inverness cape, he barged out of the office.

Standing by the closed door, Goldstein drummed fingers on his belly. "I have this sudden sinking feeling that this case has become like ordering a meal in the Greek diner around the corner from my apartment, where the menu lists the soup of the day. Now, apparently, you are offering me the motive of the day. First, it was a mob hit, possibly tied in with the Mancuso suicide."

"Only because we found Janus's book in Mancuso's room. Until that is explained, I can't rule out a connection between the two deaths on the same night."

"Then it was something to do with Janus's mysterious visits to a guy named Jake Elwell."

"That seems less likely, but it's still on the table."

"Or maybe the motive is buried in files of Janus's cases."

"I'll be sending Leibholz and Reiter up to the ranch today to go through the files."

Goldstein settled behind his desk. "Now, you are adding to the bill of fare the possibility that Janus was killed by someone at the Black Orchid Banquet."

"Or someone who was not there."

Goldstein tilted back in his chair drummed his fingers on his belly. "It's like the poem I read by a man named Hughes Mearns:

As I was going up the stair
I met a man who wasn't there.
He wasn't there again today.
I wish, I wish he'd stay away."

"I'm sorry," Bogdanovic said. "Poetry is not my cup of tea."

Goldstein's chair came up straight. "I know. Neither is the body of work by Rex Stout."

"Am I about to hear more words of wisdom from the corpus?"

After thinking a moment, Goldstein answered, "No, John, but your fascinating and diverse menu of motives does bring to mind a Nero Wolfe title: 'Eeny, Meeny, Murder, Mo.' "

"Which of the suspects did Wolfe catch by the toe?"

"Now that I think about it, that case also had a legal angle. The secretary of the law firm of Otis, Edley, Heydekcer, and Jett wanted Wolfe to find out why one member of that firm was observed where he ought not to have been, engaging in a conversation with an opposing counsel that the two men obviously wanted kept secret."

"I presume Wolfe solved the case then and there without ever getting up from his chair."

"Wolfe happened to be in the orchid room at the time. He ordered Archie to send the woman away. However, he abandoned work on his flowers quickly after the secretary was found dead. In the time it took for Archie to speak to Wolfe, she had been murdered. As if it were not bad enough that she had been killed in Wolfe's house, the killer had the temerity to strangle the woman with one of Wolfe's expensive neckties. Wolfe found that to be, as he put it, *insupportable*."

"So who done it?"

"I never give away endings. You'll have to read the story. However, I will tell you that the suspects were three men."

Bogdanovic grunted a laugh. "There you go again. Or rather, there goes Rex Stout again. What was it with that guy and his fixation on the number three?"

Goldstein's jaw went slack in astonishment. "How could you possibly know about that?"

"Maggie Dane pointed it out." As he spoke, his face took on a worried expression. "Geez, I wonder if she's seen that picture in the *Graphic*. Damn! I should have called and warned her."

"Maggie's a prosecutor. She's seen crime scene photos."

"Yeah, but the guy in this one was a friend."

"A point well taken. Give her a call. Then pay a visit to the

Graphic and employ your charms on Jerry Abelman to get him to explain how he got his grubby mitts on the photo in question."

"May I take Maggie along?"

Goldstein grinned. "Only if she promises not to punch out Abelman's lights."

27

Kill Now—Pay Later

"THE LAST TIME I laid eyes on Jerry Abelman was five years ago at an Inner Circle dinner," Dane said as an elevator took her and Bogdanovic to the top floor of the ancient building that had been headquarters of the *Graphic* since the halcyon days of New York journalism in the 1920s, when the city had more than a dozen newspapers. "You do know what the Inner Circle dinner is?"

"It's the annual banquet when the press puts on a show to mock the mayor and other politicians and the mayor puts on his own show in response."

"Five years ago Abelman did a number in drag in a gown that made him look like the great white whale in *Moby Dick.*"

"Wait till you see him now. He must be twice that size. One of these days his body will be as big as his ego."

"MAGGIE DANE," ABLEMAN bellowed as she entered his office. "I expected Bogdanovic to call, but not you. Have you finally come to your senses and returned to New York? Are you now at work in the vineyards of District Attorney Vanderhoff? Please have a chair and tell me all about it."

"Let's just say I'm on a busman's holiday, Jerry."

"When my photographer at that dinner Saturday night told me that the country's top lady prosecutor was looking awfully chummy with the ace sleuth of the NYPD, I thought you two might be on the way to becoming an item for our 'Page Nine Togetherness' feature. Now, here you are in my office. But why do I sense that you are not here in the company of Sergeant Bogdanovic to inform me personally of pending nuptials?"

"You know damn well why we're here, Jerry," Bogdanovic said. "So let's cut to the chase. We want to know all the circumstances surrounding the picture on today's front page, which you say is a *Graphic* exclusive."

Ableman winked. "Have you seen it in any other paper?"

"No cameraman from any newspaper got anywhere near the crime scene. So how did the *Graphic* get the picture? Is this another example of pocketbook journalism? Was this a case of kill now and cash in later?"

"As you well know, Johnny, I am not obliged to tell you how I got the picture."

"Yeah, yeah. First Amendment! Only what we're talking about is not freedom of the press. We're talking about your impeding an investigation, and quite possibly your being an accomplice after the fact in a case of murder in the first degree."

"By what stretch of even your highly flexible imagination might I be regarded as an accomplice in Janus's murder?"

"That picture did not come from one of your photographers, nor any other newspaper's cameraman. Neither was it leaked by somebody on my side. And it sure as hell wasn't taken by someone who just happened to be passing by. So tell me, Jerry. Who does that leave?"

Abelman's tone was taunting. "The killer, perhaps?"

"Very good, Jerry. I repeat my question. How did your paper get hold of that picture? Who sold it to you? And don't get up on your high horse about the First Amendment giving you the right to refuse to tell me, because if you do, I'll have to report your refusal to District Attorney Vanderhoff. He'll haul you before a grand jury which will certainly cite you for contempt. You know what they say about grand juries. They will indict a ham sandwich if the DA asks them to. And then Vanderhoff will find a judge who has no love for the *Graphic* and who will be delighted to slap you into the slammer for as long as it takes to persuade you to reveal where you got the picture."

"Of all your legendary charms, Bogdanovic, the one I admire most is your subtlety. First, the *Graphic* did not pay for it. I have no idea where it came from."

"It just flew in the window?"

"In a way. It was hand-delivered to the receptionist," said Abelman, opening a drawer of his desk and withdrawing a manila clasp envelope. "A young guy dropped it off in this. As you can see, it is addressed to me, with the word *urgent* on it big black letters. I'm not a fool, Johnny. When I opened it and saw what it contained, and knowing that you'd kept cameras away from the crime scene until after the body was removed, I figured that when the picture was published, you or one of your henchmen Leibholz or Reiter would come around, sooner or later."

"I also want the original picture."

"Of course you do. You will find it in the envelope. And just to prove what a high-minded citizen I am, I've also included the negative."

Bogdanovic's eyes went wide open with amazement. "This guy also sent you the *negative?*"

"It was obviously his way of proving to me that the print was legit. He thought he was being smart. But sending the negative was probably a big mistake, perhaps a fatal one."

Dane leaned forward and asked, "Why do you say that?"

"When he cut that one frame from the strip of film, he also clipped off a small portion of the frame he'd exposed before he made the shot of Janus's body. Being of an inquisitive nature, I had our photo lab print and enlarge that snippet. It's also in the envelope. I had hoped it might turn out to be a nice second-day front-page pic. Unfortunately, it's unusable. All it shows is a part of Janus's left shoulder. It seems to have been taken at the news conference Janus and Maggie held before that dinner. But don't count on finding fingerprints on the negative. The guy handled the film by the edges, wearing darkroom gloves."

"Fingerprints would have been good to have," Bogdanovic said as he took the envelope from Abelman, "but the portion of a frame taken at the Gramercy Park Hotel and the next one showing Janus dead is enough to argue to a jury that the person who took them murdered Janus."

"When you arrest him, I shall expect a gesture of gratitude for my assistance in this matter in the form of a telephone call from you so that a *Graphic* photographer will be on hand to snap an *exclusive* picture of the murderer being led away in cuffs."

"That's fine, but only if you give me your word that nothing about this meeting gets in the paper until I've made an arrest."

"You know me, Johnny. I'm always ready to sit on a story, as long as it serves my purpose."

"Then we have a deal," Bogdanovic said, standing to extend a hand to Abelman.

Dane also stood. "Good to see you again, Jerry."

"Now, tell me, kiddies, off the record," Abelman said as he accompanied them to the door, "is there or isn't there something going on between you two in what the late godfather of the gossip colum, Walter Winchell, liked to call the moonlight and roses department?"

"Our only connection to flowers," said Bogdanovic, surprising Dane by looping an arm around her waist, "is by way of a fat man who cultivates orchids."

28

In the Best Families

LOOKING UP FROM a gratifyingly thin report on the number and nature of crimes that had been committed in the confines of the five boroughs of New York City during the past twenty-four hours, Chief of Detectives Harvey Goldstein greeted the arrival in his office of Bogdanovic and Dane with a proud smile.

"It appears that the forces of law, order, and righteousness continue to enjoy the upper hand against the bad guys," he said, tapping the report with a fingertip. "Yesterday's overall felony stats are down six percent from the same date a year ago. Homicides yesterday? Four. Off by three."

His eyes shifted to what appeared from across the room to be a large manila envelope in a clear plastic evidence bag clutched in Bogdanovic's right hand.

"What have you there, Johnny? Equally good news, I hope."

Bogdanovic laid the envelope on the desk. "Possibly. What's in it could be the solution to the Janus murder. It's the original of the picture that was in the *Graphic*. And the negative."

"Well, well. Our camera-and-gun-toting killer certainly is a brave soul, isn't he?"

"He was also careless. When he clipped the negative of the photo of Janus from the film strip, he also snipped off part of a picture taken at the press conference that Janus and Maggie held just before the Black Orchid Banquet."

"That was very sloppy of him, indeed. It's better than having a confession. A clever lawyer like Maggie Dane could get a confession thrown out on any number of technicalities. But one picture, as the saying goes, is worth a thousand words. Dare I hope that either the picture or the negative will produce a set of finger-prints?"

"The killer was sloppy, but he was not stupid. According to Abelman, the photo lab experts at the *Graphic* found no prints on either the picture or the negative. The killer wore gloves. The picture and negatives were delivered in the envelope that's in the evidence bag, but I'm not counting on finding the killer's fingerprints on it."

"Even without fingerprints," Dane interjected, "the envelope may still connect him to the crime. It was sealed, so it's likely that he sealed it by licking the flap. If so, testing of the saliva and comparing its genetic markers to DNA in a sample of the suspect's will tie the killer to the envelope. That will allow a DA to lead a jury to the inescapable conclusion that whoever sent the envelope to the *Graphic* murdered Theo."

Goldstein beamed. "The mind of a prosecutor at work! Johnny, it is a beautiful thing to behold at work, especially, in the words of Shakespeare in *Henry V,* 'When blood is their argument.' "

"Shakespeare?" Bogdanovic exclaimed. "Chief, I'm surprised. I was all set to hear a pithy, on-point quotation from either the canon of Sherlock Holmes or the corpus of Nero Wolfe."

"Not to disappoint you, John," said Dane. "I refer you to a short story in *Trouble in Triplicate* titled 'Blood Will Tell.' Of course, that was 1949, decades before the discovery of DNA."

With a chuckle of delight, Goldstein looked at Bogdanovic. "Any testing for DNA in this case is for the future. Meanwhile, Johnny, even though we're not likely to find fingerprints on any of the objects you brought from the *Graphic,* send them to the lab anyway. Maybe we'll get lucky. And while that's being done, where do these fascinating photographic clues leave you in regard to your various theories of the case?"

"They appear to rule out all those involving this having been a gangland killing. The mob doesn't rub out someone and then send a picture of the corpse to a newspaper. And I find it hard to see how Janus's murder is connected to Mancuso's death."

"What about Janus's book on Mancuso's nightstand?"

"The book with its inscription may have provided the impetus for Paulie to jump out the window. But there is no evidence that Janus was involved. We may never know how that book got there, or why. Nor the reason for Paulie's jump."

"Are you proposing that we leave the Mancuso investigation solely to Cornelius Vanderhoff's people?"

"Why not? They had no problem in cutting us out of the loop in that matter. Why get in bed with them now? I personally feel no obligation to pull their irons out of the fire. Let them stew in their own incompetence. I say, tough titties. Let 'em sink or swim. They made that omelette. Let them eat it."

Goldstein directed a mischievous look at Dane. "Maggie, I believe Sergeant Bogdanovic has just set a record for using the most metaphors in a single argument in favor of the dereliction of duty."

With veins standing out in his neck, Bogdanovic angrily demanded, "Since when have I been employed to fix the mistakes of the district attorney's office?"

Still looking at Dane, Goldstein said, "Maggie, I haven't witnessed such an outburst of indignation since Sherlock Holmes defended himself for letting a guilty man go by pointing out to Dr. Watson that he was not retained to supply the deficiencies of Scotland Yard. Have you, Maggie?"

"No, Chief, I haven't."

Goldstein's eyes turned to Bogdanovic. "Of course, Holmes was right. He was not an official detective. He had the luxury of picking his cases and, if he chose, dropping them. And what the hell if a crime went unsolved?"

Bogdanovic took a deep breath, sank into his customary chair, and with a measured cadence said, "There is nothing to indicate, other than writing in a book of what might or might not have been a threat against Mancuso's family, that Mancuso's death was not exactly what it appeared to be, a suicide."

"Yet this very morning in this office," Goldstein replied, "you recited for me a number of theories concerning the murder of Theodore Janus, each of which *appeared* to be viable. Now you say that you've changed your mind. All your theories, like Mancuso, have gone out the window, save one. You have come to this conclusion that the deaths of Mancuso and Janus on the same night were a fluke of timing and a coincidence."

"Pardon me, sir, but—"

"Watch out, Maggie," Goldstein interjected. "When Johnny addresses me as *sir,* the scene that follows is not pleasant. You may wish to leave the room."

As Dane rose to leave, Bogdanovic exclaimed, "You just stay put, Maggie. No ducking out in the middle of a little squabble. They happen in the best of families."

Dane's questioning look at Goldstein was answered with two downturned palms gesturing to her to resume her seat.

"As to my instincts, Chief," Bogdanovic continued quietly, "they have served you very well so far."

Goldstein responded in a restrained tone that seemed to Dane like a father's to an unruly child. "Those instincts have indeed served me well. That's because they were invariably followed by evidence. All I am asking is that you show me the evidence that will back up your instinct that there's no relationship between Janus's killer and what happened to Mancuso."

"How do I prove a negative?"

"Excuse me, gentlemen," said Dane, "but dare I point out an observation by the man who is at the center of Theo's murder? I refer, of course, to Nero Wolfe."

Bogdanovic threw up his arms in dismay. "Why the hell not? All I've heard since this friggin' case started is the apparently endless wisdom of an overweight sleuth who never existed."

Goldstein's smile was as benign as his tone. "Go ahead, Maggie. What did Wolfe have to say?"

"He said that a negative can never be established. You can only establish guilt."

Bogdanovic grunted. "Brilliant! Apparently, the man was an expert at recognizing the obvious."

Unperturbed, Dane continued, "My point is that when you find out who took that picture and have him in custody, you will know who killed Theo. Having established guilt in one case, you will be in a position to learn whether Theo's murder and the death of Mancuso were related. Fortunately, Theo's killer has provided you the means to track him down. Shakespeare was right when he wrote that murder, though it have no tongue, will speak with most miraculous organ. In this instance, that most miraculous organ was a camera. I don't know why Theo's killer felt he had to record the deed on film and send it to the *Graphic,* but in being so bold, he made a mistake that planted the seed of his undoing. That little piece of negative showing that he had been in the Gramercy Park Hotel has reduced the field of suspects to those who were in the lobby when Theo and I met the press before dinner."

"Granted," interjected Goldstein. "But there must have been more than a hundred people in that lobby, not including newspaper photographers and TV news crews jostling with each other to point their lenses at your faces. I even saw one TV cameraman shooting you and Janus from behind."

"The ubiquitous reverse-angle shot," Dane said, stoically, as she looked at Bogdanovic, slouching and listening with what seemed to be indifference. "During the big trial, I quickly got used to seeing the back of my head on the six o'clock news."

Bogdanovic lurched out of his slouch. "Reverse-angle shot. Chief, would you by any chance recall what station's camera was shooting Maggie and Janus from the rear?"

With closed eyes and fingers drumming his belly, Goldstein looked at Bogdanovic and said, "I'm not positive, John, but I have a vague memory of the number eleven on the side of the camera. The guy handling it had a gray walrus mustache."

Bogdanovic bolted to his feet. "Chief, your memory serves you well. The cameraman was Bobby Fields. He and I know each other from who knows how many crimes scenes."

"That's good. Need I suggest that you head up to the station's studios at Forty-second and Second Avenue right now and get your friend to show you his handiwork?"

"While Maggie and I are on the way," Bogdanovic said, "let us pray that it hasn't been erased."

29

Black Orchids

THE NAME ENGRAVED on a brass plate on a desk littered with paper and stacks of video cassette boxes was Elaine Rose.

As Bogdanovic inquired of her into the availability of the video tape, Dane noted with pleasure and pride that the news director of the television station was not only a woman, but a person who could not be impressed or intimidated by a man bearing a detective's shield.

"Our policy regarding turning over our news tapes and out-takes to the police, or to any other government agency, is to refuse to do so unless we are served with a subpoena," Rose said firmly. "And then only on the advice of the company's attorney that we must comply."

"I'm not asking that the tape in question be turned over," Bogdanovic asserted. "I merely want to look at it here and now."

"The effect is the same."

"The *effect* of your refusal, Ms. Rose," Bogdanovic said in a bristling tone of voice, "might be construed by District Attorney Vanderhoff as illegal interference with a murder investigation. A further effect could be a contempt citation with your name on it. You could find yourself sitting in a cell in the Women's House of Detention on Riker's Island until I'm allowed to see the tape."

Rose turned to Dane. "I fail to grasp what relevance a video tape of a news conference with Mr. Janus and you, Miss Dane, has to the investigation of the murder."

"I'm afraid I'm not at liberty to divulge the relevance. I can only tell you that Sergeant Bogdanovic's viewing the tape at the earliest possible moment may be crucial to solving the case."

Rose allowed herself a slight smile. "What do you expect to find on the tape, Sergeant? Might it be a shot of the murderer?"

"All I can say about that," Bogdanovic replied quietly, "is that if there is a shot of the murderer, you've got yourself one hell of a hot piece of tape. That picture would be an even bigger scoop than the one the *Graphic* bragged about in today's edition."

Rose scowled. "I must admit that shot of the corpus delicti with the cigar in his mouth was quite a coup. Did you know that Abelman had the damn thing copyrighted and then had the balls to demand twenty thousand bucks for permission to use it?"

"As a matter of law," Dane said, suppressing a laugh, "the copyright does not belong to the *Graphic,* unless Abelman bought the rights from the person who took the picture."

Rose's eyebrows arched. "May I gather from what Ms. Dane just said, Sergeant, that you suspect the person who took the picture was the murderer?"

"No comment."

"Since you trashed the First Amendment by keeping the press away from the murder scene until after the body was gone, it is logical to conclude that the person who got that amazing photo must have committed the murder."

Bogdanovic grinned. "Nice try, Ms. Rose."

"Try this, Sergeant. Why shouldn't I conclude from your interest in seeing our video of the news conference that the person who took the picture—namely the murderer—might have been caught on our tape of the news conference?"

"As I said, if he is, you've got a valuable tape. I imagine that the proper hype before you run it on your ten o'clock news would result in a healthy boost in the show's ratings. You might even turn the tables on Abelman by charging him for the right to lift a picture of the murderer from your tape."

"You know Jerry Abelman as well as I do, Sergeant. The rat would pirate the picture."

"All this conjecturing is moot, unless I see the tape and it leads to identification and arrest of the murderer."

"For that to happen, you will need more than a look at the tape. You'll require a copy of it so that you and your experts at One Police Plaza can study it. Therein lies the rub."

"Then I suggest you pick up your phone and dump the rub in the lap of your legal eagle. If he says I may see the tape, the issue is settled."

"My legal eagle is a she."

"Should *she* say nay, I'll take the matter to the district attorney and he can thrash it out with your lawyer. But keep in mind that if they fail to reach an accommodation, it could be you who lands in the pokey."

"Sergeant Bogdanovic, in the course of my career in news I have been caught in the crossfire between Serbs and Muslims in Bosnia and Israelis and Palestinians in Manger Square in Bethlehem. I was also held hostage for a day by leftist rebels in Peru in conditions that would make sitting in a cell at Riker's Island a cakewalk. So you can rattle your detective's badge at me all you want. I stand behind the shield of the First Amendment, unless the station's lawyer tells me otherwise. Now, while I place the call to her, you may wait outside. There are coffee and soda machines in the newsroom."

A few moments later, Dane selected a diet cola.

Mindful of the curious looks directed at her by the men and women in the newsroom. Bogdanovic whispered, "How's it feel to be a celebrity prosecutor, Maggie?"

"I'll be glad to get back to blessed anonymity."

"I'm afraid that's highly unlikely. Television let the genie out of the bottle and there's no putting it back."

"How can you be so certain they're not looking at you?"

"Because at least half of the people in this newsroom have known me for years. The rest pride themselves on spotting a cop a mile away, so I'm just another flatfoot. But you are the woman who won a moral victory over Theodore R. Janus in what they and their like across the nation branded the trial of the century. You are the darling of the press."

"Elaine Rose didn't seem to share that opinion."

"Only because you caught her off guard by showing up with a guy who is determined to trample the First Amendment."

"You have to admit she is a gutsy woman."

"In keeping me from viewing the video tape, that gutsy woman is inhibiting a murder investigation. Were you the DA on this case, you would be hightailing it to a judge's chambers to apply for a subpoena, and if Ms. Rose didn't fork over the tape forthwith, you'd lose no time in ordering me to slap on the cuffs."

"True. But I'd still admire her guts."

As she spoke, Rose stepped from her office and signaled them to return.

"That didn't take long," said Bogdanovic.

Stepping aside as they entered the office, Rose said, "Because we have no desire to delay the apprehension of a murderer, and in as much as there is a possibility that our raw tape of the news conference may provide a clue to the killer's identity, you may review the tape at this time, Sergeant. However, should you decide that you need a copy of the material, you will be required to present a subpoena. Locating the tape and setting it up will take a few minutes. You're in luck, by the way. The man who shot the tape is on the premises."

"That would be Bobby Fields?"

"Yes. I gather you know him."

"We're old friends professionally."

"I expect you'll find him not quite so friendly. Because of your dirty trick of keeping cameras away from the scene while you spirited away the body, we had to run the murder as the second story on last night's broadcast. The decision to keep the cameras away until the body was removed thwarted the basic precept of TV news. If it bleeds, it leads. We were forced to use file footage of Janus and a small portion of the video of the news conference. With all due respect to you, Ms. Dane, it wasn't very exciting."

WEARING A RED-AND-BLUE plaid shirt and faded blue jeans and seated before a row of television screens and a bank of video tape machines, the portly cameraman gently stroked the walrus mustache with obvious pride, turned slowly in a red swivel chair, fixed ice blue eyes on Bogdanovic, and said, "Well, well, if it isn't Mr. Screw-the-First-Amendment."

Bogdanovic made a slight bow. "It's nice to see you again, too, Bobby."

Lifting himself slightly from the red chair, Fields gave a nod of greeting to Dane. "It's only because you are here, Miss Dane, that I'm restraining myself from fulfilling the desire of every cameraman in this town to let this guy have it in the jaw for keeping us away from that crime scene till there was nothing worth getting on tape. I presume that it is too optimistic of me to expect that an apology might be forthcoming for his outrageous conduct early Sunday morning in Gramercy Park."

"Bobby, I believe you have the same rule in the news trade that we coppers live by," Bogdanovic said. "Never apologize. Your friends don't need it, and your enemies won't believe you."

Fields picked up a video cassette and shook it at him. "You owe me for this, Johnny."

"Duly noted, Bobby."

The tape went into a playback deck. "If you'll tell me what you're looking for, it might save us a lot of time."

Bogdanovic said, "I'm looking for shots you may have gotten at the news conference in the hotel lobby of anybody who had a camera."

"Practically everybody had one."

With the punch of a button, Fields started the tape.

"I'm interested in thirty-five-millimeter cameras," Bogdanovic said. "Ones equipped with a flash."

Fields pondered this a moment, then exclaimed, "I get it! It's that picture in the *Graphic*. You think somebody at the news conference followed Janus to his car, shot him, photographed the corpse, and sent it to the *Graphic*. I wondered where that picture came from. It never dawned on me that it might have come from the killer. Does that take the cake for chutzpah, or what?"

The screen above the tape deck filled with a shot of Wolfe Pack members milling on the sidewalk in front of the hotel.

"As soon as I arrive at a story," Fields explained, "I get an establishing shot. I was hoping to catch Janus and Miss Dane as they arrived, but they were already inside the lobby."

Onto the screen came a close-up of a sign:

BLACK ORCHIDS BANQUET
SECOND FLOOR DINING ROOM

"Oh my gosh," Dane said. "How could Wiggins have missed that mistake?"

With a puzzled look, Fields asked, "What mistake?"

"It's Black Orchid. Singular."

The screen showed the crowded lobby with Janus's white hat seemingly afloat on a sea of backs of heads. Then came a jiggling shot of the lobby's carpet.

"Ever since I didn't have my camera ready and missed getting a shot of Bobby Kennedy being gunned down in that hotel kitchen in Los Angeles," Fields said, "I always keep the camera rolling whenever I change position."

Next on the screen was the news conference itself with rude reporters asking rude questions.

Throughout these questions and the answers, Fields's lens remained on Janus and Dane. But now he changed his position, moving behind them for the reverse angle.

"This is the shot I'm interested in," Bogdanovic said.

A young man with a camera slung from a shoulder and grasping a traditional reporter's notebook who politely addressed Janus as *mister* was asked by Janus, "Is my father here?"

As the crowd laughed, Fields's lens zoomed into a close-up of the unamused youth as he demanded, "How do you sleep at night?"

"I sleep in the raw!"

"What I meant was, how can you sleep at night knowing that you make it possible for so many guilty people to go free? Do you ever think about the feelings of the people who loved the victims of these criminals that you got off?"

"I don't free anyone, young man. Juries do. And when they have rendered their verdict of not guilty, I sleep with the clear conscience of a baby."

The broad back of Wiggins thrust into the picture. "Time for only one more question."

A young woman asked, "Theo, were you surprised to find out that you'd be getting this award from Maggie?"

Janus tipped back his hat as he replied. "To paraphrase Nero Wolfe, there are two ways for a man to ruin a friendship. One is to lend a pal a lot of money. The other is to question the purity of a woman's gesture."

The picture widened to show the crowd dispersing.

"And that is all of it," Fields said. "Did you find what you were looking for, Johnny?"

Bogdanovic's eyes were still directed to the screen. "Could you show me the reverse-angle shot again?"

"I'm glad to. It was the best part of story," Fields said as a touch of a finger restored a picture to the screen and sent it spinning crazily backward. "It got Janus at an angle for the best of the questions—the one that wanted to know how Janus slept at night after getting a guilty person off."

The tape stopped, then ran forward at regular speed.

"Even from behind you can see by Janus's body language that he was really irritated," said Fields, touching the screen.

"It was a nasty question," Dane said, "and obviously one the reporter intended to use to embarrass Theo."

"I wouldn't know about that," Fields said, stopping the tape and freezing the scene on the screen. "But if that's what the kid had in mind, he blew the opportunity. When he asked his question he didn't have his camera ready to get Janus's angry reaction."

"Have you ever seen that reporter at other news events?"

"Nah. And I'd be surprised if he was a reporter. He's certainly not a professional photographer. Look at his camera. It's what you'd take with you on vacation. It shoots thirty-five millimeter, but the lens is fixed. And then there's the flash. It's built right into the camera. No pro would go on assignment with that. My guess is this kid was staying at the hotel, or maybe he was passing by. He also could have been a student at the School of Visual Arts. It's only a block from the hotel. He could have seen the crowd and the press outside the hotel and decided to get in on the excitement by pretending he was a reporter. It's ironic that he asked the best question of the night."

"I may need a copy of this tape, Bobby."

"If you want your own copy, you'll have to get in the ring and duke that matter out with my boss. But don't be misled by her size. She looks like a lightweight, but she packs a wallop."

"Having had a preliminary bout with Ms. Rose, I am not looking forward to a rematch. But if I have to go to the mat to get this tape, I will."

"What's on it that's so important? Is it some kind of clue?"

"Possibly. So please take care that it doesn't get erased."

WHEN THEY REACHED their car Bogdanovic said, "Maggie, I'm going to take you to lunch at my favorite restaurant, and then I'll try my hand at telling a mystery story."

"Why shouldn't you? Everybody else seems to be doing it."

"Of course, as a storyteller I am not in the same league as Arthur Conan Doyle and Rex Stout," he said, starting the engine. "Or Marian Pickering Henry, for that matter."

"Who the hell is? May I assume that your story will be based on one of your actual cases?"

"It will be part fact, part conjecture, part imagination."

"There was a very good mystery in which the detective—a sergeant, by the way—said that it is not logic that a policeman needs, but imagination. He held that the only difference between a policeman and a criminal is that the cop uses imagination to solve rather than commit crimes. The book by Patrick McGinley was called *Bogmail*. That's Irish for blackmail."

"There's a coincidence. The place we're going to for lunch is an Irish pub on East Fifty-seventh Street. Neary's."

The car stopped at Forty-second Street and First Avenue as a traffic light permitted a throng of children in parochial school uniforms to cross for a visit to the United Nations.

"As to detectives using their imaginations," Bogdanovic said, "a few years ago a retired Scotland Yard inspector who was in town on a visit told me the same thing. His name was Colin Whicher. He was a big help in solving a string of murders that were committed to cover up the one that counted to the killers. Fortunately, your friend Janus was engaged in other cases at the time. The murderer and his accomplice were convicted and their life sentences upheld on appeal."

"Proving that justice can prevail in life as it always does in the final chapter of a mystery," Dane said as the car proceeded up

First Avenue. "Everyone who reads a detective novel has no need to worry about some slick lawyer stepping in to screw up the ending by finding a loose end the detective failed to tie up."

"That's what I want you to do after I tell you my story. I expect you to use your expertise as a reader of mysteries, and as a prosecutor, to point out loose ends."

Ten minutes later, as a pretty red-haired waitress with an Irish lilt in her voice led them past a long bar at the front to a corner table draped in a heavy red cloth, Dane said, "What a delightful spot."

Looking around the long, dimly lit room, she found maroon leather banquettes and dark wood-paneled walls decorated with pictures of Irish castles and many autographed photos of Irish politicians, including Ronald Reagan and Senator Ted Kennedy. On a staff fixed to a wall hung the orange, green, and white banner of the Republic of Ireland.

"It's the quintessential New York restaurant," she added, "with just the right overlay of lace-curtain Irish!"

Bogdanovic blushed and looked around to see if she might have been overheard.

"Don't worry, John," she said, grinning as she patted his wrist reassuringly. "I'm allowed to say that because lace-curtain Irish is what I am."

"The lunch menu is on the blackboard," he said, pointing to it on the wall above the doorway to the kitchen. "If you don't care for what's there, you can choose from the regular menu. You can never go wrong with Neary's lamb chops. We eat first. But no discussing the case. Then we'll have Irish coffee while I tell you my story."

30

Plot It Yourself

"PROPER IRISH COFFEE is made with brown sugar," Bogdanovic lectured. "The cream must be freshly whipped and added gently to the top, not stirred in. Serve in a warmed, fluted glass."

Lifting hers, Dane said, "I offer a genuine Irish toast. May you be dancing with the angels in Heaven half an hour before the Devil even knows you're gone."

Bogdanovic clinked his glass against hers, "And this is a Croatian toast:

> Here's to lying, cheating, stealing, and drinking.
> When you lie, lie to save a friend.
> When you cheat, cheat death.
> When you steal, steal a maiden's heart.
> When you drink, drink with me, my friend."

Their sips of the coffee left thin mustaches of cream on their upper lips.

"Now, Miss Dane," he said as they patted them off with large white napkins, "are you ready to hear my story?"

"It had better not begin, 'It was a dark and stormy night.' "

"Actually, it begins in a courtroom where a man is on trial for murder. The case has been dragging on for months, thanks to the clever maneuverings of the defense lawyer. It is now time for him to deliver his summation to the jury. Watching from the front row of the audience, as he has done every day of the proceedings, is a young man whom I shall call Vic."

Dane smiled. "I see. As in *vic*-tim?"

"Actually, Vic is the son, or perhaps another relative, of the person the defendant is accused of having murdered. It was a killing that in no way can be justified. Although the evidence is circumstantial, the prosecution has presented a very strong case. But the defense lawyer has lived up to his reputation as the best mouthpiece in the country. He has punched holes in every piece of what the prosecution called in its summation a mountain of proof of guilt. The jury retires to deliberate, and after a couple of days returns with a verdict of not guilty."

Dane took a sip of coffee. "Vic is understandably outraged."

"Of course he is. And why not? First, his relative was murdered. Now, because of what he regards as legal trickery, he has been made a victim a second time. He trusted in the law and the law let him down. Justice has been denied him. But even worse, in Vic's mind, is the image of the killer's lawyer going about his business, apparently untroubled by getting a murderer off. Over and over in his mind, Vic asks the lawyer—"

Dane cut him off. "He asks the question posed by the young man at the press conference. How can he sleep at night knowing that he makes it possible for so many guilty people to go free? Does he ever think about the feelings of the people who loved the victims of these criminals that he got off?" She paused with a look of horror on her face. "Good lord, John, is it possible that if Janus hadn't said that he slept with the clear conscience of a baby, the kid might not have shot him? Might that kid have been hoping for some sort of public apology?"

"It wouldn't have mattered how Janus replied. The kid's mind was set on punishing Janus. He went there intending to kill him. If an opportunity hadn't presented itself that night, he would have kept trying until he succeeded."

"You are assuming he was the person who took that shot at Theo at his ranch."

"This is where my detective's imagination comes in. Suppose the shot hadn't gone awry. What if it had been intended to miss him? Imagine a scenario in which the kid wanted Janus to know he was being hunted. Imagine further that the shot was putting Janus on notice that someone was determined to kill him in an act of retribution, so that in the instant when Janus was facing death he would know why he was being killed. I expect that a search of the files at Janus's ranch will turn up evidence that he had been put on notice that he should expect to die and that when the moment came he would recognize his killer and the reason. I think that is why the killer asked those questions at the press conference. He wanted Janus in the last moment of life to remember him and, perhaps, also realize as he looked into the killer's face that he'd seen it many times before in a courtroom."

"Okay. The kid brought a camera to the press conference in order to blend in with the press. What I do not understand is why he snapped that ghastly death photo and sent it to the *Graphic*."

"This is conjecture, but I think it's likely that he thought it was important to record his achievement. If I may stretch my imagination even further—"

"It's serving you well so far!"

"I think it is possible that Vic wanted the photo published in order to let others who perceived themselves as the victims of miscarriages of justice know that a score had been settled with the symbol of a legal system that puts rights of criminals ahead of those of victims. Does that explanation make sense to you?"

"It certainly does."

"So, what do you think of my little murder story? Do you see any loose ends?"

"The only thing missing is the actual name of the murderer."

"I can't give you that until we search Janus's cases for the one that fits my plot."

"Have you given your story a title?"

"How about 'The Phony Cameraman'?"

"That's not bad. But might I suggest you plagiarize a Nero Wolfe title? There are two that fit your story: 'Counterfeit for Murder' and 'Disguise for Murder'."

"Dare I try out my yarn on a certain chief of detectives?"

"With the possible exception of the proprietor of the Usual Suspects bookstore and yours truly, I can't think of anyone more appreciative of an imaginative mystery story."

LOOKING UP AT them as they came into his office, Goldstein said, "You look like a couple of cats who ate the canary. I trust you found something useful on the channel eleven videotape."

"As a matter of fact," Dane said, "John has come up with a nifty piece of deductive reasoning equal to anything demonstrated by Sherlock Holmes and Nero Wolfe."

Bogdanovic blushed. "Maggie is much too generous."

"I'll decide that," Goldstein said. "Let's hear it."

As Bogdanovic sat on the edge of his chair in a posture so erect he looked like a marine at attention, Dane imagined he was Archie Goodwin reporting findings to Nero Wolfe in a brownstone on West Thirty-fifth Street. The only things lacking to complete the scene were a bottle of beer clasped in Goldstein's hand, a vest straining to contain an extra one hundred and fifty pounds around Goldstein's middle, and four additional inches in height to bring Goldstein equal to Wolfe's five feet eleven inches. Nor did his pale blue shirt with a button-down collar arrest her eyes as would Wolfe's invariable bright canary yellow.

When Bogdanovic ended his story, Goldstein said, "I think you are on to something, Johnny. Your reasoning about the killer pretending to be a member of the press is sound. It's a damn lucky thing Bobby Fields captured the guy's face on tape."

Bogdanovic grimaced. "To get a copy we'll need a subpoena."

Goldstein shrugged. "Consider it done. What's next?"

"I intend to take Leibholz and Reiter up to Janus's ranch to help locate a file Janus was keeping of the threats he received from people who didn't care much for his record as the great defender."

31

Die Like a Dog

"YOU PROBABLY DON'T remember, Miss Dane," said Detective
Al Leibholz from the front seat of the car, "but I was a witness in
one of your trials a few years ago. It was the big child murders
case. You put the perp away for three consecutive life terms."

"I remember the case, of course," Dane said. "Horrible! But
there were a lot of police witnesses."

"Fifteen of us, actually. My partner at the time was Officer
Scott Gordon. We were working radio patrol and found the third
of the victims, an eleven-year-old boy, in a vacant lot on the Lower
East Side. Our testimony was all cut-and-dried, so there was no
reason for either of us to stick out in your mind. That's just the
way it is with uniforms. One cop looks like every other one."

"A situation which you and Red have corrected by creating
your own inimitable styles," Bogdanovic teased. "Detective Leibholz in Armani suits and silk ties by Fabienne and Red Reiter in
custom-made duds from the Urban Cowboy."

Driving the car, Reiter said, "That's right. The same place
where Janus bought his outfits. I saw him there once. He was
being fitted for boots. He ordered six pairs that had to have cost
him the equivalent of my salary for a couple of months."

"Proving that crimes pays," Bogdanovic said, "if you are a defense lawyer by the name of Theodore Roosevelt Janus."

"So that's what the middle initial stood for," Reiter said. "I
never knew he was named after Teddy. Now I understand why he
went for the western look clothing wise. I suppose he figured it
helped boost his reputation with juries as a tough character if he
looked like a Rough Rider. The funny thing, though, is that I always thought he looked more like the star attraction of Buffalo

Bill's old-time Wild West shows. You know, all hat and no cattle, as they say out in Texas."

"I believe you will change your opinion," said Dane, "once you've seen Theo's ranch. And there was nothing phony about his admiration for Teddy Roosevelt."

PRESENTLY, THEY PASSED beneath the Little Misery sign and up the driveway, watched by half a dozen horses behind white fences.

As they arrived in front of the house, David Kolker ambled toward them from the stables. "Back again, Miss Dane. Are you making progress in finding out who killed Mr. Janus?"

"I believe so," she said. "We need to get into the house."

"Go right ahead. The door's open."

As they walked down the long corridor toward the office, Leibholz's eyes explored the pictures of Janus drawn by courtroom artists and said, "There's no doubt whose house this is."

Stepping into the large room that was both an office and a museum to Janus's namesake, Reiter let out a low whistle as he looked at youthful Teddy Roosevelt as Dakota Territory cowboy. In a suit, vest, and lank bow tie, he struck a formal pose beside the desk he had used, and which had been passed on for the use of every police commissioner who followed him as Teddy moved onward and upward.

Gazing at these artifacts, Reiter said to Dane, "I see what you mean about Janus's fondness for Teddy being genuine."

Standing before the portrait of Janus, Leibholz said, "He was pretty fond of himself, too."

"We're not here as sightseers, folks," Bogdanovic grumbled. "So let's get down to work."

Leibholz looked at the rows of file cabinets. "The man must have saved every piece of paper he ever touched. Talk about your search for a needle in a haystack!"

"It won't be that bad," Dane said. "The files are arranged chronologically. Each file cabinet contains one year's papers. They are subdivided into months and weeks and those folders are then arranged alphabetically by subject."

"Be that as it may," Leibholz replied, "there are lots of years to plow through."

"Not really, Al," said Bogdanovic. "Theo had the windows of his car bulletproofed after he returned from the trial in Los Angeles. The trial ended in July, so I think we can safely assume that he was reacting to a threat or threats received since then. That's months of files divided between us. It shouldn't take that long to go through them."

Leibholz went to the file for the current year and pulled open the top drawer. Joined by Reiter, he began withdrawing thick folders. As the two detectives emptied the six-drawer cabinet and stacked the files on a long table, Bogdanovic quickly sorted them according to month.

Finished with the transfer of material, Reiter asked, "What are we hoping to find?"

"Look for threatening letters and notes."

Dane added, "Also look for any memorandums Theo might have written concerning threats. When I worked with him he was always dictating memorandums for the files. He also might have gotten threats on tape. Or there could be recordings of threatening phone calls. Theo had an automatic phone taping system."

Reiter opened a slender file labeled August 1–7. "Shades of Tricky Dicky Nixon's White House."

Leibholz held a thick file as if weighing it. "Didn't this guy ever hear of a paper shredder?"

"He was an attorney," Dane answered, taking a file for the first week of September. "He was strict in obeying the first rule of practicing law: The papers you discard today may be the ones you'll need tomorrow. Law is based on precedent. The first thing you do when you get a new case is dash to the law library to find out how a similar case was decided. Theo was also keenly aware that the only memory you can trust is the one that was written down, especially when you get around to writing your memoirs. That's why I'm certain that every threat or angry letter he ever got will be in his files."

Settling into silence, they each picked up and studied a file and moved on to the next.

"Here's one that gets right to the point," Leibholz said, holding up a sheet of paper with a ragged edge. "Torn from a notebook, obviously. 'For what you did in that big trial I hope you die like a dog.' It's unsigned, of course."

Bogdanovic studied the note. "The writing is feminine. We're looking for a man."

As they worked, the only sounds in the room were turning papers, an occasional clearing of a throat, or a weary sigh as one of the searchers lifted a head, yawned, or rubbed eyes.

Presently, Reiter startled the others with, "Hey! This looks promising. Listen. 'Because of you, the people who killed my father got off with little more than a slap on the wrist. I've waited too long for you to admit you were wrong. Now you will be made to pay.'"

Bogdanovic took the letter. "It appears to have been done on a computer with a laser printer."

With Dane looking over his shoulder, he read:

> The armored car guard that radical gang shotgunned to death was my father. Because you made those creeps into victims of society instead of cold-blooded killers, that woman got off scot-free. She should have been executed. One of these days I am going to make you pay the price she didn't have to. And I will make sure the whole world knows about it!

Dane said, "This obviously refers to the aborted stickup by the gang of radicals who botched that robbery of the armored van and killed a guard."

Bogdanovic nodded. "What did you say his name was?"

"Lawrence Newport."

"You said he had a son?"

"Two years old at the time."

Bogdanovic read the letter again. "Maggie, what would you estimate was the age of that young man with the camera at the press conference?"

"I'd guess he was twenty something!"

Bogdanovic stared at the letter. "Do you happen to remember the son's name?"

"No, but I'm sure it's in the case file."

"There may be a quicker way to check," Dane said. "The son's name is probably mentioned in the chapter devoted to the case in *Janus for the Defense.* There should be a leather-bound copy of it and his other books on the shelf below his portrait. Try looking up the name Newport in the index."

Leibholz located the book, thumbed through the pages at the back, and said, "Here it is. Newport, Lawrence. Just above it is another Newport. Alice."

"That was his wife. She created a hell of a ruckus when she barged into a press conference Theo called to announce that there would be no retrial of Victoria Davis. She had the kid with her. It's the only time I ever saw Theo upstaged."

"Here's the son in the index," Leibholz interjected. "His name was William."

Dane smiled. "Good old index, to quote Sherlock Holmes, who was another fellow who never threw away a piece of paper."

"To hell with files on paper," Bogdanovic said as he all but leapt to his feet. "I expect we will find what we need to know about William Newport in somebody's computer. As soon as we get back to the city, we are going to commence a search in every mainframe we can access. Someplace, sometime, somebody keyboarded all there was to know about William Newport, entered it, and saved it. All we have to do is find it."

32

Too Many Detectives

LOOKING STARTLED AS Bogdanovic and Dane shattered the quiet of his office by bursting in, Goldstein peered over the tops of half-moon reading glasses, regarded their smiling faces, and said, "Evidently your outing in the country was fruitful."

"Very productive," Bogdanovic said, beaming. "I think we've got ourselves a prime suspect. I believe he's the son of a security company guard who was killed in an armored car robbery that went wrong up in Stone County. Janus got the convictions of the perps overturned on appeal. The motive was revenge."

"Rather long in coming," Goldstein said.

"The dead guard's son is named William Newport. He was only two years old at the time of the holdup."

"I see. When he was a little kid and someone asked him what he wanted to do when he grew up, Willie said, 'I intend to avenge the death of my old man, not by killing the people who gunned him down on the job, but the lawyer who took their case on appeal.' "

"That's exactly it," Bogdanovic retorted. "We've got letters to prove it. One of them specifically references the holdup and says the guard who was killed was the writer's father."

"If this guy sent threatening letters and *signed* them, he's already laid a pretty strong foundation for a defense based on a claim of diminished mental capacity."

"I think I can show that he was at Janus's press conference prior to the Wolfe Pack dinner."

Goldstein whipped off the glasses and tossed them onto a sea of paperwork. "You think? You believe? This is not evidence, and neither are those letters, until you can place William Newport at the scene of the crime. I'd feel a lot better if you told me you were certain."

"I am hopeful that I will soon have a picture of Newport and that it will be a match with the young man in Fields's video."

"Hopeful! There you go again, Johnny. I hope you can bring me evidence in the form of the gun that killed Janus, with William Newport's fingerprints on the trigger. Regarding that tape, while you were rooting around in Janus's archives I persuaded Vanderhoff to draw up a subpoena to get a copy. You can pick it up at your convenience."

"We might not need it. When we locate William Newport we can put him in a lineup and have Bobby Fields take a look at him. I'm confident Bobby will make a positive ID. We may find others who were at the dinner who can put Newport there. How soon that will happen depends on how soon we locate Newport in somebody's computer files."

Goldstein retrieved his glasses and slipped them on. "Well, don't let me detain you."

Leaving Goldstein's office and striding down the corridor toward his own, Bogdanovic said, "This may sound disingenuous to you, Maggie, but at moments like this I actually feel sorry for today's criminals. When I got into police work, it was a human enterprise. Cops versus crooks. One or two homicide detectives wearing out shoe leather to track down a killer. It was brains combined with legwork. A morality drama. A good guy going after a bad guy. Very personal. A test of wits and wills in which the bad guy had a fifty-fifty chance of getting away. Computers have changed all that. The misbegotten felon is trapped in a world in which there are just too many detectives."

Opening the door of his office, he found Leibholz and Reiter seated at tables with eyes already focused on two of the office's four computer screens.

"Good old data banks," he said, gleefully. Pulling off his jacket, he sat at his desk, rubbed his hands eagerly, and winked at Dane. "Pull up a chair, Maggie. The game is afoot!"

"I don't know what rules the police department has set out as to who is authorized to use its computers," she replied. "But I can't help noticing one of yours sitting idle. There is no way for you to have known this fact about me, but I also know how to navigate cyberspace. I was on the team of prosecutors that was consulted in setting up the computer system in Vanderhoff's office. I also had input in upgrading the operation in the district attorney's offices in Los Angeles."

"Well, don't just sit there, woman! Boot up and log on. We have a lot of territory to explore. The Motor Vehicles Department for a driver's license. Parking Violations Bureau. Social Security for a number. Bank accounts. Internal Revenue Service. Voter registration lists. He may have a rap sheet in our own files."

Reiter looked away from his screen and announced, "No luck there, John. I've checked. William has never been arrested in the city of New York and there are no wants or warrants on file from anywhere else."

Bogdanovic asked, "What about the FBI?"

"I was just about to tap into them. I'll be more than happy to turn the G-men over to Miss Dane."

"Please call me Maggie," she said. "As the housefly said to the spider, 'Since we're in the same web, we might as well be on a first-name basis.' "

Leibholz grunted a laugh. "That's a good one, Maggie."

"If you don't mind, Red, I'll pass on the feds," she said as she sat at the idle computer. "Having spent a year working frauds in Vanderhoff's vineyards, I thought I'd try to get in touch with a friend from those days who now works for an all-knowing, all-powerful gatherer of every American's most intimate information."

"Good idea," said Bogdanovic. "The dreaded IRS."

"I refer to an even more efficient organization," she said, switching on the computer. "My old friend is the chief of security for a credit reporting agency."

"Maggie, that is brilliant idea."

Turning away, she muttered, "Let us all pray that my friend of old is reachable at his old e-mail address, and that he'll do a data search for me."

"My prayer is that Mr. Newport is a resident of the Empire

State," said Bogdanovic. "I hate it when I have to go to a court to request extradition."

As he scrolled through a roster of persons with delinquent parking fines, the office fell into a silence broken only by fingers on four computer keyboards and the occasional blare of an automobile horn from the direction of the ramps to the Brooklyn Bridge.

Finding the parking fines file unavailing, Bogdanovic was about to try voter registration lists when Dane shouted, "My friend is indeed at his e-mail address. He's searching the firm's records. It shouldn't take long."

Reiter paused in his combing of driver's license files to say, "Let us all hope that William Newport is not one of those incredible consumers who manage to make their way through life on a policy of cash and carry."

Staring expectantly at the blank computer screen, Dane said, "Come on, baby. Don't disappoint. Speak to me."

In the next instant as the screen filled with data, Dane exclaimed, "Fellas, I believe we've found the murdering twerp!"

Bogdanovic lurched away from his desk to roll in his chair to Dane's position and read aloud, "Newport, William. Two hundred forty East Twenty-fifth Street."

"Easy walking distance from Gramercy Park," said Reiter.

"Occupation: faculty member, School of Visual Arts," Bogdanovic continued. "That's on Twenty-first Street, east of Third Avenue. Three blocks from the murder scene! Care to guess what visual art he teaches?"

Dane said, "He's got credit cards for Bloomingdale's, Brooks Brothers, and Paul Stuart. His overall credit is rated A-plus."

"Obviously, William has quite a few bucks," said Leibholz.

As Dane hit the Print button, Bogdanovic said, "He's going to need it to retain the caliber of lawyer he'll be needing to defend him against a charge of first-degree murder. We have him dead to rights."

Dane asked, "Do we, John?"

"We have the threatening letters and the picture in the *Graphic* puts him at the scene. We have two bullets—the one that killed

Janus and the slug that Wiggins brought us. Motive, opportunity, and means!"

"The letters, the tape, the photograph, and the bullets are worthless without the gun he used," Dane said. "If he's as smart as he appears to be, he'll have gotten rid of it. Unless it flew away like the gun with wings in a Nero Wolfe story, I'd venture that within minutes of Theo's death it went in the East River. Unless you can produce an eyewitness to the murder, you have a circumstantial case that Theo could turn into Swiss cheese."

"Fortunately for the cause of justice," Bogdanovic replied brusquely, "Janus is not around to appear in anybody's defense."

33

And Be a Villain

With his right ear to the apartment door, Reiter drew his Glock and whispered, "Somebody's home. I hear movement."

Gripping his pistol in his right hand and using his left to loudly thump the apartment door, Leibholz bellowed, "Police! We have a search warrant! Open up or we break down the door."

As it swung open, William Newport exclaimed, "Don't worry." Backing into the room, he raised his arms. "I am not going to resist. I'm not stupid."

Bogdanovic stepped into the room. "Are you William Newport?"

"Yes I am."

"You are under arrest for the murder of Theodore Janus."

"I expected you people to show up sooner or later. Frankly, it's a great relief."

As Reiter continued to brandish his weapon, Leibholz pulled down Newport's arms and snapped on handcuffs.

"Before we ask you any further questions," said Bogdanovic, "you must understand that you have the right to remain silent. Do you understand?"

Newport looked toward Dane with a quizzical smile. "You're the lady prosecutor from California. Why are you here?"

"Theodore Janus was my very dear friend."

Newport's young face wrinkled with puzzlement. "Really?"

Bogdanovic continued, "Anything you say can be used against you in court. You have the right to talk to a lawyer."

Newport giggled. "That's funny. What irony. You need not go on, sir. I understand all my rights."

"Do you wish to invoke them?"

"I'm not a hypocrite, sir."

"May I interpret that as your consent to submit yourself to questioning regarding the murder?"

"I welcome the opportunity to explain what I prefer to call an act of righteous retribution."

Signaling Reiter to holster his gun, Bogdanovic said, "Very well, William, we're listening."

"I presume by your presence that you have a pretty good idea of my motive. I hope you will do me the courtesy to tell me what I did to lead you to me so quickly."

"In a nutshell," Bogdanovic said, "you should have left your camera at home."

"But that was impossible. I needed it to prove that Janus's death was not mere happenstance. The camera was the means to show that his murder had been planned, and to make it clear that he'd been made to pay for his sins."

"I grant you that the picture showed premeditation. But how was anyone to know by looking at it that Janus had been called to account for what you considered to be sins?"

"I intended to send the newspaper a second photograph, along with a letter of explanation. Alas, you arrived before I had time to deliver them. They're in an envelope in the darkroom."

As Reiter went to retrieve them, Bogdanovic asked, "We know that you killed Janus because he was reponsible for freeing the people who murdered your father. But that was years ago. Why did you wait so long?"

"I was only two years old when my father was killed. I had some growing up to do. That was not so easy, in as much as my mother died a year after Janus got my father's killers off. She died of a broken heart. That was another sin for which Janus had to pay. Of course, a three-year-old child is not in a position to go out seeking revenge. As the years went by, I was busy being a kid and a teenager, and then there was college and getting my life started. I was willing to wait. I watched that trial in L.A. The more I felt that Janus was likely to get that killer off, despite your efforts, Miss Dane, the more I despised him. And the more I saw pictures of the mother of the woman he'd butchered, and how she suffered, the more I realized the time had come for Janus to suffer for all the pain he caused my mother, me, and all the other victims of all the criminals that Janus's legal trickery had kept from getting everything that they deserved under the law."

Dane asked, "Why did you send him letters?"

"I wanted him to know he was being hunted. I could easily have killed him with that shot I fired at him at his ranch, but I aimed away just enough to miss him, yet close enough for him to know somebody had tried to kill him."

Bogdanovic asked, "How did you know where he lived?"

"I found out all I could about him by reading his books and every newspaper or magazine article I could find. His books were exactly like the man I saw on television: smug and arrogant and filled with conceit. Then I read in a newspaper about his getting some award and that the presentation dinner was to be held at the Gramercy Park Hotel. It was as though fate was on my side. I decided that the perfect time for him to die was shortly after he'd received his award."

"Why did you masquerade as a reporter?"

Newport smiled proudly. "I thought I pulled that off well."

"You certainly did," Dane said, "One of the TV news cameramen thinks you asked the best question of the night."

"You probably won't believe me, Miss Dane, but when I asked him how he could sleep after all that he'd done to hurt so many people, I hoped he would say he was sorry for the pain he caused. If he had answered that his conscience had bothered him *once,* I might not have killed him. But he was the usual arrogant, self-centered Theodore Roosevelt Janus. So I hung around until the dinner was over, waiting for my chance. But I couldn't shoot him right away because he was talking to people coming out of the hotel. He was playing big shot with his award under his arm and lighting up a cigar."

"So you followed him to his car."

"Yes, but at a safe distance. For a while, I thought he might not make it."

Dane asked, "Why did you think that?"

"He started staggering as if he was drunk. But he got to the car all right, so I rushed up to it before he could drive away. But he didn't. He sat smoking his cigar. I could smell it through the open window as I walked up. When I found him at the wheel with that expensive cigar in his mouth, I told him my name and who my father was, and that he was going to die. But he just sat there looking straight ahead as if I didn't exist. That pissed me off. The indifference! I pointed the gun at the side of his head and shot him once. He didn't even flinch!"

"Why did you take that picture of him?"

"I didn't want the police to assume he'd been killed in an attempted robbery. I wanted it known that it was a premeditated act. And I wanted to show all his victims that Janus had finally gotten what he deserved. I hoped it would bring them closure."

"Where is the gun?"

"I threw it in the river."

"Where did you get the gun?"

"It was my father's. It was one of two he was carrying the day he was murdered. He had a thirty-eight and a twenty-two. But they never gave him a chance to draw either of them. I used the thirty-eight to shoot at Janus and deliberately miss him. Both are in the river."

Reiter stepped from the darkroom. With the corner of a large clasp envelope held between the thumb and forefinger of his left hand, he asked. "Is the second photograph in this?"

Newport nodded. "You won't find fingerprints. I wore gloves."

34

Not Quite Dead Enough

"WHILE YOU WERE arresting William Newport," Goldstein said as Bogdanovic and Dane entered his office, "there was a message for you from our friend Dr. Hassan Awini. The autopsy on Janus has been completed."

Bogdanovic sank into his usual chair. "What does the distinguished medical examiner want from me? My congratulations for finding the obvious? We always knew how Janus died, and now we know who did it and why. The good doctor is a little late. All we lack is the gun Newport used."

"Nonetheless, Awini said that before he sends the bullet that he got from Janus's head to ballistics for comparison to the slug that Wiggins brought in, he needs to speak to you."

Bogdanovic glowered. "Did he tell you why?"

"I didn't talk to him. I was on the horn with Vanderhoff at the time, telling him that you'd solved the Janus murder. Officer Sweeney took the call. You can ask her. Or you can call Awini yourself. Use my phone."

When Bogdanovic picked it up, Goldstein punched a button to put the call on the speakerphone.

The voice of the medical examiner was a cheery contrast to the nature of his work. "Johnny!"

Bogdanovic sat on the corner of Goldstein's desk. "I'm told you want to talk about the slug you got from Janus's head."

"That's right. Very interesting. It's a twenty-two caliber, fired at fairly close range, and certainly it was capable of having killed Mr. Janus."

Bogdanovic stood and glared at the speakerphone. *"Capable?* What the devil does that mean?"

"It means the man was not shot to death."

"What? Of course he was," Janus insisted. "I have just come from booking the killer. He confessed to shooting Janus."

"Johnny, I did not say that Mr. Janus was not shot. I said that he was not shot *to death.* You may recall that when I examined the body at the scene of the crime, I remarked that there was very little blood. That is because Mr. Janus's heart ceased to pump blood before he was shot."

"Just a darn minute, Doctor," Goldstein interjected, "Are you telling us Janus died of *natural causes?"*

"Hello, Harvey," Awini said, sounding surprised. "I did not know you were on the line. What I am saying is, the bullet was fired after Janus's heart stopped. I've said nothing about death by natural cause. Quite the contrary. Now, I did find evidence of severe coronary arterial blockage. The man was definitely on his way to having a massive heart attack. But the cardiac arrest he suffered was not the result of his heart disease."

"So what killed him?"

"Pending the toxicology and serological analyses, it is my opinion that the cause of death was poisoning. But this is very puzzling to me, because my preliminary examination of the stomach contents disclosed nothing indicative of a poison being present in anything Mr. Janus either ate or drank. Only the toxicology report will provide the answer."

Bogdanovic asked, "When will you have it?"

"I've assigned it the highest priority, John, but with all the budget cutbacks imposed on my office, I've had to reduce the overtime costs."

"Damn the overtime, Hassan," blared Goldstein. "Forward the bill to my office."

"I'll require a memo to that effect, Harvey."

"You'll have it in the morning, which is when I'll expect to see the toxicology report."

Bogdanovic switched off the speakerphone.

"This is certainly a first for me," Goldstein grumbled as he drummed fingers on his desk and looked toward Dane with a frown. "Maggie, have you ever heard of someone being murdered twice?"

"That's an impossibility."

"Well, somebody apparently believed once was not enough."

Slouched in his chair, Bogdanovic pouted. "There is no way that William Newport could have poisoned Janus. So, if Janus was not shot to death, if he was *poisoned,* I have been running around in circles like a dog chasing its tail. First, I looked for a mob connection, then some link to Paulie Mancuso, and when none of that added up, I dreamed up a story of a revenge-minded stalker."

"You were right on that score," Dane said.

"Except for the fact that Newport didn't kill Janus. While he was plotting his revenge, someone else had murder in mind, but with the distinct advantage of being able to get close enough to Janus to slip a little poison into him."

Goldstein said, "He certainly ate a great deal, but we all ate the same food."

"Maybe the poison was in a drink. There wasn't a moment when Janus didn't have a glass in his hand, or within easy reach."

"I recall one moment," Dane said. "He bumped into a waiter and dropped his glass."

"That's just great," Bogdanovic said as he returned to his chair. "The butler did it."

"No need for sarcasm, Sergeant," Goldstein snapped. "Maggie is on our side."

"What about you, sir? Did you by chance see anyone who might have slipped a fatal Mickey into Janus's glass?"

After pondering a moment, Goldstein answered. "There was a young woman who asked him to autograph a book. She could easily have dropped something into Janus's martini."

"Did you notice if she happened to be wearing a ring that might have had a hallowed-out compartment for a dose of poison?"

"The chief and I share your frustration, Johnny," Dane said, sympathetically. "But we have no evidence that Theo was poisoned at the Black Orchid dinner. It could have happened much earlier. There are slow-acting poisons."

"Maggie is right," Goldstein said. "I propose that we wait till the toxicology report is in. Awini could be mistaken."

With a morose expression, Bogdanovic shook his head. "When was the last time you heard of Awini being wrong? The ugly truth is that I've wasted all this time tracking down a young man who didn't kill anyone, and in the meantime the actual murderer has every reason to think he's in the clear. He has to have seen the picture of Janus with a bullet wound in his head."

"I see that as a plus," Goldstein said. "A killer who's certain someone else is being hunted as Janus's murderer is not going to feel the necessity to be on alert."

"That feeling will evaporate the moment the news media reports the fact that Janus was poisoned."

Goldstein smiled impishly. "Who says the newspapers have to know that we know Janus was poisoned?"

"They'll know when Awini releases the autopsy results."

"Hassan is not about to report on the autopsy until he has received the toxicology report. And who knows how long it might take him to get around to reviewing it?"

"Excuse me, Chief, but you told Awini you expect to have the report first thing tomorrow. Once we have it, we have the legal obligation to immediately turn over possibly exculpatory material to Newport's lawyer."

"Has Newport exercised his right to have a lawyer?"

Dane answered, "He waived it at the time of his arrest."

"That is true," Bogdanovic said, "but he still has the right to speak to an attorney anytime he chooses. When he finds out he didn't kill Janus, he'll be screaming for a lawyer."

"Of course he will, "Goldstein retorted. "But until he has a lawyer, and as long as Awimi is not through with his work, we are under no obligation to reveal anything beyond the charge against Newport. Which is what?"

"First-degree murder."

"Amend the charge."

Bogdanovic grunted. "Change it to what?"

"*Attempted* murder."

"The kid confessed."

"He confessed to shooting Janus."

"In addition to attempted murder," Dane said, "Newport can be charged with unlawful discharge of a firearm and possession of a gun. District Attorney Vanderhoff might also choose to tack on the associated offense of attempted assault with a deadly weapon. There's also failure to report a dead body. And there is even a law against abusing a corpse."

"Newport did not know he was pumping a bullet into somebody who was already dead."

"It doesn't matter. His *intent* was to commit murder. Give me a moment to refresh my memory of New York's criminal statutes by going through a copy of the Penal Law and Criminal Procedure Law handbook and I may come up with further offenses."

Goldstein folded his hands upon his belly. "That's what I love about the criminal laws. If you're not sure you've got the grounds to make one charge stick, you can look up another one that probably will."

"What can we expect to gain by changing the charge?" Bogdanovic demanded.

"I expect us to gain time," Goldstein said. "Time for you to look for the real killer. I will begin by issuing a statement to the press that, pending further investigation, Newport is being held on a variety of charges, including those Maggie listed—all of which are eminently supportable. I will also let our friend Hassan know that, in view of the pressures on him to hold down costs, I have changed my mind and that there's no need to hurry the completion of his autopsy report. You then proceed on the basis of Awini's *preliminary* report that Janus was poisoned."

"If Newport gets himself a lawyer and the lawyer finds out about this subterfuge, he will raise unholy hell," said Bogdanovic.

"I'm confident that by then you will have arrested the true killer. I can't envision any defense attorney complaining about police methods that cleared his client."

"And consider how sweet it will be for you, John," said Dane cheerfully, "and how surprised the true murderer is going to be, when you show up at his door to execute an arrest warrant."

Goldstein came upright in his chair. "There was another message that arrived while you were arresting Newport," he said as he rummaged in papers on his desk. "Marian Pickering Henry has invited the three of us to a Christmas party on Saturday evening. Sounds like fun. Can you make it, Maggie?"

"I'd be delighted to attend, after I call my son in California."

"Good. I'll give her a call and accept for all of us."

PART SEVEN

Please Pass the Guilt

35

Murder Is No Joke

WEDNESDAY MORNING, WITH a feeling of satisfaction, Bogdanovic sat at his desk and again read the thrilling front-page headline of the *Graphic:*

JANUS MURDER CASE SENSATION!
POLICE SAY YOUTH THREATENED,
STALKED FAMED DEFENSE LAWYER
Charge Is Attempted Homicide
While Investigation Continues

An hour earlier he had stopped at a newsstand, bought the paper, read the headline, and turned to the story on page three to read:

Less than three days after famed defense lawyer Theodore R. Janus's body was found with a single, fatal gunshot wound in the head as he sat in the front seat of his Rolls-Royce on posh Gramercy Park East, police sources report that a suspect, William Newport, a teacher of photography, is being held on a charge of attempted murder, pending further investigation.

"We have no doubt that charges against Newport will be amended to conform to the true nature of his crime," said Chief of Detectives Harvey Goldstein in a statement released late yesterday. "In the meantime, our investigation continues."

Now, as Dane entered his office carrying the newspaper, Bogdanovic sat with the *Graphic* in his lap and his feet crossed at the ankles on his desk. Beaming with delight, he said, "Maggie, my boss is the master of obfuscation." He opened the paper to page three and read aloud, " 'We have no doubt that charges against Newport will be amended to conform to the true nature of his crime.' Is that brilliant, or what? There's not so much as a hint that Janus was not shot to death and that the continuation of the investigation depends on what turns up in a toxicology report. I can hardly wait till the chief gets into the office so I can congratulate him."

"Harvey's not here? I thought you two were inseparable."

"He called me late last night to tell me there was to be a big meeting—last minute, very urgent, and only the top brass—at seven this morning in Vanderhoff's office about the Mancuso fiasco. Rather than have me pick him up, he grabbed a cab. He said, and these are his exact words, 'No use you sitting on your ass at One Hogan Place when you should be sitting on your ass at One Police Plaza, in case the written toxicology report comes in.' "

Dane dropped a large handbag on a chair and sat in another. "A sound management decision. But obviously, you have not gotten Awini's report."

He removed his feet from the desk. "No, but I've been giving a lot of thought to Awini's preliminary opinion that the cause of death was poisoning. If that's true, we have an entirely new ball game. To poison someone, you have to be close to the victim."

"Poisoning would certainly narrow the circle of suspects."

"Do you buy the old saw that poison is a woman's weapon?"

"Like everything else that's been said to put women down," Dane answered, "that slur has to have been coined by a man."

"Really? Look at history! The wife of Caesar Augustus, the amazing Livia. And what about Lucrezia Borgia? And there was a delightful English dame in India who got tired of her husband and said in her confession that the only way out was to put poison in the soup. The pages of encyclopedias of crime are crammed with members of the fair sex who murdered with poison, like the dizzy old sisters in *Arsenic and Old Lace*."

"I can name outstanding poisoners of the masculine gender."

"Even Marian Pickering Henry admits that females are more likely to use poison than men. What did she say to me at the Wolfe Pack dinner? Something to the effect that with poison, a woman doesn't have to mop up the blood. She even showed me how easily she could have slipped a something lethal into me."

"So could any of the men at our table. For instance, Nicky Stamos. Anyone who has ever heard of Aristotle knows Greek men knew all about hemlock. Then there's the lovely Ariadne. She is from the Balkans, a very poisonous region. Oscar Pendelton knows about poisons by virtue of publishing the doyenne of the dollop of cyanide. What about our purveyor of crime books, Wiggins? Or members of the steering committee who were against Theo's getting the Nero Wolfe Award? And there's me, of course."

"What possible motive could you have?"

"As with every possible suspect I've named, and those I have overlooked, it's for me to know and you to find out, Detective."

He leaned back as if to study her and said, "You don't look like a poisoner to me."

"What does a poisoner look like?"

"She looks like the hag with the apple in 'Snow White.' The wicked witch in *The Wizard of Oz*."

The phone rang.

Dr. Hassan Awini demanded, "Put Harvey on, Sergeant."

"He's involved in a powwow at the DA's office. Won't I do?"

Awini sighed. "Very well. I will summarize the toxicological report. Take notes. You will have it in writing as soon as I can round up a messenger."

Grabbing a pen, Bogdanovic also put the call on the speakerphone. "Ready to copy, Hassan."

"If this is on the speaker, I must know who is with you."

Dane answered, "Maggie Dane. I can leave, Doctor."

"Not necessary. Toxicological tests revealed the presence of a substance that is a derivative of the yellow oleander, a tropical plant. It is a cardiac glycoside."

Bogdanovic asked, "How do you spell it and what is it?"

"I assume you can spell cardiac. Glycoside is g-l-y-c-o—."

"I follow you. Glycocide as in homicide."

"Exactly. In laymen's terms, it triggers a heart attack. The inner portion of yellow oleander fruit contains two kernels. Five or six yield enough thevetin to kill within twenty-four hours."

"So Janus could have gotten the cardiac glycoside into him as long as a day before he died?"

"I said it could kill within that time. But if it was administered to someone with advanced heart disease, as in Mr. Janus's case, the effects would be felt much quicker. But there is more to this, Sergeant. The toxicologist also reports the presence of taxine. Shall I spell it?"

"No need. Does that mean Janus had *two* poisons in him?"

"Taxine derives from the taxus plant, better known as the yew tree, or the ground hemlock. It is found in almost all areas of the United States. The bark, needles, and seeds contain large amounts of alkaloid taxine. The symptoms of taxine poisoning include muscular weakness."

"The person we have arrested in this case said he thought Janus looked wobbly, as if he'd had too much to drink. Would that be consistent with symptoms of taxine poisoning?"

"It would. But for a man such as Janus, with acute coronary artery disease, taxine would kill rather quickly."

"If there was no evidence of these substances in the food he ate, how were they administered? In a drink?"

"Absolutely not. Both substances have distinct and powerful flavors and aromas that would be noticed immediately—unless they were masked by something equally strong in both flavoring and aroma."

"Such as?"

"Do you have at hand the photos of the crime scene?"

Hurriedly, Bogdanovic opened a drawer, withdrew a slim sheaf of photographs, fanned them on the desktop like a winning hand of cards, studied them, and exclaimed exultantly, "His *cigar.*"

"To be certain, I had the butt analyzed. It contained large concentrations of both substances. And it contained an amount of nicotine that far exceeded what one would expect even in a strong cigar. This suggests that a highly concentrated dose of nicotine had been added."

Dane asked, "Were you able to determine how all these deadly additives got into the cigar?"

"They were liquified and injected."

"Pardon my ignorance, Hassan," Bogdanovic said, still gazing at the photos. "How the hell would you turn the leaves, bark, and needles of plants into a liquid?"

"In the same manner in which whiskey is made. You chop up the plant, cook it in alcohol, and distill it. You could do it in a coffee percolator."

"Then what?"

"You put the distillate in a syringe and inject it into the cigar. Naturally, I examined the cigar butt under a microscope, and, to my surprise, found no such a hole. Then I got what I can only call a brainstorm. I observed that the band was in place."

Dane said, "Theo never removed the band."

"When I took the band off," Awini continued, "I discovered a small puncture in the wrapper leaf consistent with a syringe. As the cigar was being smoked, the toxins were drawn into the mouth and absorbed through mucous membranes and saliva in the same manner, and as rapidly as the nitroglycerin in the tablets taken by a person suffering an episode of angina pectoris."

Bogdanovic's voice quivered. "This is absolutely unique."

"I concede that it is unusual," Awini said, "but you might recall that the Central Intelligence Agency was alleged to have planned to eliminate Fidel Castro by either poisoning his cigars or planting an explosive in them. Years ago, when I was a child, you could go into a novelty store and buy explosive devices to insert in cigars as a joke."

"An exploding cigar may have been funny, Hassan," Bogdanovic said, "but murder is no joke."

"Indeed not. As I said, Harvey can expect a detailed written report by messenger."

"He's the only one who gets it, right? This report is just between us?"

With a little cackle of a laugh, Awini asked, "What report?"

36

Death of a Demon

"As to slipping a little lethality into a cigar, it seems to me that only a cigar smoker would think of that," Dane said as she sat and Bogdanovic stood at the window and peered into the middle distance. "Were I you, John, I would concentrate on the cigar aficionados in Theo's life. Unfortunately, there were many."

"But how many would have had been alone with his private stash of prized Cubans—and inject them with that poisonous concoction?"

"Theo also kept a supply in a special travel humidor in his car's glove compartment."

"The killer would still face the problem."

"Perhaps there was no need to raid Theo's humidors. The lethal one could have been a gift."

"If the poisoned cigar had been a gift," he said, turning away from the window, "Janus would have smoked it immediately. A man offers a cigar to another man when they talk business or are in a social situation. After a good meal, for instance. It would be rude to accept a cigar and stick it in a pocket for later."

"Very well, someone gave Theo the cigar at the Wolfe Pack dinner, knowing he would smoke it then and there."

He returned to his desk and sat. "Janus was the person who handed out the cigars and passed them off as having come from his private trove of rare Havanas."

"Frankly, I don't see how anyone can tell the difference between one cigar and another. To me a cigar is just a cigar. And I think this reverence for cigars that come from Cuba is snobbishness based on the fact that there is an embargo on their importation. I'd bet that the mystique of Cuban cigars would disappear if they were not so hard to get."

"Would you happen to know where Janus obtained his?"

"I presume he got them where they are readily available. He flew to the Caribbean frequently. He often went to Europe on business. And he took two weeks' vacation in London every year."

"In other words, he smuggled them."

"How difficult could it be to sneak in a box of cigars?"

"Especially if you fly your own plane to the islands."

"Even if Theo flew commercially, I can not imagine him being stopped by a customs official with a demand that he open his bags for a search."

"That is an advantage of being rich and famous."

"I fail to see the importance of where he got his cigars."

"What's important is that whoever killed him had to be very well informed on the subject of his Cuban cigars."

"I told you his passion for them was common knowledge."

"Yes, but how common was it for someone to have such easy access to those cigars that he had no problem poisoning one? He kept them at his ranch, right?"

"Correct. Plus the few in the travel humidor in his car."

"That means that whoever poisoned one of the cigars had to have access to either his house or that car. Such an individual had to be regarded by Janus as a friend. I am not talking about social friends and acquaintances. I mean people he might invite up to the ranch for a weekend, or sit up with, talking, sipping brandy, and sharing his prized cigars to the wee hours of the morning. Intimate friends." He looked up from the notes. "How many people belonged to that select company?"

"Very few. But I haven't been a member of Theo's intimate circle for several years. During that time he might have made new friends, or even dropped some. Living in California, I have not felt the need to keep abreast of matters concerning Theo's personal life. For that you'll have to talk to someone more atuned to the current and recent gossip."

Abruptly rising, he said, "And I know just the person!"

"Shouldn't you wait for Harvey to return?"

"By the time he gets back, he'll have the written report."

HANGING SLIGHTLY ASKEW against the background of a green window shade, the sign advised:

HOURS: NOON TO MIDNIGHT
IF CLOSED AND YOU *MUST* HAVE A BOOK
THIS MINUTE, KNOCK VERY LOUDLY

Below, a smaller placard read:

THANK YOU FOR NOT ASKING
THE PROPRIETOR NOT TO SMOKE
WIGGINS

Three thumps resulted in the door's being opened a crack by a young man who seemed to have been routed from bed. Rubbing bleary eyes, he asked, "Yes?"

"Tell Wiggins it's Sergeant Bogdanovic."

From deep within in store, Wiggins's voice was a blast from a foghorn. "It's all right. He is not here to make a pinch. The sergeant isn't with the vice squad. You may admit him."

The youth shouted, "There's a lady with him."

Wiggins's voice was closer now. "It's still all right."

As the door swung wide, the youth reached to his right and threw a switch that first produced a stuttering of fluorescent tubes above a milky white ceiling and then total illumination of the bookstore and its gigantic owner. A figure in a long scarlet robe, he resembled and moved with the deliberate gait of a cardinal advancing toward the altar, except that the center aisle of this cathedral was formed by cases of books exalting the sixth of the Ten Commandments.

"Congratulations, Sergeant B.," Wiggins boomed as he neared, "on your quick success in the Janus case." The huge head turned toward Dane. "It must be a great relief to you, Maggie."

"It's very satisfying."

Wiggins flashed a smile and returned his attention to Bogdanovic. "So, Sergeant B., what brings you tap, tap, tapping at my door, like Mr. Poe's pesky raven?"

"You know me. I'm just looking for any loose ends."

Deep in the fleshy folds of his smiling face, Wiggins's black eyes sparkled. "As the hangman said to the condemned prisoner, I do know you, Sergeant. I know you so well that I recognize when a game of detection is still afoot. May I presume, this morning's newspapers notwithstanding, that the case against the young man you have locked up is not as airtight as it seems? Are you harboring a doubt about his being the culprit? Are you worried that you might not have nabbed the right suspect?"

"I assure you that there is no doubt in my mind that the guy we have in custody fired a bullet into Janus's head."

"I take your point. I should mind my own business! However, I can not suppress my fascination with the fact that, in spite of the young man's being detained, you have paid a call on me. Surely it is not to purchase for Goldstein a book for Hanukkah. Why, then, are you in my humble emporium?"

"Have you forgotten that you are a material witness?"

"Ah, yes! The errant bullet. Have you matched that slug with the one that killed Theo?"

"The ballistics tests aren't in yet, and there's no guarantee there will be a match. That's why you are a material witness. You are the only one who can testify that Janus was being stalked. I need to get a deposition."

"Really, Sergeant B., you are a tease. This stuff about your being here because I am a crucial witness is, to quote Mr. Nero Wolfe, flummery. All that was needed to obtain my deposition was a phone call to tell me when and where. Yet here you are with Maggie at your side when I was about to enjoy a leisurely breakfast in my office. There's more than enough for three. Join me, please. Perhaps a taste of a scrumptious raisin scone with clotted cream will entice you to divulge the true purpose of your surprising but welcome visit."

As they sat at a long table, the young man who had opened the door served the food.

"I'm sorry to bring this up while we are eating, Sergeant B.,"

Wiggins said, "but I need to know when the M.E. will release the body."

"You'll have to ask him. Why?"

"To my astonishment," Wiggins said, lathering a scone with a giant glob of cream, "I have been asked by Theo's attorney to assist in making the arrangements for the funeral, as well as deliver the eulogy at a memorial service, the date and place to be announced presently."

Dane asked, "Why were you astonished?"

"Perhaps that's the wrong word. I should have said that I was shocked and saddened to realize he could think of no else."

"That doesn't shock me," Bogdanovic said. "Judging by what was said about Janus by the guests at my table during the dinner, Janus was not exactly drowning in a sea of friendships. Except for Maggie, everyone at my table seemed to see Janus as some kind of demon. Do you know why?"

"In spite of my deserved reputation as a notorious gossip and disher of dirt, I hesitate to relate unpleasantries regarding Theo in Maggie's presence."

"It's all right, Wiggy," Dane said, patting him tenderly on his massive shoulder. "I can handle it."

"Very well, I shall begin with the Greek shipping tycoon."

"That would be Nick Stamos," said Bogdanovic.

"Nee, Niarchos Aristotle Stamopolous."

"What about him?"

"The story I got is that this latter-day demigod of Athens found himself the prime target of a very-much-under-wraps federal probe into drug trafficking. The dope originated in the poppy fields of Turkey and made its way to the Bekaa Valley of Lebanon. There it was transformed into heroin. The product then made its way across the Mediterranean Sea to the port of Athens."

"On Nick's ships."

"Via his private yacht, *Ariadne,* named after you know who. Then the goods proceeded via Nicky's cargo fleet to the streets and back alleys of the New World. When all this appeared to be headed to a federal grand jury, Nicky sought out Janus for legal assistance. The retainer was millions of dollars in bearer bonds, which were placed in a safe-deposit box in Theo's bank in the Cayman Islands."

"That's what Stamos meant at the dinner when he called Janus the three-million-dollar man."

"In the event Theo succeeded in plucking Nicky off the hook, he was to keep one-third of the bonds. Theo got Nicky off, but he refused to give back the other two million. Nicky was, shall we say, disgruntled? But what could he do?"

"A civil suit would have exposed the drug smuggling," Dane said, "perhaps giving the federal government an opportunity for a second bite of the apple."

"I presume the Internal Revenue Service might also step in," Bogdanovic said.

"Yes, so taking Theo to court was out of the question," said Wiggins. "All Nicky could do was quietly fume. But the funny part is that the person who was most distressed was Ariadne."

"I can see why," Bogdanovic said. "Those millions could have bought several ropes of perfect pearls at Cartier to adorn Ariadne's lovely, swanlike throat."

"True, but Ariadne is the type of woman who would have preferred to tighten a real rope around Theo's bull-moose neck. When Ariadne feels wronged, watch out!"

"Dangerous, huh?"

"In the extreme. When I saw Theo's photo in the newspaper I immediately thought of Ariadne, but I just as soon dismissed that interesting notion."

"Why?"

"She would never chance spattering her dress with blood, unless the dress was red. The one she wore at the dinner was pale blue."

Dane asked, "How come you didn't suspect her husband?"

"Nicky would never kill anybody himself. He'd hire someone."

"Having eliminated them from your list of suspects," Dane said, "did you consider others who were at the dinner?"

"My dear, I considered most of them, starting with that old reprobate Judge Simmons. He has never forgiven Theo for winning a reversal of the verdict in the Victoria Davis trial. I do not expect to see Reggie's countenance among the mourning faces at the forthcoming memorial service. Nor do I anticipate attendance by those on the Wolfe Pack steering committee who objected to Theo's receiving the Nero Wolfe Award. James Hamilton will stay away, just as he shunned the dinner."

Bogdanovic asked, "Who else would you *not* expect to see?"

"I'd be surprised to look out from the pulpit and find Oscar Pendelton weeping in a front pew."

"Surely Theo's publisher will go," Dane said.

"You are out of touch, Maggie! The Janus-Pendelton author-publisher relationship was severed months ago."

Dane exclaimed, "How did that happen?"

"It was at Theo's initiative. He found a publisher with the deeper pockets required to meet Theo's demands for the advance on his book on the trial in which you played a starring role."

"Theo never told me he was planning a book about the trial."

"The irony is that the book was Oscar's idea. Unfortunately for him, Theo promptly took the idea elsewhere. Oscar was irate. That's why I wondered, fleetingly, if he might have decided to prevent Theo from writing the book for anyone."

"I can't imagine Oscar turning to murder," Bogdanovic said.

Wiggins dipped a scone into a mug of coffee. "No? I seem to recall that Oscar ranked high on your list of initial suspects in the Mystery Writers murder case."

"I didn't know Oscar at that time."

The scone went into Wiggins's mouth, delaying his reply.

"Oscar was quite thrilled at being suspected, as was I," he said, dabbing a napkin to his lips. "But in this instance, Oscar got his revenge as only a book publisher can. He got his book by signing up Marian Pickering Henry."

"Marian has never been known for nonfiction," Dane said. "She built her reputation grinding out thrillers."

"Think about it! A book about the trial of the century with Marian Pickering Henry's name on the jacket! Oscar is looking at sales numbers that Theo's tome could never have matched. The man was a legal nonpareil, but his books read like the *Harvard Law Review*. Marian's work will bring in millions of dollars from readers who automatically buy any Henry title. Oscar is a publishing genius. So, unless there is a definitive book on the trial forthcoming from Maggie Dane, or the man who got away with murder decides to tell all, Mysterious Doings Books faces no serious competition."

"Hooray for Oscar," Bogdanovic said.

"Quite so," Wiggins said as another chunk of scone dipped into the coffee. "What all this talk has to do with loose ends escapes me, Sergeant B. Is there more here than meets the eye?"

"There is one loose end you may be able to tie up for me," Bogdanovic said. "Did you observe Janus as he left the hotel?"

"I accompanied him to the door."

"How did he seem to you?"

"What do you mean?"

"He'd been drinking a good deal. Did he look as if he were in his cups?"

After thinking a moment, Wiggins smiled, then broke into a laugh that traveled through his huge body as though it had been racked by an earthquake. "Excuse the black humor, Sergeant B., but he was as sober as a judge!"

"Count on you to come up with a witticism," Bogdanovic said through a forced smile.

Dane asked, "Do you recall if Theo was smoking a cigar?"

Still quaking, Wiggins asked, "Wasn't he always?"

"Try to remember," Bogdanovic said, forcefully. "It could be important to the case."

The slits of Wiggins's eyes narrowed to the point of disappearing. When they popped open, he said, "He had just lit up one of those odious black Havanas. He took it out of a pocket case, silver, with his initials on it. The cutter was small scissors. He lit it with a long wooden match. Then he went through the revolving door and stood awhile under the marquee, smoking like a chimney and chatting with a few of the Wolfies. That was the last I saw of him, until I found that horrible picture in the *Graphic*. I immediately brought that mutilated bullet to you. I hope it gets that young punk of a killer strapped into the electric chair."

"Evidently you are not one of Janus's detractors."

"Oh, I share the view that he was a devil. But I happen to like such people. They make great characters in books. Without them, how could I possibly earn a living? Despite what you have heard, crime pays."

"One other loose end, if I may, Wiggy?"

"Of course."

"Since you know so much about Janus, would you happen to know which of the people he regarded as friends might have been guests at his ranch?"

"Except for my recent visit, I had never been to the place. However, may I offer a suggestion?"

"When Wiggins talks, Bogdanovic listens!"

"As Maggie can aver, Theo was a man who believed in keeping detailed records. That's why his autobiography made such fascinating reading. He obviously discarded nothing. He must have kept a diary or other such aide-mémoire. Have you looked for a calendar, appointment book, or other such daily record that might contain references to vistors to his upstate Valhalla?"

"I have his appointment book. That's how I knew of your unusual visit to the ranch, even before you informed me of how extraordinary it was. Thanks for your help. Sorry for interrupting your breakfast. We'll leave you to finish it in peace."

As they rose to leave, Wiggins said, "I do hope I will see both of you at Marian Pickering Henry's annual holiday fete."

Bogdanovic halted in the doorway. "How the hell did you find out that we were invited to that party?"

"It's elementary. Marian phoned and asked how to go about reaching you. I found it very amusing that the leading light of crime writing did not know the address of the most famous police headquarters this side of Scotland Yard."

"Would you happen to know who else has been invited?"

"Sergeant B., you've known me long enough to appreciate that I go to only three kinds of parties—those which I give, those at which I am the guest of honor, and those given by others who give me veto power regarding the guest list. Marian not only allows me to approve the invitations each year, but honors me by insisting that I emulate none other than Nero Wolfe in the story "Christmas Party" by dressing up as Santa Claus. If you cross your heart that you've been a good boy, I'll see that you get a swell present."

"You can give me mine now," Bogdanovic said, tracing an *X* on his chest. "I'll take the list of Henry's guests."

With the list tucked into an inside pocket, Bogdanovic said, "I'll see you at the party, Wiggy."

"Why do I have a feeling, Sergeant B., that Santa Claus will not be the only one there with a surprise in his pack?"

Unanswered, he returned to his breakfast.

"EVEN THOUGH I'VE never read a Nero Wolfe story," Bogdanovic said as he and Dane left the store, "I can not picture a man of Nero Wolfe's apparent dignity getting into a Santa Claus outfit."

"The situation was dire. Archie had tricked Wolfe into believing that Archie was about to get married. He even showed him a marriage license."

Opening the car door for her, Bogdanovic said, "What business was it of Wolfe's?"

"Everything about Archie was Wolfe's business," she said, getting into the car, "especially if it involved the peace and quiet of a certain brownstone on West Thirty-fifth Street."

When Bogdanovic got behind the wheel, she continued, "You see, Archie carried his joke further by telling Wolfe he planned to settle down with the wife in Archie's quarters in the house. To get a glimpse of the bride-to-be, Wolfe managed to attend a Christmas party by persuading the host, a recent client by the name of Kurt Bottswell, to let him play the jolly old elf from the North Pole."

Bogdanovic started the engine, "I presume these yuletide festivities were marred when someone was found murdered."

"Yes. Poor Kurt. But he was not *found* murdered. He was poisoned before the eyes of the guests. The deadly stuff had been put into the Pernot he preferred to champagne. It's a wonderful yarn. I've made reading it a part of my Christmas rituals, along with a rereading of Sherlock Holmes's Christmas story, 'The Blue Carbuncle.' "

"You can celebrate Christmas with Holmes and Wolfe all you like," Bogdanovic said as he made a U-turn. "I'll stick to ' 'Twas the Night Before Christmas.' "

"If you attend Marian's party, you're going to be stuck with Wolfe. It is a tradition of Marian's get-together that 'Christmas Party' be passed among guests round-robin style, with each reading one page aloud until the story is finished. Of course, everyone tries to outdo one another in hamming it up. It's a lot of fun."

Stopping at a red light at First Avenue, Bogdanovic said, "I'll pass on that, thank you."

"I see. Participating in party games is not Sgt. Johnny Bogdanovic's style. There's too much danger of doing damage to the dignity and demeanor of the dedicated detective."

"You get an A-plus in alliteration."

"And you get a D-minus for deviousness."

Bogdanovic looked at her askance. "I have no idea what you are talking about."

"You all but came right out and told Wiggins that you suspect one of Marian's guests of murdering Theo."

"Really? When and how did I do that?"

"Why else would you ask for a list of people invited to her Christmas party?"

"It was a routine security measure. I always obtain a list of the people who will be at an affair that Goldstein is planning to attend. There are a lot of crazies out there who'd love to get even with him. Not to get a list of the invited guests would have been a dereliction of my duty."

When the light turned green, the car darted across First Avenue toward Second. "Since it is your policy to make a list and check it twice, maybe you should take the part of Saint Nick at Marian's shindig."

"Only if you sit on my knee and tell me what you want for Christmas, little girl."

"I can tell you now," she said, looking grim as Bogdanovic barely made the green to swing left to head downtown on Second. "I want to see Theo's murderer at the bar of justice as quickly as possible. And if it were in your power to grant it, Santa, I would ask you for the opportunity to prosecute him."

"Cornelius Vanderhoff has the power. Thanks to the Mancuso fiasco, he's got three openings on his staff. Apply for one."

"You are a superb detective, John, but you obviously do not have a clue into the workings of the mind of a district attorney. The reality of my recent courtroom joust with Theodore Janus, and all the attendant hullabaloo, is that there is no DA anywhere who would want me around. I have become too well known. My appearance in a courtroom would send a defense attorney running to the press to claim his client could not get a fair trial. And he would be right."

"You're not considering giving up the law?"

"I see no other possibility. I could never become a defense attorney. I realized that when I worked for Theo. And I certainly am not cut out for civil law. I find suing people, or defending those who are being sued, exceedingly boring. Nor am I a woman to bang my head against the glass ceiling of corporate law firms."

"What will you do? Write a book?"

"I have no desire to chase the fleeting glory of a ranking on the *New York Times* best-seller list. That would lead to disappointed expectations for a second book. I am not a writer."

"How about running for elective office?"

"I could make a joke about politicians being the only people held in lower public esteem than lawyers, with the possible exception of journalists."

"May I interpret that as an indication that you've also rejected the idea of becoming one of those legal analysts who seem to have popped up all over TV screens like mushrooms?"

"You may."

"What are your other options?"

"I might try my hand at teaching law. Since the big trial, I've had offers. Being on a law school faculty would give me an opportunity to try to make amends with my son for all the times I failed him as a mother."

"I don't believe that."

Turning away to look at storefronts and restaurants as the car sped down Second Avenue, she fell silent.

Bogdanovic smiled. "I'll bet when you were a little girl, you poked around in all the closets looking for the gifts your mom and dad had tried their best to hide."

"Didn't you?"

"Of course. And I found them. Even then I had the instincts of a snooping detective."

"I felt the stirrings of growing up to be a well-prepared lawyer, who, as you know, abhors surprises. Are you going to tell me how many people you suspect?"

"That is shockingly un-Wolfian of you, Maggie. You know that the primary number in the corpus is three."

37

Christmas Party

"I MUST SAY I am pleasantly surprised," declared Goldstein as Bogdanovic guided the car across the George Washington Bridge. "Here we are, dressed to the nines and on our way to a fancy dinner party, and John hasn't groused about it once. I have heard not one 'bah, humbug' concerning this party. Truly extraordinary."

"It's Christmastime," Dane said, gaily. "John is obviously caught up in the spirit of the season."

"That's right," Bogdanovic answered, turning off the bridge on the New Jersey side. "Ho, ho, ho. And as Tiny Tim said, 'God bless us every one.' Except murderers."

"Chief, I have a feeling we are misreading the mood of the man at the wheel," Dane said. "He might turn out to be the Grinch who stole Christmas."

Presently, the car rolled through a neighborhood of gated stone walls, snow-dusted lawns, and electric candles in windows of stately houses at the ends of long driveways.

As Bogdanovic turned into the lane leading to the home of Marian Pickering Henry, Goldstein said, "This is what millions of paperback sales gets you. Plus a couple of movie deals. It is hard to believe that only a few years ago the woman who resides here was a widowed suburban housewife. Now she's a millionaire."

"Hooray for her," Dane said.

Pressing a doorbell button next to a white door adorned with a giant Christmas wreath, Bogdanovic heard seasonal music within, and the unmistakable voice of Wiggins blaring, "Hold your reindeer, Santa will be there in a jiffy." A second later, the door swung open to reveal an enormous figure with a magnificent fluffy white beard that almost obscured his bulging red belly.

Turning slightly away, he shouted, "Hold down the noise, people. Somebody called the cops!"

Following him from a festive garland-draped, marble-walled foyer, they entered a massive living room rich with the pungent aromas of seasonal decorations. A hum of cheery voices was punctuated by the clinking of crystal glassware as a pair of young men dressed as Victorian butlers offered drinks from silver trays.

With a squeeze of Bogdanovic's biceps and a wink Wiggins whispered, "They are all here, Sergeant B. Nick and Ariadne Stamos. Oscar Pendleton and his wife, Ellen. Admiral Horne and the impossible wife who has been his anchor since Noah launched the ark. Judge Simmons, alone as usual. The others are neighbors of Marian's and various literary types who have no part in the drama you have in mind."

Dane asked, "What drama is that?"

"Don't play coy with me, Maggie," Wiggins huffed. "You know exactly what game is afoot here. The suspects are gathered. But please, Sergeant B., allow us to have a sumptuous dinner before you unmask the murderer."

"I don't know what you're talking about, Wiggins. I'm here because Goldstein ordered me to be."

Tightening the grip on Bogdanovic's arm, Wiggins said, "What a naughty boy you are, misbehaving by telling a fib to Santa!"

As Henry broke away from a cluster of guests, Bogdanovic's voice went low. "You're the one who had better behave himself."

"I am so delighted you could all come," Henry exclaimed.

"Your house is beautiful," Dane said. "The decorations are magnificent. The whole place smells of Christmases past."

"Thank you. It took hours to make and arrange them. But, as they say, Christmas comes but once a year. I believe you know almost everyone here. If not, I'm sure Wiggins will introduce you. If you want a drink, ask a waiter and he'll bring it to you. In case you haven't noticed, I've tried to create a Sherlockian atmosphere, as you will discover when dinner is served in a few minutes. It will be roast goose with all the trimmings, although I can not guarantee one of you will discover a blue carbuncle. After dinner, it's coffe and cognac in this room, with cigars if you wish. Then we all join in reading 'Christmas Story.' Now, if you will excuse me, I must go to the kitchen to check on dinner."

THE NEXT TWO hours passed as promised with a meal that Dane and Goldstein agreed would have delighted Sherlock Holmes, followed by afterdinner drinks and the smoking of a few cigars, culminating with Henry's presenting to Wiggins a copy of the story of Archie Goodwin's attempt to trick Nero Wolfe into believing that his trusty assistant was about to get married.

"With apologies for breaking with your cherished tradition, Marian," Wiggins said, setting the book aside, "I believe Sergeant Bogdanovic has a story of his own to tell that you may all find compelling. He's been working on it for several days. It is, of course, a murder mystery with a number of suspects and, I do hope, a few red herrings, plus a couple of surprising twists. Am I right, Sergeant B.?"

"In fact, there were so many of each," Bogdanovic said, "I was not at all sure I could come up with a believable ending."

Oscar Pendelton declared, "Obviously you have, Sergeant, or you would not have contrived with Wiggins to set up this drama."

"I confess to doing just that," Bogdanovic said, looking around the room. "But I'm content to let you all decide if I've merely succeeded in making a fool of myself. You be the judges."

"And the jurors?"

Bogdanovic smiled nervously at Henry. "May I proceed?"

"With everyone on edge, Sergeant, how could I say no?"

"Oh goodie," exclaimed Wiggins, plopping into a huge chair. "This is just like story time at summer camp when I was a kid!"

"You were never a kid, Wiggins," said Goldstein. "You and that bookstore of yours just appeared one day."

"I suspect we are already familiar with the crime in your story," said Pendelton. "Feel free to skip ahead and tell us how you tracked down the young man who killed Janus."

"Finding William Newport was easy. Routine police work. But that provided the first twist in the case."

"Don't tell me Newport was Janus's illegitimate son," said Pendelton. "Was he like Stapleton in *The Hound of the Baskervilles,* planning to come forward after a decent interval to claim an inheritance?"

"The twist was much better than that, Oscar. It came in the course of the autopsy."

"Why bother to autopsy a man who had been shot in the head?"

"He certainly was shot, but that wasn't the cause of death."

The guests gasped and exchanged incredulous looks.

"Janus was poisoned with a mixture of yellow oleander, yew, and nicotine," Bogdanovic continued as they quieted. "This stuff had been distilled into a concentrate that precipitated a heart attack. It was quite ingenious. The taste and aroma of the poison blended perfectly with the very strong flavor of Janus's private stock of Havanas. He preferred *oscuros*. Very strong."

"What a brilliant concept," exclaimed Wiggins. "Because Theo never shared his Cubans, there was no chance that anyone but Theo would light up the lethal stogie. By the way, Sergeant B., how did the poison get into the cigar?"

"It was injected with a thin syringe like diabetics use."

"Wouldn't a lot of that mixture be required to spike a whole box of Janus's cigars?" Wiggins asked.

"Examination and testing of the cigars showed that only three had been poisoned."

"You said the poison was injected," Wiggins said. "I know from personal experience that Theo inspected his cigars carefully for flaws. It seems to me he would have found such a puncture and thrown away that cigar."

"The injection was made in the part of the cigar covered by the band. The killer knew that Janus never removed the band when he smoked. The bands were removed, injections made, and the bands put back on."

"To do all that," said Judge Simmons as though he were on the bench, "the killer would have to gain access to the cigars. This would require knowledge of Janus's domestic arrangements and habits. For the cigars to be poisoned, the killer had to know where to find them, and to be certain that Janus would be away at the time they were being tampered with."

"I am talking of an individual capable of careful study and

planning, and someone with a motive so powerful that he was willing to go to great lengths to attain his goal."

"It seems to me that the culprit in your scenario," Simmons went on, "is intelligent and not without a keenly developed sense of humor. You must concede there is a delicious irony in Theodore Janus's being murdered with one of his cigars."

"As ever, Your Honor, you grasp the essence of the matter. The murderer was someone who knew Janus very well, who possessed cunning and wit, and who had access to the cigars. All of this required, as you have so aptly pointed out, a powerful motive. But, as I noted, the murderer was an individual of almost boundless willingness to bide his time. You might even say that the killer had the patience of . . . a judge."

Simmons's gaunt face went ghostly white. "This is outrageous! I demand you retract that groundless accusation, Sergeant."

"Groundless? I don't think so, sir. Who has a more powerful motive for murder than a judge whose reputation was sullied by a humiliating reversal in a high-profile case that was expected to be remembered in the history of jurisprudence as the capstone of a long and otherwise distinguished career on the bench?"

"What utter nonsense! If you don't apologize for this slander immediately, you'll be hearing from my attorney."

Goldstein grunted. "You know the laws of libel, Reginald. Sergeant Bogdanovic is speaking as a police officer. As long as he is carrying out his sworn duty, he is protected. Besides, I'm not aware that he has accused you of anything."

"Your point about access to Janus's cigars is well taken, Judge Simmons," Bogdanovic continued. "There is no doubt that the killer had to gain access to them. This could only have been done in two places. Either the killer got into Janus's automobile and a small humidor he kept in the glove compartment, or he'd visited Janus at his ranch. I believe the former is unlikely."

Pendelton said, "I don't see why."

"The only time the Rolls could have been entered was when it was parked in a public place. If Janus left the humidor in the car, it was because he expected to return shortly. I incline to credit the killer with not wishing to run the risk of being seen breaking into the Rolls, especially if Janus might come back. If the car had been left for a lengthier period, such as in a long-term parking area of an airport, Janus would take the humidor with him. That is why I concluded that the poisoned cigar Janus smoked on the night he died had been taken from the pocket case he had on him at the dinner. Therefore, the cigar that killed him had to have been brought from his home. It follows that either the cigar had been poisoned in the house in Janus's absence or brought to the house and given to Janus by the killer, possibly as a gift."

"Pardon me, Sergeant B.," Wiggins said. "Nobody pays a visit to a cigar aficionado's home and brings only one cigar as a gift. He brings a *box* of cigars."

"I can't agree with that, Wiggins," asserted Nick Stamos. "I had an occasion to visit Janus at his ranch last year on a business matter. But I had only two Cohibas on hand at the time, so I took one along for myself and gave him the other."

"What did Janus do with his?" Bogdanovic asked.

"What do you think he did with it? He smoked it!"

"Of course he did, as he would have done with any cigar he'd been given. It would be an insult if a man stuck a gift cigar in his pocket for later. Someone with enough knowledge of cigars to know how to go about poisoning one would also appreciate cigar etiquette. He would know that if he presented Janus one cigar he would light it up immediately, as he did with yours, Nick."

"I'm glad I didn't give him a whole box," Stamos said with a smile. "Otherwise, you might suspect me of killing him."

"You could have given him a box of poisoned cigars at another time. You certainly had a motive to murder him."

"Ridiculous. I had no cause to kill him."

"Not true. You had two million reasons."

Stamos laughed scoffingly. "That matter was on its way to being resolved to my complete satisfaction."

Bogdanovic asked, "What about you, Ariadne? Were you satisfied?"

"What a charmer you are, Sergeant," she said through an icy smile. "You may have been born in Brooklyn, but your thinking is strictly Balkan in nature. Anyway, I know nothing about cigars."

"Your husband does. And you both travel regularly to places where Cuban cigars are available. I assume it would be easy for a box or two of Havanas to be smuggled into the country aboard one of Nick's ships, even his yacht, as readily, for instance, as a shipment of heroin."

"I am not the only person in this room with a yacht, and a motive to kill Janus," Stamos objected. "Have you considered a certain retired admiral?"

The stately figure of Trevor Horne jerked as if it were a puppet whose strings had been pulled. "See here, Nicky. That is a contemptible suggestion."

"There is the troubling matter of Janus's law suit against you, Admiral," Bogdanovic said quietly. "And you do take your vacations in Bermuda. Cuban cigars have always been sold there."

"I'm not alone in choosing Bermuda for vacationing," Horne retorted. "Are you aware that James Hamilton has a condo there?"

"I am indeed, Admiral."

"Are you also aware that James Hamilton despised Janus so much that he tried to stop Wiggins from pushing through the plan to give Janus the Nero Wolfe Award, and when he did not succeed, boycotted the Black Orchid dinner?"

"I am also aware that Mr. Hamilton has chosen not to attend this Christmas party."

"I can explain that," Henry interjected. "There is nothing at all sinister about it. He is down with the flu. But really, Sergeant, I think your story hour has gone too far. You appear to suspect everyone here of murdering Theo. I hope you will forgive me for saying it, but I have the impression from all this casting about that you have no idea as to who killed Theo."

"Well, you know what Nero Wolfe said: 'Any spoke will lead an ant to the hub.' In this case, the spokes were the cigars in a box of Cubans from which Janus selected the last he would smoke. There had been three poisoned cigars in the box. The question for me was not only how they came to be laced with that deadly mixture, but where, when, and how Janus had obtained them. They were Cohiba *espléndidos,* purchased at Dunhill's in London."

"Of course they were," said Oscar Pendelton, impatiently. "When he went to London, he always bought several boxes of Cubans at Dunhill's. So did I."

"When were you last in London, Oscar?"

"In January."

"Do you know when Janus was there last?"

"I have no idea."

"I do. I checked his appointment calendar and his passport. He was there October a year ago, a few weeks before he went to California to do battle with Maggie Dane. He purchased four boxes of his usual Cohiba *espléndidos*. I know this because I spoke by phone to his tobacconist."

"Proving again that you are a meticulous detective," said Oscar, "Everyone in this room knows his favorite cigar was the Cohiba *espléndido*. He was never without them."

"He kept the bands on while he smoked them," Henry said in an exasperated tone, "so everyone would know they were from Cuba."

"You are wrong that Janus was never without his Cohibas, Oscar," Bogdanovic said. "He *was* out of them at least once that I know of. He smoked his last one after dinner with Maggie in Los Angeles. Yet, he was smoking one at the time he died and he had a nearly full box of them in his office. So where did he get them?"

"Someone must have bought them for him," said Pendleton.

"Very good, Oscar! But they were not *bought* at his behest. Those cigars were a *gift* from the person who visited him at the ranch."

"Hold on there, Sergeant B.," bellowed Wiggins. "I went to see Theo at the ranch, as you well know, but I did not take him a box of poison-laced Cuban cigars. He had a humidor full. He offered me one."

"Lucky for you that you didn't take it. Marian would have had to find another Santa Claus."

"Just a minute! If Janus had been given a box of cigars by this mysterious visitor," said Wiggins, "how come he didn't smoke a deadly one before Saturday night?"

"Pure chance. As I said, only three of the cigars had been taken from the box, poisoned, and replaced. Now, this is speculation on my part, but I can't see the killer putting the three at the very top of the box and thereby running the risk that Janus would take one out, smoke it, and drop dead then and there. This very clever murderer was content to have Janus smoke a poisoned cigar at his leisure. The killer also assumed that the cause of death would be attributed to a heart attack, as it might have been at the autopsy had Janus not been shot after he was dead and the very observant medical examiner, Dr. Hassan Awini, not noticed something odd about the gunshot wound. For Awini, the lack of blood was the spoke. The hub was a cardiac glycoside by the name of thevetin, found in yellow oleander, and an alkaloid taxine from the yew tree. Plus a hefty dose of concentrated nicotine."

"It's enough to make me consider giving up my pipe," said Wiggins with a forced shudder. "But on the other hand, Sherlock Holmes is alive, well, and keeping bees in Sussex."

"The news that Janus had been killed with a gun," said Nick Stamos, "and that awful photograph in the *Graphic,* must have been a shock to the person who expected to kill him with a cigar."

With an abrupt turn toward Henry, Bogdanovic said, "Perhaps Marian would care to tell us what she felt."

Henry gave a surprised laugh. "Cheated."

38

The Second Confession

"MY NEXT EMOTION was anxiety," Henry continued. "I wondered if the police faked that photograph in the *Graphic* as part of a scheme to lull Theo's murderer into a sense of security."

"We're not that smart, Marian," Goldstein declared.

"It was a reasonable deduction," Henry said. "That the photo appeared only in the *Graphic* struck me as peculiar. It occurred to me that it might have been planted. I had to know."

"Hence the invitation to Chief Goldstein, Maggie, and me to this party," Bogdanovic said. "You hoped that one of us might let you in on what was really going on in the investigation."

"It was obviously an error in judgment that ranks up there with Nixon's refusal to burn the White House tapes."

"You made *several* errors in judgment, Marian," Bogdanovic said, severely. "The first was your decision to kill Janus. If you had a grievance, you ought to have gone to court. The second mistake was using poisoned cigars."

"I had to, Sergeant. I'm terrified of firearms."

Goldstein asked, "Why did you want to kill him?"

"I don't see that it matters. You're not obliged to present a motive to a jury."

"That's true, Marian," Dane said, "but jurors have read so many mystery novels and seen so many courtroom dramas, fictional and real, that they always expect to hear one."

"I assure you they would not hear a tale of a woman being driven to murder by love, hate, greed, revenge, or an unbalanced mind. I am afraid they would find my motive unfathomable."

"I am confident," Bogdanovic said, "that a woman who writes the country's most popular books is able to explain anything."

Henry sipped a glass of scotch. "Long before I'd met you, Sergeant, I knew of your reputation for solving complicated cases. You do not disappoint. If anyone might understand my motive, it's you."

"Thank you. I take that as high praise."

"Oh it is, Sergeant."

"About your motive . . ."

"It evolved, beginning with the trial in which Theo pulled trick after trick out of his hat to thwart Maggie and frustrate justice. At some point in the proceedings I received a phone call from Oscar. He astonished me by asking if I would be interested in doing a book on the case. I told him I would love to, but that I was a fiction writer. But Oscar pointed out that what the definitive book about the case needed was a novelist's touch. With our verbal handshake, Oscar's firm put out a press release announcing that I would write *the* book on the case."

"That's all true, Sergeant," Pendelton exclaimed.

"But there was soon a hitch," Henry said.

Looking pained, Pendleton sighed. "I'll say there was."

"Shortly after Theo returned to New York," Henry went on, "he invited me to his ranch. He demanded that I cancel my book. He said he did not want it competing with the one he was planning. He said that if I did not agree to abandon my project, he would tie up poor Oscar and me in litigation. He acted like a schoolyard bully. I recognized that it would be futile to argue with him. I told him I would meet with Oscar and cancel our deal as soon as I returned from a trip to London. But as I thought about all of this while I was away, I began to view the situation as if it were the plot of a novel. This amused me so much that I found myself thinking of a method by which the murder of a man might be mistaken as a death by natural causes. I knew about Theo's heart condition, of course, so the obvious way to kill him would be to somehow precipitate a heart attack. Then the question was how. The inkling of an answer came to me one evening as I was having dinner at the Sherlock Holmes Pub when a gentleman at the next table asked me if I would object if he smoked a cigar. Naturally, I did not. But as I watched him enjoying his postprandial smoke, I came up with the exciting prospect of poisoning one of

Theo's cigars. Later that evening, I reasoned that the only way I might achieve that goal was to poison an entire box of cigars. The next day I went to Dunhill's. I knew it was Theo's tobacconist in London because I'd bought cigars for him there on previous trips. I asked the sales clerk for a box of Theo's favorite cigars."

"Cohiba *espléndidos,*" Bogdanovic said.

"Yes. My next challenge was twofold: how to poison them and with what substance."

"You found the answer to the latter problem in your garden."

"Quite right, Sergeant. Then I got a book on cigars that explained how they were made. I visited a quaint shop in Union City where a lovely old expatriate Cuban demonstrated how hand-made cigars are produced. Fascinating! A true art! That was how I learned that in a premium cigar the end that goes in the mouth has to be cut open. This was a crucial discovery, because I had formed a plan to inject a poison into the tips of Theo's cigars. I saw immediately that Theo might notice a puncture. I confirmed this by inserting a needle into several of the cigars that I bought from the man in Union City. The holes I made were quite plain to see. To test my hypothesis, I visited several of the cigar rooms that seem to have sprouted everywhere. In observing the rituals of men smoking cigars, I found to a man that they did, indeed, examine their cigars before trimming them. I also noticed that some of the men removed the bands and others did not. I learned from one man that the on-or-off issue is quite a controversy. As it happened, he preferred the band off. In demonstrating how easily one can be removed, he expressed his opinion that smokers who did not remove them were nothing but show-offs who needed everyone to know that they smoked only the best cigars, meaning the most expensive brands. He ventured that the prime example of this phenomenon was invariably found in those who smoked Cuban cigars, because of the distinctive black and gold bands. I left him knowing exactly how to poison Theo's cigars without fear of his becoming suspicious. And I knew where to get poison that would not be detected."

"That was another error. The substances you chose narrowed the field of suspects considerably. Very few people are familiar with the toxic qualities of yellow oleander and the yew tree. Those are exotic touches one expects to find in mystery novels. The wreath on your front door contains yew branches and leaves."

"In literature, Sergeant, that flaw is known as hubris. It is also a fault in gardeners. My compliments on your powers of observation and your knowledge of plants."

"I'm afraid that when it comes to knowing about agriculture, I looked up yellow oleander and yew in a book on poisons."

"Just to be sure I have all this straight," said Goldstein, "your motive for killing Janus was to prevent him from suing to stop you from writing a book?"

Pendelton answered, "By suing, Janus would have tied Marian and me up in the details of litigation. The result would have been to delay the publication of her book long enough for his to hit the bookstores first. It was the preemptive strike of an author who was also a lawyer."

"Be that as it may, Oscar," Bogdanovic said, "I don't buy it as a motive for murder. It certainly is not what I'd expect to read in the final chapter of a Marian Pickering Henry novel."

"Approximately two million dollars were at stake."

"I can see how millions of dollars in royalties could be a powerful motive for an ordinary author," Bogdanovic replied. "Certainly it makes sense for a publisher. Or even for a Greek shipping tycoon, or his wife," he continued, turning and bowing slightly in the direction of Nick and Ariadne Stamos. "I can see someone killing out of revenge. A judge who felt his reputation had been besmirched, for example. But I find it difficult to accept the proposition that Marian Pickering Henry murdered to ensure herself a little more income. It is my impression that she has more than she could ever spend."

"You've turned the tables on me, Sergeant," Henry said. "Now I'm the one on the receiving end of high praise, both as author and murderer. Of course I was not motivated by money. And not by a thirst for vengeance, though I might have been at first, because I was also offended by Theo's manner. He wasn't a pleasant man. When he demanded that I give up writing a book on the trial, he was brutal. As I said, a schoolyard bully. But kill him for being a nasty man?"

Dane leaned forward urgently. "Then *why?*"

Henry's eyes sparkled and the corners of her lips twitched with an incipient smile as she looked to Bogdanovic. "Would you care to venture a guess, Sergeant? Or do you, like Mr. Sherlock Holmes, never resort to guesswork because it is destructive to the logical faculty?"

"When I guess, I'm usually wrong."

"It's the same thing."

"I will offer you a hypothesis. I propose that you did it to find out if you could get away with it."

"Unfortunately, the case was assigned to a detective whose imagination was sharper than mine."

"That's very kind of you, Marian. If it's any consolation, you almost succeeded."

"You know what the man said, Sergeant."

"If the man was Nero Wolfe, I don't."

"No, you won't find this quotation in Theo's Nero Wolfe encyclopedia. The man said, 'Close, but no cigar.' "

EPILOGUE

And Four to Go

"The chief will be a little late in joining us at Neary's," Bogdanovic announced as Dane got into the car. "He's tied up at the DA's office in another big meeting. The brass is trying to put as good a face as possible on the Mancuso debacle. In short, it's cover-one's-ass time."

"The case has been solved?"

"No thanks to the DA's office. Goldstein unleashed Leibholz and Reiter and ordered them not to come back until they found out what the hell happened in that hotel room."

"Evidently they did."

"It turns out that the three assistant DAs who were minding Mancuso decided to break the monotony by having a little fun at poor Paulie's expense. One of them came up with the loony idea of making Paulie believe he was not long for this world. They got Janus's book and one of them wrote the inscription about Paulie doing the right thing. The trouble was, Paulie did not find it at all amusing. So it was *sic transit* Paulie, right out the window. And now it is *sic transit* that zany trio out the door with the outline of Cornelius Vanderhoff's toe imprinted indelibly on the tails of their Calvin Klein suits. And right behind them will go the deputy district attorney who was in charge of keeping Paulie alive and well until he testified. You know what that means."

"Of course. Four careers in law are over."

"The hell with them. What it means is that Vanderhoff is in need of a new deputy. Someone of such standing, and with such an exemplary reputation, that her arrival at One Hogan Place will set the local press atwitter with excitement and hosannas of praise for Vanderhoff. I refer, of course, to yourself."

"The closest I intend to get to a courtroom is supervising moot courts in a law school. I am headed for the quiet groves of academia."

"There are too many law school graduates already. Furthermore, Vanderhoff can't go on in that job forever. Who better to take over for him after he retires or dies than you?"

"The office of district attorney is not inherited, Sergeant. Whoever succeeds Cornelius Vanderhoff will have to be chosen by the people in an election."

"You've already got my vote. Plus Goldstein's. And Leibholz and Reiter think you are the cat's pajamas. That's four. Yours is five. You're on your way to a landslide!"

"This is very flattering, but I'm afraid my answer has to be one of Nero Wolfe's favorite phrases: *I will not be hounded.*"

ABOUT THE AUTHOR

A former broadcast journalist, H. Paul Jeffers has published nearly forty books. His most recent nonfiction includes *The Good Cigar* and a history and guide on the subject of spiritous drinks, *High Spirits.* In addition to the Sgt. John Bogdanovic series of novels, he is author of the Arlene Flynn mysteries, also from St. Martin's Press. He smokes, drinks, and writes in Manhattan.